The Art of Sin

Alexandrea Weis

This is a work of fiction. Names, characters, places, and incidents are products of the author's imagination or are used fictitiously and are not to be construed as real. Any resemblance to actual events, locations, organizations, or persons, living or dead, is entirely coincidental.

Weba Publishing May 3, 2015

Cover: BookFabulous Designs
Editor: Maxine Bringenberg
Editor: Karen Hrdlicka

Chapter 1

The shadow of the imposing French Quarter mansion towered over the handsome stranger standing before its decorative black wrought iron gate. The home's etched glass and dark oak front doors beckoned, while the weight of the man's suitcase, garment bag, and duffle bag weighed him down. Struggling to balance his cumbersome luggage, he pressed an elbow into the buzzer next to the gate.

While he waited for a response, the muscular blond turned his attention to the stately three-story home. The façade of large french windows complimented the wrought iron-wrapped second and third floor balconies, while a round, white cupola sat atop the steeply sloping roof. Painted a dark shade of yellow, with dark green shutters for protecting the front doors and windows, the structure had all the classic detail of a Creole townhouse. One pair of french windows on the second floor of the grand home was open, and a soft spring breeze was billowing a sheer pair of white curtains just inside.

His brawny arms were growing weary with the heavy luggage, and after uttering an aggravated grunt, he smacked them down on the uneven sidewalk.

"Son of a bitch. Where is everyone?"

Standing back, he gazed up at the open french windows, and was considering calling out for assistance, when a sultry female voice came over the intercom speaker by the gate.

"Yeah?"

He pressed the reply button. "I'm Grady Paulson, the new tenant for apartment C. I'm supposed to be getting a key from—"

"Oh, you're the new guy," the tantalizing voice interrupted. "I'm on my way down."

Minutes ticked by and his impatience grew. He was about to press the intercom button again when he saw the front doors of the home open.

A well-endowed blonde appeared, wearing only a thigh-high, silky pink nightgown with a flimsy, short pink robe that highlighted all of her assets. She was the epitome of a centerfold pinup. When she came down the front steps and saw Grady standing on the sidewalk outside of the gate, she gave him a show-stopping smile.

Grady's sharp blue eyes greedily devoured her figure and he smiled back at her.

I think I'm gonna like it here.

As she made her way down the short walkway, Grady could feel his cock coming to life when he recognized the long, toned legs and slender hips of a dancer. However, when her face came into focus, her features held none of the youthful appeal of her figure, making Grady's lustful intentions quickly fizzle out. If anything, she was more careworn than fresh and vibrant. The folds alongside her slender red mouth were deep, and her skin was more sallow than pale. Even her empty brown eyes seemed hard and suspicious, as if a lifetime of second-guessing the intentions of others had taken its toll.

"I'm Suzie," she said in a breathless, Marilyn Monroe-esque voice. "It's Grady, right?"

"Grady Paulson."

While admiring his chiseled cheekbones and square jaw, Suzie flashed a set of silver keys in her manicured hand. "I'm to show you to your place and give you the ground rules."

Grimacing, Grady ran his hand through his short-cropped blond hair. "Ground rules? You're kidding?"

Suzie reached the other side of the gate and turned the handle. "Wish I was, but Little Al's kind of picky about noise, probably since she's the only one with a day job around here, whereas all the rest of us work nights in the Quarter." She pushed open the black gate. "She's got a nice place here, so she likes to make sure it stays that way."

Grady lifted his luggage from the sidewalk. "Who's Little Al?"

Suzie held the gate open as he passed through to the walkway. "Allison Wagner … we all call her Little Al; tiny thing, but real smart. She owns the place."

With a glint of lust in her deep-set brown eyes, Suzie checked out Grady's body beneath his tight blue T-shirt and baggy jeans. Licking her red-painted lips, she paid special attention to his thick arms, wide chest, and broad shoulders.

"Are you gonna work in one of the clubs?"

"Yes, The Flesh Factory." He headed for the steps, struggling with the luggage. "I've got a four-month gig as a guest dancer."

"Heard that's the new hot spot for the boys in town. My agent says a lot of clubs are gettin' out of the girls and goin' for the boy shows. More money, you know?"

Grady climbed the steps. "Men's strip shows are all the rage." He made it to the porch and stood before the double doors. "I just drove in from a gig in Chicago."

Suzie shut the gate. "I danced there for about a year at The Monte Carlo Club. Real money town, Chicago."

Grady waited at the front doors and glanced back at Suzie. "Yeah, hated to leave, but my agent said New Orleans is an up and coming place for men to dance."

Suzie snorted as she came up the steps. "Honey, New Orleans is far from up and comin' for anythin'. Real strange city this is, and I've been here damn near a year."

Grady arched a single blond eyebrow at her. "Strange how?"

Suzie held the right side of the front doors open for him. "They've got more holidays and reasons to throw a party down here than any place I've ever been. Just be thankful you're not dancin' during Saints football season. Whole damn town shuts down for a Saints game."

Grady maneuvered his bags through the doors. Out of the corner of his eye, he saw Suzie blatantly checking out his ass.

He chuckled to himself. Women and their obsession with men's butts; he could never understand it.

Grady stepped inside a brightly lit entrance foyer, with a flight of dark oak stairs with a thick banister climbing to a second floor. In the ceiling was a plaster inlay medallion of rose vines with a beaded drop chandelier hanging from the center. To his right was a dark oak-paneled hallway, and beside the massive glass doors sat a walnut table engraved with intertwined vines and a collection of unopened mail atop it.

Suzie motioned down the hallway. "Doug is in apartment A. He's a bartender at Pat O'Brien's." She pointed to another door closer to them. "Lydia lives there. She dances at the Fleur De Lis on Bourbon." Suzie started up the stairs. "You'll be on the second floor along with me, Donna Maria, and Randy. Donna's in apartment E—she dances with me at the Flying Aces. Randy is in F, and he dances in the show at Harrah's Casino."

Keeping an eye on Suzie's fine ass, Grady struggled to balance his luggage and duffel bag while he followed her up the steps.

Halfway up the stairs, he asked, "What about the third floor?"

"No tenants above the second floor. Al lives on the third floor."

"What about the cupola? Can we go up there?"

"No one is allowed in the cupola." Suzie took the last step to the second-floor landing and turned to him. "And don't be botherin' Al about it. She gets real testy if anyone starts askin' questions about the cupola."

Grady made it up the last step. "Why?"

Suzie turned from him and proceeded along a landing that led to another open hallway. "All I know is, it's one of her ground rules."

As Grady trudged along the hallway, fighting with his bags, he eyed paintings of riverboats and the New Orleans riverfront from the late 1800's. Several of the pieces appeared to be very old, and he figured were probably worth quite a bit of money. An ornate mahogany bench with dark green velvet upholstery sat between two white cypress doors with the letters D and E on them.

"What are the rest of these ground rules?" he inquired, taking in a beautiful round, orange stained glass window at the end of the hallway.

"No loud music, no loud televisions." Suzie came to another cypress door at the end of the hall with a brass C on it. "No obnoxious parties, no playin' of loud musical instruments, no pets, no smokin', no barbequin' in the rooms or on the balconies." She put her hand on the brass doorknob. "If you are goin' to paint or redecorate your room, you have to check with Al first." Suzie placed the key in a shiny brass lock. "Some devil-worshipper a few years back painted his rooms all black, and Al said she had a hell of a time repaintin' that apartment. So, if you feel the urge to change your décor, let her know. Ain't no animal sacrifice allowed in any of the rooms, neither. The devil-worshipper was plannin' on killin' a goat one night until Al found out and ran his ass out of the place."

Grady grinned. "No animal sacrifice. Got it."

Suzie turned the key in the lock and pushed the door open. "You got a car?"

He nodded to the front of the house. "Honda Accord. I parked it out front."

"There's off street parkin' available in the courtyard in back, but let Al know you're parkin' back there. Al gets all the cars she don't know towed away." Suzie stepped into the apartment. "The rent is due on the first of the month, and left under Al's door. Everyone usually pays her cash, but she takes checks, too."

When Grady entered the apartment, and dropped his bags on the worn oak floor, he found himself in the center of a cozy living room. The furnishings were simple with only a round coffee table and dark brown upholstered sofa. Two long french windows facing Esplanade Avenue took up most of the adjacent wall, with a faux wood entertainment center placed between the windows. Atop the entertainment center was a modest flat screen television and cable box.

Grady went to inspect the walk-in efficiency kitchen across from the entrance.

"If you have anythin' that needs to be fixed, leave Al a note under her door," Suzie related behind him.

He ran his fingers over the white Formica countertops, and then opened the white refrigerator.

"There's a convenience store two blocks down, on Decatur," Suzie remarked when she saw him inspecting the empty refrigerator shelves. "If you want fresh fruits and veggies, there's the French Market at the end of Esplanade."

Grady pulled out a few of the plain pine drawers and glimpsed the paltry flatware and utensils left inside. In the cabinets above the metal sink, he discovered a few mismatched dishes of various shapes and colors, two blue mugs, and a few old-fashioned glasses. He opened the white range oven and found two pots and one frying pan.

"Most of us eat out around here. That's one thing this city has got tons of … good places to eat."

"So I hear." He turned on the cold-water tap and a steady stream of water flowed from the sink faucet.

"The water, electricity, and gas are factored in with your rent," Suzie informed him.

Stepping out of the small kitchen, he made his way across the living room. "That's very helpful."

"Al has been rentin' to our kind for years. She knows none of us stay too long in one place and tries to make it easy for everyone. She even has washin' machines and dryers for the tenants in the carriage house across the courtyard."

"I'm glad my agent was able to get me in here. Seems like a nice place." Grady entered the adjoining room.

The bedroom had a king-sized sleigh bed set in the center, already made up with a blue bedspread and two pillows. Next to the bed was a nightstand, and along the far wall, beside another tall french window, was a single chest of drawers. The room was painted a light powder blue with a single painting of the Mississippi River hanging above the head of the bed.

He stuck his head in the very small bathroom done in the same powder blue. There was only room for a single sink and vanity, toilet, and a narrow shower stall. Three folded white towels, waiting on a rack next to the glass shower stall, caught his eye.

"This Al seems to think of everything," he commented, turning from the bathroom. "I'll have to thank her when I run into her."

Suzie snickered from the doorway. "Good luck with that. Al may be all helpful with her tenants, but she's never around much. She's always workin'."

"What does she do?" Grady asked, coming back into the bedroom.

Suzie furrowed her smooth brow. "What do you call those people that put you to sleep for operations?"

Grady's eyebrows went up. "An anesthesiologist?"

"Well, aren't you a smarty?" She regarded him anew, making sure to stick out her ample bosom. "No, not one of those. The kind that is a nurse and does that."

"You mean a nurse anesthetist."

Suzie pointed a slender red-manicured finger at him. "That's the one. Al is one of those," she bobbed her finger up and down at him, "… nurse thingies."

"How does a nurse anesthetist end up running an apartment house for dancers?"

Suzie pouted her thick lips and shrugged. "Beats me." Her eyes hungrily lingered over his physique. "You're in real nice shape. How long you been strippin'?"

"Four years." Grady's eyes gravitated toward Suzie's plentiful bosom. He briefly pondered how her big tits would feel in his mouth. "Where are you headed next?"

Her flirty grin fell. "I've been waitin' for my agent to get me another job, but things are slow, you know?"

Grady gave her a sympathetic smile. There was always plenty of work for good looking young women in the business, but for those who were approaching middle age, there were a lot fewer gigs. He guessed that plastic surgery, and a whole lot of Botox, was helping to keep Suzie attractive, but her days of high-paying shows were behind her. Washed up at thirty-five was unheard of in any other business, but in stripping it was the norm. Grady had often wondered about his own longevity in a profession where big muscles, chiseled features, and a tight ass were prized.

"I'm sure you'll get another job, real soon," he declared, heading to the bedroom door.

Suzie's seductive smile was back and she rested her shoulder against the doorframe, blocking his way. "You think so?"

Grady ogled her deep cleavage. He could feel his cock stirring, and just as visions of getting his hands on her firm tits started filling his head, his common sense kicked in.

You came to New Orleans to dance, not fuck, Grady.

"I should get settled in," he muttered,

Suzie eased up to him, grinning, and then pressed her hand into the crotch of his jeans. "Don't tell me you bat for the other team?"

Grady licked his lips, tempted, but determined to refuse her advances. He moved her hand away. "No, I just don't like to get involved when I'm on tour. Makes things messy."

Suzie frowned and shimmied out of his way. "Shame. Could make our time here interestin', you know?" She handed him the keys, letting her long nails gently graze his skin. "I'm in apartment D, just down the hall, when you change your mind."

She turned from the door, gave him one last come-hither glance over her shoulder—the same one he had seen a hundred times before on the stage—and went to the apartment door, accentuating the roll of her hips as she walked.

After she had left, he leaned against the bedroom doorframe and blew out a frustrated sigh. "She's the last thing you need in your life."

Beggars can't be choosers, his pesky inner voice returned.

Angrily pocketing his keys, Grady went to his luggage on the floor in the living room. Snatching up his suitcase, garment bag, and duffel bag, he marched into his bedroom and tossed them onto the bed. Peering down at the crammed bags, Grady clenched his fists. This was not what he had envisioned for himself at thirty-two.

Unzipping his suitcase, his anger bubbled over. "Here you are still traveling the country, dancing for tips, and being hit on by strippers, with no hope of having a normal life with an honest woman." He began to remove piles of T-shirts, socks, jeans, and briefs from his suitcase.

After putting away his everyday clothes, he kicked the chest of drawers. Eyeing the garment bag on his bed, he silently chastised himself for his temper tantrum and then hastily unzipped the bag.

He carefully removed his black tuxedo costume, with its crisp white shirt and black bow tie, from the bag. While wiping away the wrinkles that his black pants had acquired during the long drive from Chicago, he took it to the small closet next to his bathroom door.

Returning to the garment bag, he pulled out a pair of black leather chaps, a black whip, and a black cowboy shirt with sparkling silver thread swirls. Next, he removed the silver-sequined cape, silver-satin pants, and bright, silver-sequined shirt. With a sick churning in his stomach, he inspected the sequins and noted their dingy appearance.

The costumes were his livelihood, but now he looked on them as a painful reminder of the life he had been forced to return to. With a wistful grimace, he placed the shiny, sequined costume in his closet. Unzipping a side-pocket on the garment bag, he retrieved a selection of G-strings, including the silver-sequined one he hated because it always scratched his balls.

When the last of his clothes and toiletries had been put away, his stomach rumbled. Eager to get something to eat, he reached into the front pocket of his jeans and pulled out the keys Suzie had given him. Tossing the keys in the air, he caught them firmly in his hand and then checked the stainless steel watch on his wrist.

Heading for the front doors, he figured he had plenty of time to take a walk around before he had to check in at The Flesh Factory. After all, this was New Orleans, and he wanted to see some of the famous landmarks before he got caught up in work. Once his show schedule kicked in, he would have little time left for sightseeing. Grady suddenly yearned to be like all the other tourists that flocked to the Crescent City: to enjoy a few hours of sunshine before he became trapped behind the unrelenting curtain of night.

Chapter 2

Urged on by the gnawing in his stomach, Grady strolled along the shady sidewalks of Esplanade Avenue, heading toward the Mississippi River and the famous French Market. When he came to an open-air market by the riverfront, he turned to the collection of stalls and the flurry of people inspecting the various goods for sale.

Navigating through the tables of crafts, antiques, and second-hand clothing, he stopped along the way to take in knick-knacks that caught his eye. The hum of activity around him was infectious as people laughed, socialized, and marveled at the European style open-air market.

Leaving the flea market behind, Grady soon found himself standing before long trays of fresh fruits and vegetables. His stomach complained louder than before when he caught sight of an appetizing row of rich red strawberries from the nearby city of Ponchatoula. While searching for the perfect carton of big, round berries, his mouth watered. Further down the long aisle, he spied apples, oranges, and raspberries with equal appeal.

"They're three ninety-nine a carton," a very short man with gray-sprinkled brown hair and a white apron clarified next to him.

Grady held up two fingers. "I'll take two."

"Good decision," a melodious female voice uttered behind him.

Grady slowly pivoted around and saw a petite blonde with her long hair pulled back in a ponytail. She was wearing dark sunglasses, and her thin lips were curled back in an intriguing grin.

She nodded to the display. “Best berries around.”

Grady was taken aback by her confident stance, and then he noticed her green medical scrubs. She was attractive and had a toned body, but it was that grin that was getting the better of him. He felt that stirring of excitement in his cock while images of taking her, and her sassy grin, from behind inundated his mind.

“The best around?” He eyed her small breasts. “Really? I find that hard to believe.”

Her grin stretched into a hearty smile. “I promise you won’t be disappointed.”

“Eight fifty-six,” the merchant said, distracting him.

Grady pulled his wallet from the back pocket of his jeans and hastily handed the merchant a ten-dollar bill. When he spun back around to talk to the blonde, she was gone. He eagerly scanned the market area, but there was no sign of her.

“Hey, you want your change?”

Grady took his change and a brown paper bag of berries from the merchant’s outstretched hands.

“Thanks,” he mumbled, still surveying the aisle.

A finger tapped his right shoulder.

“She went into the flea market,” the merchant pointed out with a wink.

“Thank you.” Grady took off toward the flea market.

Right after he crossed the threshold that separated the produce section from the flea market, he spotted the woman’s long blonde ponytail as she perused an assortment of old postcards on a vendor’s table. He hastily walked up to her, formulating an opening line that would grab her interest. Reaching into the brown bag he had clutched to his chest, he came alongside her, and poised a red berry in front of his lips.

“You were right. Juicy and sweet,” he proclaimed in a sultry voice.

Nonplussed by his comment, the slender woman continued to search the postcards on the table before her.

“You were right about the strawberries,” he said a little louder, hoping to get her attention.

She turned to him, but he could not read the expression on her face behind the dark sunglasses. All he could detect was the slight smirk on her thin, pink lips.

"Yeah, they are pretty good this year." She went around him, heading to a table displaying homemade scented candles.

Grady followed her, taking in the way the green scrubs clung to her small, tight ass. He liked her ass. It was the perfect size … for him, anyway.

"Are you a doctor?"

"Hardly." She removed her sunglasses.

When he saw her eyes for the first time, Grady felt as if the air had been sucked out of his lungs. There was something captivating and disturbing about her deep gray orbs. It was not their round shape or the way they complemented her pale skin, high cheekbones or round chin … it was how they looked at him. It was an intense expression of distrust that almost seemed to contrast the welcoming smile on her lips.

"Where are you from?" she asked, scrutinizing his snug blue T-shirt, jeans, and dingy tennis shoes.

"Connecticut."

Grady tried to figure out how old she was, but her appearance exuded an interesting blend of youthful charm with a hint of worldly sophistication, as if she were an old soul cloaked in a little girl's body.

She replaced her sunglasses on her face. "Connecticut? Interesting. What brings you to New Orleans?"

Grady froze. It was the one question he was not prepared to answer. Plenty of women got turned on when they discovered he was a male stripper, but more often than not, the women he was attracted to were repulsed by his job. He always found it an interesting irony in his life that the women who appealed to him were never the kind to frequent his clubs.

"I'm working on my MBA at Tulane," he lied, knowing that would be a whole lot more alluring to a woman like the one before him.

She tilted her head to the side and studied him for several seconds without saying a word. Grady's antiperspirant was failing him miserably as he began to sweat beneath the scrutiny of her sunglasses.

"That's funny?" she finally spoke up. "I don't see you as a grad student."

"Well, I'm only going there part-time. I also work as a bartender in the city while I'm getting through school."

Her eyebrows went up. "Bartender? Where?"

He remembered what Suzie had told him about another tenant in their building. "Pat O'Brien's," came out of his mouth before he could stop it.

Grady knew he was only getting in deeper trouble, but like so many times in the past, he could not help himself. He never liked telling anyone what he did for a living, feeling any lie was more palatable than the truth.

He gave her one of his well-rehearsed smiles and held out his hand. "My name's Grady."

The smile fell from her lips. "Grady?" She took his hand and gave it a curt shake.

Instantly, he sensed the change in her. It was as if her dislike for him had taken a turn for the worse.

She removed her sunglasses and carefully scrutinized his body with those disconcerting eyes. Grady found he liked the feeling he got from her intense scrutiny. Puffing out his chest slightly, he wanted to make sure she got a real good look at him.

"Sure you're not a male stripper? You definitely have the body for it," she voiced in a condescending tone.

Grady's stomach shriveled to the size of a walnut. His blue eyes furiously darted about the flea market.

Shit! How did she know?

He suddenly wanted to get away. Searching for an excuse, he nervously checked his watch.

"I should get going. Thanks for the tip about the strawberries." He turned to go.

"Grady Paulson, isn't it?"

Grady slowly faced her. Her smile was back, but now it resembled more of a coy smirk than a heartfelt gesture. That long held fear, of being recognized from his shows hit his gut with the force of a high caliber bullet.

"Ah, have we met?"

She took a step closer to him. "I'm Al Wagner, your new landlord."

Relief tunneled through him, making Grady let go a light chuckle.

That would explain everything.

He dropped his grin and raised his head to her. "I was given the impression that you were never seen by any of your tenants, Ms. Wagner, and only communicated via notes slipped under your door."

Al folded up her sunglasses and looped them over the waistband of her green scrubs. "I see Suzie exaggerated everything, as usual. I hope she at least gave you the ground rules."

Grady nodded and held his bag of strawberries against his chest. "Forgoing my weekly animal sacrifice may be a bit hard, but I think the rest of your ground rules should be pretty easy to follow."

"A comedian and a stripper. How unique."

He took a few steps back from her. "I try my best to entertain the ladies."

"I guess that's part of your job description."

Grady muted his desire to be sarcastic, and tried to remember that this woman was going to be his landlord for the next four months. "I should thank you for the extra amenities, like the towels and bed linens. Most rentals I've stayed in don't provide you with anything but a bed and cable television."

"I know a lot of people in your business are on the road most of the time and having a place feel more like home than a hotel helps."

He dipped his head to her. "It was appreciated."

She came alongside him. "Are you heading back to the house?"

He viewed the setting sun over the rooftops of the French Quarter cottages. "Yeah, I've got to go to my new club and check in."

"I'll give you a lift. My car is right over there." She motioned to a line of cars parked next to the flea market.

"That's all right. I can walk."

He was about to turn away when she reached for his arm. "I'm sorry, but I suspected it was you from the moment I saw you standing in front of the strawberries. I should have said something sooner."

Her touch ignited his curiosity. "How did you know it was me?"

Her hand fell away. "Burt Conroe, your agent, emailed me a publicity picture of you. He does that with all the renters he sends me. He likes to give me some info on his people. About you, he told me very little."

"Well, what did he tell you?" Grady questioned, with a hint of aggravation in his voice.

"That you were straight, clean, and a little bit lost."

His eyebrows went up. "Lost? Why would Burt say that?"

"I don't know. Why don't you tell me?" Al headed to a red BMW 325i, parked next to a table of antique mirrors.

He followed her to the car. "Look, I don't know what Burt told you, but I'm not lost. I'm simply here for a job."

She put her hand on the driver's side door. "If that's the case, then why hand me that bullshit about studying at Tulane?"

Grady eased right up to her, taking in her shrewd gray eyes. "Because a lot of women may like going to see a male stripper dance in a club, but they don't want to associate with one."

"Did you think I was one of those women?"

He contemplated her green scrubs and white clogs. "I thought you were the kind of woman who would be more impressed by someone going to Tulane, rather than stripping on Bourbon Street."

Her pink mouth turned downward into an impish frown. "That's rather prejudicial, don't you think? I might have thought your being a male stripper was pretty damned sexy. Ever consider that?"

An excited fluttering gripped Grady's insides. Great, this was all he needed. Not even two hours in the city, and he was already getting turned on by his landlord.

He tried to picture cold showers and fat female strippers to cool his ardor. "Let's just forget it."

"No," she persisted, opening her car door. "Why did you lie? Or does lying about what you do make it easier to forget their names in the morning?"

He leaned back from her and redirected his eyes to the crowds in the flea market. "Maybe I should just jot down my reasons on a Post-it note and slip it under your door, Ms. Wagner."

The smug grin on her face was disconcerting as hell. Grady always loved a bit of mental sparring with a woman, but something told him tangling with this woman was a real bad idea.

"I'm sure all those reasons would just about fit on a Post-it note," she shot back. "Tell me something, Grady Paulson, are you always this way with women?"

"What way?" he cautiously returned.

"Angry."

Grady suppressed the urge to laugh out loud; instead he simply narrowed his blue eyes on her. "Thanks for the tip about the strawberries."

Undeterred, she casually removed the sunglasses from the waistband of her scrubs. "Avoiding my question only confirms my suspicions about you."

He let out an aggravated sigh. This was going nowhere. "Your suspicions? Look, Ms. Wagner, I just came here to get something to eat, not get evicted on my first day in the city, all right?"

"Fair enough. And it's Al, for the record. No one calls me Ms. Wagner, unless they're trying to hustle me."

"Which I would never do … Ms. Wagner."

Al shook her head, appearing amused. Pushing the sunglasses back on her face, she said, “One day, I would like to know why you didn’t want to tell me the truth about being a stripper.”

“The truth?” Grady fought like hell to stay mad at her, but he couldn’t. She was just too damned adorable. “Quintus Septimius once said, ‘The first reaction to truth is … hatred.’”

“Is he a stripper?” she posed with a straight face.

“No, he’s a ….” Grady snickered, shaking his head. “Forget it.”

“You know, Grady, I might have been different from all the other women. If you never give a woman a chance, you might never know how she really feels.”

“How do you really feel about me, Ms. Wagner?”

Al nodded to the passenger side of the car. “Get in and perhaps I’ll tell you.”

Blowing out an irritated breath, Grady went around to the passenger side door and opened it. Remembering to play it cool, he climbed in the car, still clutching his bag of strawberries.

While Al turned over the engine, he took in her profile. “If you hadn’t known it was me, would you have still talked to me?”

She put the car in gear. “No. I don’t make it a habit to talk to strange men.”

“What about talking to men you’re attracted to?”

She waited a few beats before saying, “I’ve never run across one of those.”

Her words were like an automatic challenge to him. Instantly, he was desperate to learn all he could about her. Grady kept his eyes on her profile as she drove.

“Al is short for Allison, right?”

She nodded and merged with the traffic at the end of Esplanade Avenue. “I detest the name Allison. So if you want to stay on my good side, don’t call me that.”

“Who called you Allison?”

She gave him a wary side-glance. “What do you mean?”

“I find if someone detests a name, it’s usually because someone they disliked either called them that or had that name.”

“What are you, a stripper moonlighting as a psychologist?”

Putt off by her wisecrack, he shifted his gaze to the large homes along Esplanade Avenue. "I minored in psych at Yale. I was even considering going on to do some graduate study in it."

"Yale? I'm impressed."

"Are you going to tell me who called you Allison?"

She returned her eyes to the road ahead. "My father called me Allison until I was seven, then he walked out on me, my mother, and my older sister, Cassie."

"After that you insisted on being called Al. I understand."

She pulled to a stop at a red light. "Tell me something. How do you go from being at Yale to dancing in a strip club in New Orleans?"

"What, that wasn't in the info Burt sent you?"

Her hands tightened on the black leather steering wheel. "I shouldn't have made that crack about Burt saying you were lost. He actually said you were a real stand-up guy, hardworking, and had run into some bad luck after the economy fell apart."

Lowering his defenses, Grady relaxed in his seat, and his grip on his bag of strawberries eased. "I was working at Lehman Brothers as a stock analyst, prior to the crash."

The light turned green and the car eased forward. "How did you get into stripping?"

"My roommate at Yale was working as a stripper for a club close by the campus. He introduced me to the owner. The money was great and all the girls from the college went there."

She veered the car toward the right as the deep yellow mansion appeared just up ahead. "You ever try to go back to Wall Street?"

"You know the answer to that one. I'm one of millions, but at least I'm gainfully employed."

"Perhaps, but you don't like doing what you do … that's obvious." She swerved the car into a narrow driveway beside the dark yellow mansion. "A man happy in his profession doesn't care what other's think, he only cares about what he does."

"Where did you learn that?"

"My father," she declared, as the car slowly eased through the side entrance. "He was a musician, who worked in about every jazz joint in the city."

"What about your mother?"

"She came from an old New Orleans family. This was their home." She gestured to the house. "She died when I was sixteen. After that, my older sister, Cassie, took care of me and the house."

When the car entered the courtyard in back, high, red-bricked walls rose on either side, while dull, gray cement covered the ground. Along the walls, empty flower beds seemed to cry out for some form of decorative vegetation, while at the rear a single story cottage stood with a hipped, black shingle roof and the same deep yellow plaster that was on the main home. The green shutters on the cottage were closed, giving the building the same abandoned feel as the empty flowerbeds.

"Where's Cassie now?" Grady probed, taking in a beat-up blue Volvo to his right.

She parked the car in a spot behind the rear entrance. "She went west."

"Where west? L.A.?"

Al smiled, but the light of sorrow in her eyes gave Grady pause. "I'm not sure." Turning off the engine, she quickly added, "You got any family?"

He reached for his door. "A brother in Denver. We don't talk much. His wife likes to keep him on a short leash."

"Yeah, marriage can be a real bitch," Al proposed, opening her car door.

Grady stood from the car and gazed across the roof at her. "You ever been married?"

"No," she told him, collecting a blue backpack from the rear seat. "I don't want a husband. Never have."

"Then why the bad opinion of marriage?"

She slung the backpack over her shoulder. "I've heard enough horror stories to know I don't have any interest in writing my own."

He went around to the front of the car and waited for her. "Maybe it isn't all bad. Might be nice to have someone to lean on."

She slowly sauntered up to him. "The only person you have to count on is you. To other people, you will eventually end up as a burden."

"That's an awfully pessimistic attitude." He considered her intense gray eyes, trying to fathom the reason for her cynicism. "I thought working in the medical field would give you a kinder opinion of the human race."

She pulled a set of keys from a pocket on the outside of her blue backpack. "No, working in the medical field gives you a realistic view of the human race." She walked to the back door of the house. "Your world and mine aren't so different, Grady. We get to see the ugly reality of life, not the fairy tale."

He came toward her, wearing an upbeat smile. "In my world, the fairy tale is what we sell. It's the fantasy of having a dancer for the night. If it weren't for the suspended disbelief of my customers, I would be out of a job."

Al opened the massive solid cypress door that filled the rear entrance. "They know what they're getting, Grady: a little flash, a little bump and grind. Then, it's time to go back home and crawl into bed with men they have learned to put up with for the sake of money, children, or because they are too afraid to make it in the world on their own." She pushed the heavy door open.

Before she could step inside, Grady stretched his thick arm across the doorway in front of her. "Who was he?"

Her gray eyes angrily whirled around to him. "Who?"

"The guy who made you so bitter about relationships."

Al pushed his arm out of the way, and then smiled seductively. "What makes you so sure it was a guy?"

She glided in the doorway. Grady stood behind her with his mouth slightly ajar.

"Well, that would explain a hell of a lot," he muttered.

Inside, a narrow hallway was paneled in dark oak with occasional framed drawings of old New Orleans decorating the walls. Sconces of brass shaped like lilies occasionally appeared from the rich wood, lighting their way. Eventually the corridor opened up, and to the right the staircase Grady had used when first entering the house rose up alongside them.

Before they reached the beginning of the staircase, Al stepped up to a formidable man with short-cropped black hair, rugged features, and a very well-defined torso. Standing by a table just inside the front doors, he was taller than Grady and probably a good twenty pounds heavier. He was wearing a blue T-shirt, jeans, and in his hands were an assortment of envelopes.

"Hey, Doug." Al sorted through a few envelopes. "Is this today's mail?"

Doug looked up and Grady noticed the blackness of his eyes. They had a sinister appearance that was compounded by his olive complexion, the thick black stubble on his chin, and his prominent carved cheekbones. His jaw was square and added a brooding quality to his face.

"Hey, Little Al." He handed her a few of the envelopes. "Yeah, I was looking for my check."

Al pointed to Grady. "Doug Larson, meet Grady Paulson, new tenant in C."

Doug shoved a stack of envelopes under his arm and stretched out his free hand to Grady. "Welcome to the dorm."

Grady shook his hand. "The dorm?"

Al rolled her eyes, turning to Grady. "Doug's way of making fun of my ground rules."

"Well, you do have a lot of them, Al." Doug retrieved the envelopes from under his arm.

"I don't see you leaving," Al quipped.

Doug shrugged his broad shoulders. "Hey, I love it here." He removed an envelope from the pile. "There," he said, handing it to Al. "Light bill."

She took the envelope and added it to the stack in her hand. "The mail comes jointly, Grady. I don't use mailboxes because people come and go so frequently. If you need anything shipped or mailed, just put your name and apartment number above the address." She waved to a brass mail slot in the lower portion of one side of the double oak and glass doors. "First person to pick up the mail on the floor gets to sort it."

"Which is usually me," Doug piped in. He handed Al another envelope. "Cable bill."

Al read the address on the envelope. "Grady's dancing over at The Flesh Factory."

Grady eyed Al suspiciously. "I never told you I was dancing there."

"No, but Burt did."

Doug smiled at Grady. "Heard that's going to be the new hot spot in town."

Al eased toward the stairs. "I'll see you two later."

"Thanks for the ride," Grady called to her.

Al careened her head around. "Enjoy the strawberries," she added, waving to the bag in his hand.

The two men stood in silence, seemingly mesmerized by Al's ass as she jogged up the steps.

Letting out a low whistle, Doug returned his gaze to the envelopes in his hand. "Hell of a woman, huh?"

"A very interesting woman," Grady expounded.

Doug snorted. "Don't even think about it, man. That is one smart lady. She also never gets involved with her male tenants."

"Just her female ones, right?" Grady asserted with a grin.

Doug let out a heartfelt roar of laughter. "You fell for that line, too." He shook his head. "She tells every new guy that walks into the place that she's into girls, but she's not, trust me."

"How do you know?"

Doug placed the last of the envelopes in his hand on the walnut table by the door. "She's been dating some older guy for a few years now. He's got a key. I've seen him coming and going at odd hours."

"Then why give me that line about being interested in women?"

Doug shrugged. "To put you off. She never gets involved with her tenants. One of her ground rules."

Grady should have trusted his instincts. From the moment he had peered into her eyes, he felt that stirring of interest from her.

Now he was beginning to understand why he had sensed such animosity from her. She had been attracted to him, too, but never wanted to entertain the notion of breaking her steadfast rules.

Grady fixed his eyes on the imposing man beside him. "Suzie told me you work at Pat O'Brien's."

"Yeah. I started out dancing like you, but then the gigs dried-up and I got the job at Pat O's. It's steady, tips are great, and the female companionship … even better." He studied Grady's blue eyes and good looks. "How long have you been dancing?"

"Started in college, quit when I graduated, but thanks to the economy, I got laid off. I had to go back to it four years ago."

"Damned economy is killing everyone. I've got a financial planner and a CPA working behind the bar with me. Both of them got laid off and turned to tending bar to pay the bills."

"Yeah, there are a lot of us out there, nowadays," Grady agreed.

Doug slapped the envelopes in his hands against his thigh. "How long you here for?"

"Four months."

"When you get done at your club, you should stop by Pat O's one night, and I'll buy you a drink. I work the main bar from eight to two every night except Monday."

"Thanks, Doug. I'll do that."

"See you later." Doug turned down the hall.

As Grady climbed the steps, he watched the impressive figure of Doug Larson slip inside his apartment door. Directing his attention up the stairs, his mind once again returned to the image of Al's slender hips sashaying suggestively up the steps. He grinned as he thought of her petite figure and wondered how it would feel having her beneath him in bed.

He had always yearned to be with a tiny woman with slim hips and a supple body. The closest he had come was a nameless face he had encountered one night during a show in Phoenix. She had been a pretty brunette—barely a size two—but the allure of bedding the hapless fan was nothing in comparison to his sudden desire for Al. He did not know what intrigued him more, her sharp wit, her demure little girl looks, or her damned eyes. Whatever it was, Grady figured it would make for an interesting few months together.

Once inside his austere living room, he tossed the bag of strawberries to the round coffee table and then plopped down on the brown sofa. He wistfully glanced around the room as an overbearing sense of sadness engulfed him.

"Another town, another empty room," he mumbled. "How many more years are you going to do this to yourself?"

The silence in the room was a deafening reminder of his plight. Disgusted with his mood, he grabbed for the bag of strawberries and went to the kitchen. At least, he reasoned, there was something different in New Orleans for him to look forward to. He would be counting the hours until he saw the elusive Allison Wagner again. Only next time, he was going to be a little bolder and get her to commit to a cup of coffee or a drink.

A wry smile crossed his lips as he thought of her reply.

"She'll hate me for asking, but she'll go. Damn woman is just as interested in me as I am in her. She just doesn't know it … yet."

Chapter 3

The Flesh Factory was located on Bourbon and St. Ann Streets, in the heart of the French Quarter. Once Grady entered the establishment, the heavy cigarette smoke and smell of stale beer hit his nose. Sitting just inside the doorway was a burly bouncer with bored brown eyes, a face like a pit bull, and the body of an NFL defensive lineman.

"Ladies only, man," he said in a voice reminiscent of a ship's foghorn.

"I'm one of the new dancers. Grady Paulson."

The bouncer thumbed a thick red leather door to his right. "Matt Harrison is the manager. Go to the bar and ask for him. They'll point him out for you."

As soon as Grady pulled the red leather door open, the thumping beat of dance music pounded against his body, and the high-pitched screams of a room filled with turned on, drunken women accosted his ears.

After heading inside, it took a few minutes for his eyes to adjust to the low light. Then, he saw the brightly lit stage located behind a row of round white columns. He stepped from the darkness behind the columns and looked across the room filled with candlelit tables and packed with women.

On the stage, a well-cut dancer, wearing a lab coat and white G-string, was grinding against the hips of some unsuspecting doe from the audience. The woman was gushing and blushing, while the dancer went through his routine of rubbing everything he had against her to elicit that desired "Oh my God" response, or as the dancers affectionately called it … the orgasm. It was what every male dancer went for when he pulled a woman onto the stage.

Grady watched the woman scream with exhilaration when the dancer rubbed his cock against her face. It was all part of the show. It also helped a performer connect with his audience. Grady always tried to spot the most innocent-looking woman in the crowd to bring on the stage when he went for his orgasm every night.

Each dancer had a type they searched for in the pit—what the dancers in the business affectionately called the area before the stage where the women gathered. Some guys went for the refined women, others the excited ones, and the newer guys always went for the pretty ones, hoping to get lucky. With experience, Grady had learned that the prettiest girls in the audience were not the best to bring on stage. Time had taught him that finding a woman other women could relate to made a show a hell of a lot more successful.

At the bar to his left, an array of beefy bartenders were standing around, wearing only skimpy silver shorts and silver bow ties. He stayed along the outskirts of the room, wanting not to be seen by the customers. Grady knew entering the pit, when women were in the throws of being entertained, was as good as handing yourself over to an out-of-control mob.

One of the servers saw him waiting by the bar and came over. A bartender with black curly hair and black mustache inspected Grady's thick arms, chest, and shoulders.

"You looking for Matt?"

"Grady Paulson. New dancer."

The bartender held out his hand. "I'm Nick Davies. Matt is backstage." He motioned to a door at the end of the bar with the word Private embossed in gold across it. "Go through that door. It will take you to the backstage area."

Before Grady slipped behind the backstage door, he explored the faces of the women in the pit. There were all kinds gathered there. The old, young, pretty and not so pretty, but all the faces had the same frenzied look he had seen a million times from the stage. It had always reminded him of his days at the New York Stock Exchange. The screaming women waving their hands about resembled the buyers and sellers on the floor of the Stock Exchange. He thought it curious how the hunger for sex and money appeared exactly the same on the human face, making it hard sometimes to determine which one was more important.

Behind the door, the thud of the dance music and screams of the women were not as pronounced. Grady welcomed the respite. The backstage area was compact, stuffed with scenery and props set against the back wall with ropes tied off to a pin rail. Above, a batten that housed several stage or trooper lights hung along with extra rigging for background scenery. A few men, scantily dressed in G-strings with oiled bodies and shiny silver boots, were standing about on the dusty hardwood floor drinking from white paper cups or talking on their cell phones.

There was an almost bored look on many of the faces of the toned and buff men waiting backstage. All the chaos out front dramatically contrasted against the almost relaxed atmosphere behind the scenes.

Not looking where he was going, Grady accidently ran into a well-built man apart from the group. He was wearing a snug gladiator costume and waving his wooden sword about.

"Hey, watch it," he grumbled at Grady.

The haughty look in the man's green eyes seem to challenge Grady. There was something about him that made Grady uncomfortable, as if he sensed the guy was trouble.

"You lost, buddy?"

Grady held up his hands. "Sorry. You know where I can find Matt Harrison?"

The gladiator looked him over, his eyes filled with disdain. "Who's asking?"

Grady bit back his curt reply and simply smiled. *No need to make enemies on the first day.*

"I'm Grady Paulson, the guest dancer."

The man's uncanny eyes softened a bit. "Colin Caffranelli. I'm one of the headliners here."

Grady wanted to groan out loud. He hated headliners. In every club he had worked, from Philadelphia to Portland, the headliners always treated the travel dancers like shit. Just because they had a long-term gig in one club, they thought they were better than the guys who had to constantly move from club to club.

"Do you know where can I find Matt?" Grady asked, anxious to get away from the rude man.

Colin tilted his head to his right. "Matt's at his desk."

Grady followed his eyes to a wooden desk located against a red-bricked wall in the corner of the backstage area.

"Ah, thanks," he said to Colin, before turning away.

Sitting behind the desk, talking on a phone and waving his hand furiously about, was a scrawny man, dressed in a tailored gray suit, with a pockmarked, pasty face, gray-streaked, wiry black hair, and coal black eyes. He had a wide mouth, and his crooked nose appeared as if it had been broken more than once.

When he spotted Grady eyeing him from across the backstage area, he beckoned to him and instantly ended his call.

"Are you Paulson?" he asked, in a craggily sounding smoker's voice.

Grady nodded and held out his hand. "Mr. Harrison?"

"Matt," Matt Harrison corrected. He stood and took Grady's hand. "Burt said you were a real showstopper." He waved down Grady's body. "I can see he was right. The all-American, California look is big with these women." He put his cell phone in his jacket pocket and nodded to a door to his left. "Let me show you the dressing rooms and we can get you settled."

Grady followed Matt as he led him to the plain wooden door set into the red-bricked wall. After stepping into a dimly lit, yellow-tiled hallway, Matt shut the door with a bang.

"Damn, that's better," he said, taking in the almost peaceful stillness of the hallway. "I swear, I hear screaming women in my sleep."

"I know what you mean," Grady concurred.

"My wife told me I was an idiot for opening this place, but she stopped saying that after I bought her a new Mercedes last week." Matt came to a wooden door to his right with an A sloppily painted on it. "Ed, who is out on stage right now, shares this with Colin. They're assholes, so steer clear of them.

Grady smirked. "Yeah, I just met Colin."

"Just keep your distance. He's got a short fuse and a mean right hook."

"I'll keep that in mind."

Matt moved ahead to the other door, further down the hall. "I'm going to put you in the smaller dressing room with Lewis. He's my other traveling dancer."

Grady followed him down the hall. "Burt told me six days a week, two shows a night."

"That's right," Matt affirmed. "Tips off the stage are yours. Whether you want to share that with the waitstaff, I leave up to the dancers … though most guys do." He paused before the last door in the austere hallway. "I pay for your drinks, as long as it ain't call brands or champagne." Matt rolled his eyes. "I had a French guy here, a few weeks back, who insisted on champagne every night before a show. Needless to say, he didn't last long. Damn champagne cost me more than his show brought in." He pushed the door open.

After stepping inside, he hit a light switch to the left, bathing the room in a dull, yellow glow.

Grady took in the four bare red-bricked walls, two wooden chairs, and a dressing table complete with one slightly cracked mirror. Above, a ceiling fan with three light bulbs behind an amber bowl illuminated the room.

"It ain't much, but what else do you guys need?" Matt Harrison told him with a raspy chuckle. "I ran women's strip clubs for years. The demands they had for dressing room décor and furniture almost drove me as batty as their backstage catfights. You guys have been an absolute dream compared to the women."

Grady entered the room and caught sight of the bare hooks on the wall and the dust-covered dressing table. "I know some owners that wouldn't agree with you."

Matt put his hands in the pockets of his black trousers. "The women out front are a big pain in the ass. The screaming and carrying on gets to me. With women strippers all the drama is backstage, but with the men the drama is in the pit."

"Wherever the women are, there goes the drama," Grady professed.

Matt shrugged his narrow shoulders. "Yeah, but such is the art of sin."

"The art of sin?"

"Years ago, in a club I ran on Bourbon, a stripper named Mary Hightower called stripping the art of sin. She said, 'Anybody can take off their clothes, but only a stripper could turn such a sin into an art.'" He shook his head. "So many guys I see going out on the stage just bump and grind, flash their washboard abs, and think it's enough. In the old days, those women could have taught you boys a thing or two about the art."

"'Illusion is the first of all pleasures,'" Grady mused.

Matt furrowed his brow at him. "I don't get it."

"It's a quote from Oscar Wilde." Grady contemplated Matt's uneven skin, the deep lines on his forehead, and the dark circles beneath his eyes. "How long have you been in this business, Matt?"

"Thirty-four years. Got into it when I was nineteen, working as a bartender for a joint a few blocks down from here. Worked my way up through management, and opened my first club twenty-six years ago. Even met my wife in my club. She was a dancer, but quit when we got married."

Grady appreciated the warmth in Matt's eyes when he spoke of his wife. "How long have you been married?"

"Twelve years. I got a four-year-old son and a ten-year-old daughter. She's just like her mother when it comes to wanting the best of everything." He nodded to Grady. "You married?"

He shook his head. "Divorced. No kids, but I'm still hopeful."

"At least you're not gay. The gay guys in this business give me the creeps."

"Not a lot of them. The women figure it out, and they never last long on stage."

"I had to find that out the hard way with the French guy." Matt removed his hands from his pockets and clapped them together. "You've got a good place to stay in the city? If not, I can recommend a few spots I know in the Quarter."

"Thanks, but I got a nice place a short walk from here."

Matt glimpsed the gold Rolex on his wrist. "Good. I've got you scheduled to start tomorrow night. First show is at eight, second at eleven. When we have private gigs, it's a one-show night, but we don't get those too often. We only do one show on Sunday at eight. You'll be off on Mondays. If you need off for family, plastic surgery, or whatever else, try and give me a little notice so I can get someone to cover for you. Burt said you were real dependable."

"I don't like to miss a show," Grady admitted.

Matt smiled, showing off a row of yellow teeth. "Good boy. Get here by seven to oil up for the eight o'clock show. What costumes you got?"

"A black leather cowboy, tuxedo, and a flashy silver-sequined number."

Matt shook his head. "I've got enough cowboys in the show. Bring the tuxedo and that silver number. You can run those two for your routines."

Grady nodded. "Got it."

"I don't have a lot of rules. Just be on time, sober, and no girls backstage," Matt insisted. "I've got enough problems with the women out front. I don't want them starting shit back here."

"I understand."

Matt stepped through the dressing room door and back into the hallway. "Why don't you get out and enjoy a night in the French Quarter? Check out the sights before the club takes up all of your time. It's a hell of a town."

"Thanks, I think I'll do that." Grady stepped back out into the hallway, and Matt shut the dressing room door behind him.

"Looking forward to seeing your moves up on the stage. Burt said you really pack 'em in."

"I hope I can do that for you, Matt."

"Just keep them drunk and wet," Matt clucked. "That's all I ask of my dancers." He patted Grady on the shoulder with a long hand. "See you tomorrow night."

Matt Harrison strutted back toward the stage, pulling his cell phone from his pocket as he went.

Grady waited until his new boss had walked out the stage door. He shook his head and then sped down the hallway, eager to get out of the club and mute the cheap and dirty feeling gnawing at the pit of his stomach.

Another sleazy club; another slimy owner.

Once outside, Grady reveled in the sizzling lights of Bourbon Street. Everywhere he turned there were people along the seedy, smelly street, soaking up the heady atmosphere of music, drinking a plethora of alcoholic concoctions, and peeking into the open doors of the numerous strip clubs.

At one of the clubs that touted male dancers on its billboard, Grady saw bouncers the size of tree trunks luring female patrons inside. He was about to go in and check out the competition when he spied a couple walking by carrying paper cups adorned with the green Pat O'Brien's logo. Stopping once to ask directions, Grady eventually found the green and white sign of Pat O'Brien's hanging from beneath a balcony on St. Peter Street. He passed another muscular doorman and entered a red-bricked carriageway. The first open doorway he came to had a sign with Main Bar above it.

After stepping inside, a rush of cigarette smoke and noise hit him. The stale, recirculated air reeked of beer and the faint hint of bleach. The dimly lit room was decorated with hundreds of beer steins hanging from the ceiling, champagne bottle wall lamps, and mirrored bar backs bordered with ornate ironwork. The room had a cozy feel, appearing more as a neighborhood bar than a tourist-driven destination. There was even an old-time jukebox belting out favorite tunes from decades gone by.

As he made his way through the mass of people to the long bar, Grady kept an eye out for Doug. He quickly discovered his head of short-cropped black hair near the end of the bar. Dressed in a long-sleeved white shirt and red bow tie, Doug was wiping glasses and chatting with a young blonde. When he saw Grady taking a stool in front of his station, he smiled, adding a touch of brightness to his dark features.

"Hey, you came." Doug held out his thick hand to Grady.

"First night in New Orleans, I figured I better have a look at the famous Pat O'Brien's," Grady called back.

Doug motioned to the blonde. "Cathy, this is Grady Paulson, he's new in town."

The pretty blonde turned to Grady. Displaying a perfectly white smile, she had smooth, peach-colored skin, and dazzling green eyes. She was petite, but her arms appeared a little flabby in the white tank top she was wearing, and he thought her hips a bit wide for his taste. Still, he would consider her good enough to take to bed.

"So what brings you to N'awlins, darlin'?" Cathy loudly drawled.

Grady smiled at Doug, intrigued by her accent. "Cathy here is a local girl," Doug explained with a playful look in his dark eyes. "She often comes to see me."

Grady nodded with understanding. "You two are friends?" he asked, waving his hand between Cathy and Doug.

Doug vehemently shook his head. "She just visits me. Nothing else."

"Yeah," Cathy jumped in. "Doug's already got himself a steady girl. I just come and flirt like hell with him, trying to lure him away from his woman." She leered at Grady's bulging arms and chest. "But now that you're here …." Cathy suggestively smiled.

Doug snickered from behind the bar, entertained by Cathy's blatant flirtation. "What can I get you, Grady?"

Grady observed the other patrons sipping from tall, shapely glasses filled with the famous red drink. "What about a Hurricane?"

Cathy held up the tall glass filled with the red beverage. "Good choice."

Doug stepped away to mix Grady's drink, while Grady turned his attention to the blonde on the stool next to him.

"So you're a local girl." He let his eyes linger on her tight white tank top.

"Yeah, I can show you all the sights." Cathy happily watched as his eyes hovered over her breasts. "What brings you to our fair city?"

"Work. I'm here for the next four months."

"Doing what?"

Grady paused as he thought of something she would like to hear. "I work in computers. Designing software programs for businesses. I'm going to be redoing the software for a local bank."

"Wow. Sounds like a really intense job." Cathy's green orbs ravenously swept over his open white button-down shirt and snug blue jeans. "How do you know Doug?"

"He lives in the apartment house where I'm staying."

Cathy dipped her cleavage to Grady. "And where is that?"

Grady smirked at her flirtatious manner. "It's on Esplanade Avenue."

Doug returned, brandishing a tall glass filled with a deep red liquid and topped with a straw.

"One Hurricane, on the house," he announced, placing the glass on the bar. "You two getting along?" He flashed Grady a wicked grin.

Cathy reached for her drink. "Your friend's cute, Doug. Real cute."

"I think you have a fan, Grady," Doug remarked.

Grady lifted his drink, his eyes staying on Cathy. "Looks that way, doesn't it?"

Cathy giggled and then took a sip from her Hurricane glass, but her hungry green eyes never left Grady's face.

Grady's insides tingled with the prospect of a night naked next to the giggly girl.

I think I'm really gonna like New Orleans.

* * *

An hour later, Grady was fumbling with the keys to the front door of his apartment when Cathy slipped her arms around his waist and nibbled on his earlobe.

"Hurry up and get that door open, darlin'."

Grady made several unsuccessful attempts to get his key in the lock. "What in the hell is in that drink?"

"Allow me," Cathy offered, taking the keys from him.

After a few seconds of struggling, she finally pushed the door open. When she stepped inside, she browsed the living room. "You don't have much."

Grady yanked his keys from the lock. "Furnished apartment. I never pack my stuff and bring it with me. I travel way too much for that."

"Where's your computer?" Cathy asked, glancing about the living room.

Grady stared at her breasts and tossed his keys to the coffee table. "Bedroom."

Cathy came up to him and slid her arms about his neck. "I'd love to see your hard drive."

"My hard drive? You're a bad girl." He wrapped her in his arms while trying to maintain his balance.

"I bet you like bad girls," Cathy whispered in his ear. "Maybe you should punish me. Do you want to spank me?"

Not another one of those, he inwardly groaned.

"I have something else in mind," he told her, lifting her into his arms.

Grady wobbled a little. She was heavier than he thought, or it was the booze … he wasn't sure. Cathy giggled and wiggled in his arms as he carried her into his bedroom.

Grady deposited Cathy on the bed, and she immediately sat up on her knees and wrestled her tank top over her head. She was eager, he liked that.

Kissing the nape of her neck, his fingers expertly unclasped her bra and tossed it to the floor. Grady had wanted to get his hands on her firm breasts all night. He delighted in the feel of them. When his thumbs flicked her nipples, those little pink nubs became erect.

Grady always loved caressing a woman's breasts, though he had to admit these were a handful. Unlike a lot of other guys, he wasn't a fan of big boobs. He liked to take in the whole package with a woman, not just her tits.

Cathy hungrily began undoing the buttons on his long-sleeved shirt. Her frenzied movements added to his desire. Grady just hoped her enthusiasm was a prelude of things to come.

He raised his lips to her ear and whispered, "What do you like?"

She pushed the shirt over his shoulders, her eyes scrutinizing his carved chest. Running her hands over his muscular shoulders and ripped abs, she raised her green eyes to him.

"Do it real hard, don't be gentle. You can even tie me up if you want."

"I'll see what I can do," he chuckled.

She tugged at the zipper on his jeans. "Just don't leave any bruises. My dad asks a lot of questions when he sees bruises."

Her dad? That was a buzz kill. He waited by the edge of the bed while she pushed his jeans and briefs down his hips. Cathy's lips settled over his right nipple, and then she sank her teeth into him.

Grady winced slightly at her exuberant bite. Then, her mouth started traveling down his chest and stomach until she lowered her mouth over his erection. When she began licking his tip, he eased his head back and his knees settled against the bed. Before long, Cathy had her mouth riding up and down his shaft.

Christ, he loved it when a woman went down on him. Her wet mouth on his cock was better than her tits. He could feel the stirrings of an orgasm beginning. Wanting to hurry up and get inside of her, he raised her head off his cock and pushed her back on the bed.

It took a good bit of tugging to get the tight jeans down her ample hips, and all the while Cathy kept giggling. Yeah, the giggling was starting to get to him.

After he threw her pink underwear and jeans to the floor, he drank in her creamy white skin and shaved crotch. He dipped his fingers between her legs and felt her wetness.

"You're ready for me, baby, aren't you?"

Sitting up on her elbows, Cathy's saucy green eyes confronted him. "You need to put on a condom. I got some in my purse."

The mood momentarily broken, he nodded in agreement. "Yeah, hold on. They're in my wallet."

Grady climbed off the bed. He retrieved his wallet from his jeans and pulled out two foil packs of condoms.

Cathy flipped over on her stomach and then raised her hips in the air. "Fuck me from behind. Hard and fast."

Grady ripped open a condom package, watching the girl's round, white ass gyrate in front of him. After carefully slipping on the condom, Grady kneeled behind her and stroked her wet folds.

"Get ready for me," he murmured, and spread her open with his fingers.

He grunted when he entered her with one hard push. Her wet flesh molded around him. Shit, she was tight.

Cathy moaned beneath him. "Come on, baby. Do it harder."

He pulled out of her and thrust into her even harder than before. This time Cathy's body trembled.

"Yeah, that's it," she squealed.

Grady shook his head slightly, amused by the noises she was making. He pulled out and drove himself hard and fast into her once more. Cathy squealed again and Grady tried not to laugh.

He had heard of squealers, but had never fucked one before. He had fucked screamers, moaners, and the kind that never said a word, but he had never heard sounds from a woman quite like this.

As he began to ram into her with all of his might, Cathy's squeals of pleasure soon reverberated throughout the bedroom. Grady was concerned the noise would travel up to the third floor and disturb his landlord. As her squealing grew louder, Grady entertained the notion of putting his hand over the woman's mouth, but then decided to hell with it; he would just hurry up and get her out of his apartment.

Slamming his hips into her, he rubbed his fingers along her clit to get her to come faster. The squeals were getting louder, so he figured she must be close. As he felt his climax speedily surging forward, Cathy suddenly cried out for him to stop.

Confused, Grady backed out of her and watched as the girl rolled over on her back. "Now do missionary," Cathy ordered.

Slightly perturbed by her sudden change in positions, and with his balls beginning to ache, he quickly draped her legs around his waist and was about to enter her when she breathlessly said, "Tie my hands."

She placed her hands above her head, but instead of tying them, Grady just held her hands in place. "Pretend they're tied," he grumbled, and quickly thrust into her.

Soon Cathy was squealing with abandon, making Grady more determined to get her out of his apartment as soon as he could.

With one unexpected yelp, Cathy began bucking beneath him. Her outburst scared Grady to death. He was about to give up on coming at all when Cathy locked her legs around him.

"Come on, keep going, make me come again," she shouted at him.

Wondering when this night was going to end, Grady kept pounding into her and Cathy's squeals of passion returned. With her second climax, Cathy screamed into his ear, almost bursting Grady's eardrum.

Fed up with her obnoxious noises, he held her hips in place and slammed into her until he finally came. After, Grady was panting for breath with Cathy's chubby arms tightly clasped around his neck.

"That was wonderful," she praised and grabbed his ass, digging her long fingernails into his flesh.

Wincing, he pulled away from her and rolled over to his side. Terrified that she might want to go again, Grady checked his watch while formulating a lie to get her to leave.

"Where's your car?"

Cathy grabbed at him before he could stand from the bed. "How about another go?"

He inwardly cringed. "I can't. I've got an early meeting at the bank. If I you stay, I'll be too tired to do my job. Perhaps we can do this some other night, when I don't have to get up so early for work."

Cathy pouted, appearing disappointed. Seconds later, the unhappy face was gone and she shrugged her shoulders. "I'm free this weekend."

Grady put on one of his stage smiles. "I'd like that."

Cathy climbed from the bed. "I parked by Jax Brewery, in one of the pay lots."

"I'll drive you back and make sure you get to your car safe, all right?" he suggested, standing from the bed.

She nodded and picked up her tank top from the floor. "That would be great, Grady."

After dressing and ushering her out of his apartment, Grady took her hand and led her to the second-floor landing. Cathy giggled behind him when he pulled her down the stairs. Just as he was about to take the last step to the first floor, one of the front oak and glass doors opened and someone stepped inside.

He silently cursed his luck. A shadow crossed the threshold, and when the light from the beaded chandelier above illuminated the face coming through the doors, Grady wanted to curl into a ball and hide.

"Well, well," Al chirped, her disapproving gray eyes all over Cathy and Grady. "I'm surprised to find you here, Grady."

But Grady wasn't listening to a word she said. His eyes were too busy drinking in the red sheath dress that clung to her curves. The high-heeled black pumps she wore accentuated the muscular curve of her slender legs. Her long blonde hair was fashioned into a twist, and her face was tastefully made-up, accentuating her exquisite cheekbones, smooth, pale skin, and pink lips.

"Hi," Cathy spoke out, making up for Grady's silence. "I'm Cathy."

"Hello, Cathy." Al's eyes disdainfully swept over the younger woman. Then, she turned to Grady. "I'm glad to see you are making friends." She shot him a cocky grin and headed for the stairs.

Son of a bitch! Grady's humiliation was complete. The one person he had not wanted to encounter ended up coming through the front doors at precisely the wrong moment.

"Who was that?" Cathy whispered when Al was halfway up the staircase.

"My landlord." Grady pushed her out the doors.

When they walked through the black gate, Cathy worked her arm around Grady's waist and began making plans for their next date.

"Maybe we could meet up at Pat O'Brien's again, and then grab a bite to eat at this great little place I know that has the best ...." Grady tuned out the rest.

His mind was fixated on Al in that clingy dress. He did not know what affected him more: the way she had looked, the grin on her pink lips, or the condescending way her gray eyes had ripped into Cathy. He remembered what Doug had told him about Al having a boyfriend, and Grady considered if she had been coming in from a night out with him. His thoughts quickly became mired with images of the kind of man Al would prefer.

As they made their way to his car parked on Esplanade Avenue, Cathy continued to ramble on, but Grady paid her little heed. He was completely preoccupied with Al. He hated to admit it, but there was something about the woman that was getting under his skin. By the time they reached his gray Honda Accord, Grady had decided that he needed to spend a little time learning more about the prickly woman who detested being called Allison. After all, she was different from the usual flurry of women he encountered on the road. He opened the car door for Cathy and sighed. Perhaps Al would be a welcomed diversion in his life.

Grady felt that familiar kick in his gut. It was the same sensation he used to get when he was faced with an intriguing challenge. It had been a long time since something, or someone, had turned him on like that. While making his way around to his car door, Grady was relieved by the awakening of his dormant enthusiasm. Maybe things were finally starting to look up for him, and the numbing monotony that had filled his empty life for the past four years was about to change. God, he hoped so. What he wanted more than anything was a new life … and someone to share it with.

Chapter 4

The next morning, Grady spent half an hour trying to write a note to leave under Al's door, telling her of his desire for off-street parking in the rear of the house. He had written and rewritten the note on the blue sticky pad about a dozen times, but none of his drafts seemed appropriate.

"I should have paid attention in English lit." He crumpled another piece of blue paper in his hand.

Finally, after ten revisions, Grady felt he had the right amount of humor and wit in his note to appeal to his discriminating landlord. Shrugging on a fresh T-shirt, he stepped into the hallway to make the trek up the stairs to the third floor.

As he stood on the second-floor landing and gazed up the flight of stairs to the third floor, his stomach curled into knots. What in the hell was wrong with him? Never had he experienced such trepidation with a woman before. Well, that wasn't completely true. He had felt the same about his first date with Emma, his ex-wife.

While climbing the steps, he reflected back on the way he had changed outfits—about ten times—before setting out for their first dinner at some forgotten restaurant. The daughter of a Navy admiral, Emma had been funny, athletic, and tough … all the things he had craved in a woman.

"The only problem was she was also promiscuous as shit," he muttered as Al's apartment door loomed before him.

Grady stood for several minutes before Al's door, holding the blue sticky note in his hand. With one last heavy sigh, he pushed the note under the door. Unfortunately, the sticky back of the paper clung to the bottom edge of the door, making it impossible to slide it under.

"Damn it," he softly cursed, and tried to force the note further under the door.

The sticky back ended up being very uncooperative. Grady was soon on his hands and knees, trying to use his small right finger to shove the note all the way under the door. He was cursing up a storm and making the heavy cypress door shake as his hand banged against it. Suddenly, he heard the door handle turning, and before he could pull his finger away the door quickly opened.

Grady yelped in pain as his pinkie caught under the heavy door and bent painfully backwards. When the tip of his pinkie snapped, he yelled, "Fuck!"

As he was yanking back his hand, the door fully opened. Grady was grabbing at his little finger and hunched over on the floor when Al crossed the threshold.

"What are you doing?"

"What am I doing?" he shouted. "What are you doing shoving your door open like that?"

"I heard knocking. What was I supposed to do?"

He was in too much pain to argue with logic. "I think you broke my goddamned finger!"

She bent down and took his injured hand in hers. "Let me see." Her cool hands began to palpate his swelling finger. "Now tell me, what were you doing sticking your hand under my door?"

Grady sucked back a painful breath as a film of sweat broke out on his brow. "I was trying to push a note under your door, but it got stuck. Then you come along, open the door, and .... What are you doing home? I thought you would be at work."

Al could not help but grin while her gray eyes continued to examine his finger. "The doctor I work for didn't have any surgeries scheduled today."

Grady sat back on the hardwood floor and wiped his free hand over his eyes.

Be cool ... but damn, this really hurts!

"Just my luck." He took in another deep breath. "What's the verdict?"

"I'm sorry, Mr. Paulson, but your finger is broken."

He smirked at her. "Gee, thanks, Doc."

She stood up. "Come on in and I'll splint it for you."

He rose from the floor, carefully nursing his injured finger. "Maybe I should go to the ER."

Al waved off the suggestion. "Nonsense. An ER visit for a broken finger is going to cost you a couple of hundred dollars, and an entire day wasted. In the end, they won't do any more for you than I can do in the next ten minutes."

Grady swallowed back a nervous lump in his throat. "Do you know how to set a broken finger?"

Her smile added an alluring light to her deep gray eyes. "I was an ER nurse for three years before I went to nurse anesthetist school." She beckoned for him to follow her into the apartment.

What choice did he have? Grady sighed and stepped through the doorway.

Once inside, he admired the quaint, beige-painted foyer. The walls were covered with a collection of old photographs of well-known New Orleans landmarks. He perused the framed black and white pictures and became instantly distracted by the image of a high roller coaster.

Al closed the heavy front door and stooped to snatch up the blue note stuck to the bottom of it. Her eyes quickly read the note and then she frowned.

"You broke your finger to tell me you were parking your car around back?" She held the note up to him.

Grady tucked his injured hand closer to his chest. "Suzie told me to let you know I was parking back there. She said you would tow away my car if you did not recognize it."

Al crumpled the note. "I think I would have figured out it was your car parked in my courtyard."

He furrowed his brow. "How?"

"You have a Connecticut license plate, Grady."

"How did you know that?"

"It was on the application Burt sent me."

Grady's stomach sank to the floor. He had been a complete idiot. Not only had he spent an hour composing a note he did not need to write, but he also had broken his finger by forgetting about the obvious fact that he did have Connecticut plates on his car. He turned back to the pictures on the wall behind him, anxious for a distraction.

"Where is this?" he asked, nodding to the roller coaster.

She moved up next to him. "Pontchartrain Beach. It was an amusement park out by Lake Pontchartrain when I was a kid, but it's not around anymore."

He savored the delicate curves of her perfect profile. "What happened to the amusement park?"

"It closed in '83."

Grady eased his face closer to her and swore he could detect a faint hint of lavender in her hair. "Did you go there a lot as a kid?"

She shrugged and stepped away. "My sister took me. She would go to meet boys while I went on the rides. It was the only way she could date. Our mother was very strict about boys."

"I see. She used you as her excuse."

A heart-warming smile spread across Al's thin, pink lips. "Cassie always found a way to do exactly what she wanted."

"What does Cassie do in L.A.?"

Her smile vanished and Al's attention went to his injured hand. "Let's see to your finger."

"Did I say something wrong?" he posed, aware of how she had avoided his question.

"No. I just don't like to talk about my sister." Al let go of his finger and turned into the apartment. "This way."

Grady followed her into an open living room with polished hardwood floors and a picture window set along an east-facing wall, allowing the morning sunlight to bask the room in warm light. Below the window was a built-in storage bench with taupe cushions. The furniture was modest with a few antique mahogany pieces spread throughout. An inviting modern, fluffy red sofa stood next to a dark end table with intricate carvings of roses on it, while a thick coffee table with brass-covered feet sat before it. On the beige walls were more paintings of New Orleans, but unlike the other portraits in the hallway to his apartment, these canvases were ornately framed. The large room had twenty-foot high ceilings with track lighting set into the exposed cypress beams.

Grady craned his neck upward to take in the twelve-tiered brass chandelier. "You kept the best room for yourself."

"It was originally one of the master bedrooms of the home, but my mother renovated it to be a family room." She waved to an arched doorway in the far wall. "I also have the biggest kitchen in the house. It's just past the arch with a connecting laundry room, and another smaller room that I use as an office."

"How do you get to the cupola?"

Al went to an antique mahogany armoire located by the arched doorway. "The cupola is off limits."

"But not to you?"

She opened the armoire and reached inside. "I don't go up there," she firmly stated.

"Why don't you go up there, Allison?"

Al wheeled around to him, her gray eyes brimming with anger. "I thought I told you not to call me that."

Grady grinned. He liked it when she showed her anger. It filled her gray eyes with fire and made her less like a little girl and more like an Amazonian queen. "I like Allison. I know you detest the name, but I think it suits you better than Al."

She turned back to the armoire, mumbling words Grady could not make out. When Al came toward him, she had a package of gauze, a roll of white medical tape, and a pair of silver scissors in her hand. She nodded to the red, fluffy sofa.

"Have a seat there."

Grady went to the sofa, still clutching his finger. "How long have you been renting out apartments?"

Al took a seat next to him and placed the gauze, tape, and scissors in her lap. "Seventeen years now, ever since I took over the house." She rested his hand in her lap.

Despite the pain in his finger, Grady enjoyed the feel of his hand against her thighs. He pictured those slender thighs hugging his waist as he thrust into her. That excited tingle started in his groin, and he raised his eyes to the curve of her small breasts, indulging further in his fantasy.

"What are you thinking about?"

Grady snapped to attention. "Ah, I'm wondering why you only rent to dancers?"

Her cool fingers delicately felt along the edge of his swollen finger, adding to his excitement. "I haven't only rented to dancers. There have been quite a few bartenders, comedians, a lot of musicians, singers, and even a chef or two. Anyone who needs a furnished place for a short time ends up on my doorstep. I've just got a good rep among the dance crowd. After doing this for a while, I got to know a few agents, like your friend Burt, and they began to send their clients to me. Now, most of my tenants come from the dancing community, but occasionally I still get a musician or two."

"You prefer the dancing crowd, don't you?"

She gently braced his pinkie against his fourth finger. "I like that most of them are disciplined and take care of themselves." She reached for the gauze in her lap. "That's not to say that I haven't had to deal with my fair share of drug overdoses, but compared to the musicians and singers, the dancers are quieter." Al began rolling the gauze around his two fingers. "Actually, the chefs were the best group I ever rented to. They would cook and the house would fill with such exquisite aromas … I even let a few of them have access to my kitchen."

As she finished wrapping the gauze around his fingers, the light from the picture window glistened on her blonde hair. He ached to touch her hair, to feel its silkiness against his fingers.

"You know, I'm a pretty good chef," he asserted, hoping to work in an angle to see her again.

She stifled a chuckle while cutting the gauze. "You? I don't see it."

"I used to cook all the time for my ex-wife. Emma was never very good in the kitchen, so I took a few classes before we got married."

She raised her head and stared into his eyes. "You were married?"

He shrugged. "It didn't last long."

She put her scissors down. "What happened?"

As he weighed the question—wary of how much to tell her of his past—that voice in his head urged him to open up to Al.

You've told enough lies to women in the past, perhaps now it's time to start telling the truth.

"Emma worked as a paralegal for a law firm in Danbury, Connecticut, where we lived," he began. "I thought we were happy, until one day she came home and told me our marriage was over." He shook his head as snapshots of that day came back to him. "Stupid me. I thought all those late nights at the office were because she was working, not screwing one of the attorneys. After she moved out, I tried like hell to get my life together. Then, two months later, I got laid off from Lehman Brothers."

Al pulled off a long strip of tape from the spool. "That's when you went back to dancing and ended up on the road."

He casually dipped his head to the side. "I had to eat, and dancing was all I had left."

They sat in silence while Al secured the tape over the gauze holding his fingers together. Grady's mind raced, eager to find some way to keep the conversation going.

"How is your friend Cathy?" she blurted out.

Grady stiffened at the mention of Cathy. "Yeah, about that—"

"What you do in the privacy of your bedroom is your business, Grady. As long as they are over eighteen and human, I don't care." She finished positioning the tape around his fingers. "But she was a little too—"

"Young for me," he interjected.

"I was going to say simple. Not that she wasn't a nice girl—I'm sure she was—but you can do better."

Grady was intrigued by her comment. "Better?"

She took another long piece of white tape from the spool and cut it with the scissors. "Does she know what you do, or did that even come up in the conversation? Or did you even have any conversation?"

Grady chuckled at her smattering of sarcasm. "No, it didn't come up."

Al studied his blue eyes for a moment. "Why are you so ashamed of telling people what you do?"

"I'm not ashamed. It's just that when you start seeing a woman regularly, the questions begin popping up about the women in the audience, and why I have to kiss them, or rub against them. Girlfriends don't handle that you are a male stripper very well. Eventually, you're asked to make a choice between dancing and dating."

Al looped the last bit of tape around his fingers. "How many times have you been asked to make that choice?"

"Emma asked me. I gave it up for her—for all the good that did me." He sighed, letting his body relax against the sofa. "The reason why I don't tell women the truth about me is because … I really haven't met anyone I trust enough to share all those dirty little details with."

"You trust me. Why else would you tell me the truth?"

He angled closer to her. Her pink lips were so temptingly close. "You have my broken finger in your lap. I have no choice but to trust you."

For a split second, he could see the indecision in her eyes. Perhaps he should lean in a little closer and ….

Arching away, she removed his hand from her lap. "I hope you learn to trust people, sooner rather than later, Grady. You're a good man who deserves to be happy."

"What about you?" Grady inquired as she gathered up the materials in her lap. "Doug told me you were seeing some guy. Are you happy with him?"

She abruptly stood from the sofa. "I don't think that is any of your concern."

Grady sat back on the sofa, noting her rigid posture and downturned lips. "What happened to sharing all of our dirty little secrets? Come on, tell me something about the man in your life."

Al went to the armoire and returned the supplies to a shelf. "All right. His name is Geoff, and we've been seeing each other for several years."

"Does he want to marry you?"

She smacked the armoire doors closed. "No."

Grady stood from the sofa, grinning at her outburst. "Then he's no good for you."

She faced him, her mouth gaping with astonishment. "Isn't that a little old-fashioned?"

"I don't think so. Honore de Balzac said, 'One should believe in marriage as in the immortality of the soul.'"

"Maybe I don't believe in the immortality of the soul … or marriage."

He moved to her side, towering over her tiny figure. "Yes, you do."

Her gray eyes flared. "Don't think that a few short conversations gives you any insight into my wants or desires, Grady. You don't know anything about me."

He rested his good hand against the armoire behind her, boxing her in. "Why not let me get to know you? I can cook dinner for you, and we can talk about all of those wants and desires."

"No!" She shoved his arm away.

"Why not?"

She bolted from the armoire, putting some space between them. "One, I'm too old for you."

Grady laughed with astonishment. "Too old? What are you, three, maybe five years older than me?"

"What are you, thirty, thirty-one?" she demanded.

"I'm thirty-two, and old enough to—"

"I'm forty-two, Grady. Too old for you, and too old to give you what you want."

He was taken aback. At most, he had suspected five years difference between them. "You're not too old for me, Allison."

"Stop calling me that!"

"Mark Twain said, 'Age is an issue of mind over matter: if you don't mind, it doesn't matter.'"

She dashed toward the door. "Would you stop quoting all of these dead people to me? I'm too old for you, and I don't date tenants."

"I'll move out," he countered, rushing behind her.

She opened her front door. "No, Grady. In four months, you'll be on the road again, and I'll be sitting here wondering why I let you talk me into dating in the first place. I've been disappointed enough by men. I don't need to add your name to that pile."

"I'll be different," he vowed, standing by the open door.

"You'll be the same." She waved to the hall outside.

"I won't give up."

"I won't give in," she countered.

Grady inched closer and whispered, "I like difficult women."

"Good-bye, Grady."

He held up his bandaged finger. "What if I need more nursing care?"

She sagged against the door. "Grady, please. I'm flattered that you would want to be with me, but you and I both know that, in the end, I would be just like that girl you left with last night. Another nameless face you had a couple of quick rolls in the sack with and had forgotten about by the time you pulled into the next city."

"You don't know that," he argued.

"Yes, I do."

He decided that he had pushed her far enough. Shaking his head, he turned for the open door. "Thanks for the bandage."

"You need to keep those two fingers taped together for about four weeks. By then, it should be fine."

He walked through the entrance. "Thank you, Allison."

"It's Al, Grady. It's always been Al." She banged the door closed behind him.

Grady flinched when the thud of her front door echoed about the third floor landing. Making his way to the stairs, he thought of other ways of getting through to Al. He recalled how gentle she had been when wrapping his broken finger, the scent of lavender in her hair, the swell of her breasts, and the temptation of her lips.

Obviously, this is going to take a bit more effort than I had initially planned.

Trotting down the stairs, Grady realized there was another problem eating at him. He had opened up to Al about his past; something he had never done with a woman since hitting the road. The more time he spent with her, the more she was beginning to turn into something other than just a passing challenge; she was becoming a possibility. A possibility that Grady feared he may never be able to leave when the time came to pack up his car and move on.

Chapter 5

When Grady reached the second-floor landing, he heard the grand front doors smacking closed. Peeking down the stairs, he saw Doug in the foyer, still dressed in the same white long-sleeved shirt from the night before, with his red bow tie tucked into his front chest pocket.

"Are you just getting in?" Grady called, hurrying down the steps.

Doug glanced up from the envelopes of mail left on the table by the doors. "Yeah, long night."

Grady bounded down the last two steps. "What's her name?"

Doug tossed an envelope in his hand to the table. "Beverly."

"Is she the steady girl Cathy mentioned?"

"It's more like on again, off again with me and Bev." His dark eyes glimmered with a mischievous glint. "Cathy and you have fun?"

Grady leaned against the bannister. "Where did you find that one?"

"She hangs out in the main bar a lot, hoping to pick up the bartenders." He rolled his round, dark eyes. "Cathy's got a thing for bartenders."

"Well, she damn near killed me last night. A little warning might have been in order."

"I heard from one of the other guys at the bar that she likes it rough." He pointed to Grady's taped fingers. "She do that?"

Grady held up his right hand. "No, I got it caught in a door."

"You should let Little Al take a look at it."

"Already did." Grady nodded to his hand. "She's the one who taped it up."

Doug raised his eyebrows, appearing impressed. "Make any headway?"

"No," Grady grudgingly confided. "I'm still working on her."

"You do realize that she's heard it a hundred times before from every buff and tan guy that has walked through those doors." He thumbed the front doors behind him. "Myself included," he added with a wink.

"Yeah, but you struck out."

"I did not strike out," Doug sourly refuted. "I found someone else."

"If you had another chance, would you?"

Doug shook his head. "She's not my type; too smart. I like a woman who makes things simple."

"Does Beverly make things simple for you?"

Doug sighed and shook his head. "Anything but. It's been going on with Bev and me for close to two years now, and I'm still trying to figure it out."

"I don't think we're ever supposed to figure it out with women. When I was married, I did everything I could to make my wife happy, only to discover I had failed miserably. Ever since then, I've stopped trying to figure out where I stand with a woman."

Doug playfully slapped Grady's shoulder. "Yeah, but you sure knew where you stood with Cathy last night."

"I think the whole building heard where I stood with her," Grady griped.

"I was told she's kind of loud in bed. Hey, you get all kinds in this city. It ain't the Midwest." He made a move toward his apartment door. "When are you going to see her again?"

"Cathy? Never."

"No, when are you going to see Al again?"

Grady thoughtfully pressed his lips together. "I'm not sure about that."

Doug nodded to his injured hand. "You can't dance with your fingers taped up like that. You'll have to get it re-taped after every show." He grinned. "Seems to me like you'll have plenty of excuses to see her again and again."

"You could be right about that," Grady concurred, smiling.

"Man, you've got it bad." Doug headed to his apartment door. "Let me know what happens," he called out over his shoulder. "I always love a good melodrama."

*   *   *

That night at The Flesh Factory, Grady was waiting to go on stage. Decked out in his flashy silver outfit, he inspected the Velcro seams on his pants once more … nothing like a costume coming apart before the break away. Then he gingerly touched his swollen pinkie. Having removed the tape, it appeared badly bruised and worse than it had earlier in the day. The dull throb he had experienced with it taped was now turning into a continuous sharp explosion of electric jolts.

"Nervous?"

Grady turned to see Matt Harrison standing next to him. "Always at a first show in a new place."

"They're just the same hungry women you see in every strip joint, Grady. Shake your ass, flash your abs, and you'll knock 'em dead."

Grady didn't bother to enlighten the man to the fact that there was a hell of a lot more to his dances than that. Hours of choreography and practice went into each one of his routines. Luckily, his music roared to life from the speakers over the stage, saving him from any further conversation.

"Go get 'em," Matt encouraged with a slap on his back.

Ignoring the club owner, Grady shoved aside the red velvet curtains that led to the stage and strutted into the bright lights.

The screaming hit him first. Like the backwash from a jet engine, the screams vibrated against his body. The women were packed against the edge of the stage, and as he moved out from beneath the white lights, he got a better look at the pit.

Matt had been right. The faces, the screams, the whistles, all looked and sounded the same as every other town he had been in.

He had hoped this time it would be different. Why had he expected more?

Beginning his routine, he rolled his hips and occasionally made eye contact with a few of the women, searching for his orgasm girl. A small blonde, not far from the stage, caught his eye. She instantly reminded him of Al. She had the same petite figure and pink lips, but her eyes were not as sarcastic. Making a few spins, he checked out the other women, but kept coming back to the blonde.

When he pulled his silver-sequined shirt open, the motion made the pain from his broken pinkie shoot up his arm. He kept his stage smile plastered on his face, but he could feel the sweat gathering on his upper lip. To stop thinking about the pain, he focused his attention on the small blonde. He pictured her being Al, watching him up on stage. Grady could almost see Al smirking at him. This was good. It was helping him get through his routine. He focused on the blonde, all the while thinking of Al, and soon he forgot about his discomfort.

Grady began to feel he was dancing only for the petite woman. He could hear the other women in the crowd shouting for him to "take it all off," but he ignored them. He struggled getting his shirt off, and he saw the lithe blonde smile when she feasted her big eyes on his chest.

Yeah, she's my girl.

Grabbing at his clothing and doing a few of the acrobatic moves he had in his dance routine almost made him see stars as the tormenting pain returned. With only his pants to go, he went to the edge of the stage, ready to bring up the blonde. When he pointed to her, the blush on her cheeks almost made him laugh out loud. Al would never have blushed like that. No, Al would have scowled at him.

It took two of her friends to coax her to the stage, but when the little blonde climbed the side steps, Grady was disappointed. Up close, she was nothing like Al. Her features were plain: her mouth was bigger, her lips thicker, and her eyes were brown, not like Al's angry gray orbs. Giving her some encouragement to have fun with him, he lifted her hands to his chest and rubbed his hips against her.

The blonde squealed, covered her face, and did all the predictable things he expected of his orgasm girl. After he had danced around her a few times, he ripped off his pants—damn near cursing as the pain tore through his hand—then he gave her a kiss on the cheek and showed her off the stage.

A few last struts, flashing his silver-sequined G-string, and he was done. Snapping up his clothes from the floor with his left hand, he could feel the sweat pouring off him. He quickly jogged off the stage and back behind the curtains.

Out of the view of the audience, he bent over and very gently held his sore pinkie.

"Son of a bitch," he sighed. How was he going to survive a second show?

Hurrying to his dressing room, he grabbed for his towel and left his clothes in a heap on a chair by the door. As he stared at his trembling right hand, he yearned for a stiff shot of tequila. Instead, he reached for the bottle of Tylenol he had purchased from the nearby convenience store on his way into the club. He struggled to open the bottle with his left hand, and then tossed back four pills with a gulp from his bottle of water.

"You're not popping pills, are you?" a slender, but well-proportioned, brown-eyed man asked from the doorway to his dressing room.

Wearing only his white satin G-string with white boots, and white angel wings secured to his back with a harness, the intruder was carrying a white robe and white pants in his arms. His brown, curly hair was still glistening from the silver glitter spray Grady had watched him apply before going on stage.

"Matt will shit if he finds you're doing drugs," the young man warned, coming up to Grady.

Grady held up the Tylenol bottle to him. "It's Tylenol, Lewis," he explained to the dancer that shared his dressing room. "I broke my finger this morning and had to take off the tape to dance." Grady held up his swollen pinkie.

Lewis's puppy-dog brown eyes examined his finger. "Yikes, that looks bad."

"That's why I need the Tylenol. Pulling off the breakaway clothes on stage damn near killed me."

"You need ice. I'll get you some from the bar." Lewis momentarily deliberated on Grady's flushed face. "I'll get you a shot of something to go with the Tylenol," he finally added.

"Tequila would be great," Grady hinted.

Lewis quickly proceeded toward the dressing room door, still wearing his wings. "Tequila it is," he loudly proclaimed.

Grady pictured the young man going to the bar and asking for ice and tequila in his G-string and angel wings. He'd be lucky if he came back unmolested.

Carefully wrapping his towel around his hips, Grady sat down in the rickety wooden chair next to his dressing table. He hunched over and held his injured hand. Closing his eyes against the throbbing, he tried to distract himself by thinking of something pleasurable. An image of the sunlight on Al's blonde hair came to mind. He thought about the softness of her skin, how inviting her pink lips appeared, and how much he ached to hold her firm, little body next to his.

"You look a thousand miles away," a throaty, feminine voice called from the doorway.

Standing before him, Grady discovered a statuesque woman with slender hips, and long supple legs jutting out from a thigh-high slit in her fancy red silk dress. Her shoulder length brown hair was teased about her head, making her blue eyes stand out and accentuating the roundness of her creamy face. Her features were not as alluring to Grady as the rest of her. If anything, her nose was a little big for her face, her lips appeared artificially enlarged, and her prominent jaw overshadowed her sunken cheekbones.

"Grady, right?" She sashayed into the room with an exaggerated sway to her hips.

He sat back in his chair and let his eyes wander over her figure once more, debating how she could have gotten access to the dressing rooms. "My boss doesn't like women backstage."

"Your boss already knows I'm here." She came up to him. "I'm Mrs. Matt Harrison."

Oh shit! Grady quickly stood from his chair.

"Mrs. Harrison," Grady said, politely dipping his head. "I didn't realize you came to the club."

"My husband always likes my opinion on the new dancers." She gave him a fleeting capped-tooth smile. "I used to be in the business myself, so I've got a good eye for talent." She paused and her eyes hungrily devoured Grady's carved chest. "You're good. You've got good moves. You're handsome enough to make the ladies interested, but not too good-looking to turn them off. That intriguing blend of wholesome, all-American looks, with a touch of bad boy angst, works for you on the stage."

Not wanting to pick apart her critique, especially since she was the club owner's wife, Grady just smiled and bit his tongue.

"All the women in the club tonight were absolutely drooling over you." She leered at his ripped abdominal muscles. "How do you stay in such good shape?"

"Weights, running, and of course, dancing under the hot lights tends to keep you trim … but I'm sure you already knew that."

She flourished a diamond-clad hand in the air. "It's very different in the women's game. Our dancing is not quite as strenuous, and meant to entice more than to show off our muscles."

Grady started to feel uncomfortable under the weight of her lustful eyes. "It's a tougher business for the women dancers."

She took in the sparse dressing room. "I don't know how you guys put up with such drab rooms. You could use a little color in here, along with some more furniture."

"Well, we guys don't really care about color, only functionality."

She eased her way closer to him. "You know, I have a lot of influence over my husband. If you wanted to stay here, maybe even become a headliner, I could make that possible."

Grasping the suggestive nature of her offer, Grady's stomach clenched. "What would I have to do to get such a recommendation from you, Mrs. Harrison?"

She slowly ran her index finger down the center of his broad, muscular chest. “We could come up with some kind of an arrangement. I’m not a difficult woman to please. In fact, you may like what I can do for you.” Her finger skirted over washboard abs to the edge of the towel hugging his hips.

He eyed her finger. “What would your husband say?”

She was about to reply when Lewis walked into the room, carrying a black tray with a small bucket of ice and two shot glasses filled with a light golden liquid. When he spied Mrs. Harrison, he simply nodded his head.

“Mrs. Harrison, how are you this evening?”

Mrs. Harrison gave Lewis a flirty smile. “Wonderful, Lewis. Caught your show tonight.” She backed away from Grady. “Your wings were on crooked. Might want to fix that before you go on again.” She slowly glided toward the door. “I look forward to seeing you again, Grady.”

Lewis waited as Mrs. Harrison sashayed into the hallway. After she was gone, he turned his soft brown eyes to Grady.

“Let me guess.” He came toward Grady, balancing the black tray in his hands. “She promised to make you a headliner in exchange for a private dance in her bedroom.”

Grady reached for one of the shot glasses on the tray. “Yeah, something like that.” He tossed back the drink.

He winced as the tequila burned his throat. Still grimacing, he put the glass down on the table beside him.

Lewis removed the ice bucket from the tray and handed it to Grady. “She’s propositioned every new guy in the joint. Rumor has it she’s been hitting on every new male recruit her husband signs up for years, and he knows nothing.”

Grady took the bucket back to his chair and sat down. He gently eased his right hand into the ice, flinching when the cold hit his tender finger.

“Matt Harrison doesn’t strike me as a stupid man. He’s got to suspect, or doesn’t care,” he concluded.

Lewis took the other shot glass from the black tray and placed the tray on the table next to Grady. “Oh, he cares all right. Word is, two years back, Matt hired some guy to headline at one of his clubs, but blackballed him when he found him and the missus going at it in their bedroom." Lewis gulped back his shot of tequila and then sucked in a deep breath to ease the bite of the alcohol. "I heard the guy works as a bartender somewhere in the city. It's the only gig he can get nowadays."

Grady's curiosity peaked at the mention of the story. "Any idea who the guy is?"

Lewis shrugged and placed his glass and Grady's back on the tray. "Don't know his name, only his story, but you don't strike me as the stupid kind. I suspect you have no interest in taking her up on her offer."

Grady cast his eyes to the ice bucket. "No interest whatsoever. She's not my type."

Lewis picked up the black tray. "She's not anyone's type. Every guy I've known that has danced here has stayed away from her. Only guy she ever got friendly with was Francois, who worked here a few weeks back, and he was more like one of those gay husbands women like to acquire. She used to take him shopping with her. Matt wasn't too pleased about their friendship. He shipped Francois back to France as soon as he could." Lewis went to the door. "No, best thing is to stay as far away from Beverly Harrison as you can get."

"Beverly?" Grady pressed, feeling a tickle of concern.

Lewis paused at the door. "Yeah, her name is Beverly, but she prefers Bev." He nodded to the tray in his hands. "I'm gonna get this back before Matt finds out I swiped some Corona Gold from the bar." Lewis strode out the door.

Grady sat back in his chair, mulling over the gossip about Mrs. Harrison. He suspected the Beverly Doug had mentioned earlier that morning had to be the same Mrs. Beverly Harrison he had just met.

Grady knew how it felt to find your wife in bed with another man. He recalled many a night when he wanted to beat the crap out of the lawyer his wife had left him for. Sense, and a hefty fear of legal repercussions, had kept Grady from carrying out his twisted fantasy. Somehow, he did not think Matt Harrison would be the kind of man to show the same restraint if he ever discovered Doug with his wife again. The first time he had taken away Doug's livelihood. The next time, Grady reasoned, Matt Harrison would probably take away a whole lot more.

Chapter 6

The following Saturday night, Grady was leaving for the club when he ran into Al coming down the stairs from her third-floor apartment. She had on a fitted pair of casual black slacks that hugged her slim waist and hips. Her light blue silk top made her gray eyes appear even more captivating. She had swept her long blonde hair to the side, but left it free about her left shoulder. As he gaped at her figure, the silky shine of her hair, and the light application of makeup on her creamy skin, Grady felt his longing for her burn in his veins.

"Heading to the club?" Her eyes drifted to the garment bag in his left hand and the duffel bag slung over his shoulder.

Trying not to stare at her breasts, Grady cleared his throat and shifted his attention to his watch. "Ah, yeah. I've got to head over and get ready for the eight o'clock show."

"You don't leave your things at the club?"

"I learned a long time ago that costumes disappear when you leave them in a dressing room. Exuberant fans, looking for souvenirs, take them." He found his eyes returning to her outfit. "You look nice. Are you going out with your boyfriend?"

She crossed the landing and went to the steps to the first floor. "No, I have a business meeting."

He cocked a skeptical brow at her. "Business meeting? On a Saturday night? You expect me to buy that?"

She ignored him and made her way down the steps. "If you must know, the anesthesia group I work for has a meeting once a month for all the nurses and doctors they employ. Usually, our meetings are at a very nice restaurant in the city, so we will be more encouraged to attend."

"What restaurant?" he inquired, following her down the stairs.

"Emeril's Delmonico's on St. Charles Avenue."

"Fancy place, I hear."

When she stepped onto the first floor, she asked, "How's the finger?"

He halted midway down the steps and held up the shoddy bandage job he had done on his right hand. "Still hurts like hell."

She pointed to his hand. "Is that your handiwork?"

He nodded. "I have to remove the bandage for the show every night. I can't go on stage with my fingers taped together."

"Why not? What difference would it make?"

"It interferes with my performance." He took the last few steps and landed on the entrance floor. "I have to make sure the women who come to see me get what they pay for, and they don't pay to see a man with a bandage on his hand."

Her gray eyes radiated with that familiar glint of distaste. "Honestly, Grady, do you think any of those women would even notice if your hand was bandaged? I think they're paying more attention to your body than your fingers."

"You don't know that, Allison."

She rolled her eyes. "Don't start calling me Allison again, and I do know, Grady. Women who go to your kind of club don't care what you have on your hands, as long as they have an unencumbered view of the rest of your body."

He was amused by her disdain. "Have you ever been to my kind of club?"

"Of course not," she snapped.

"All these years you've been renting to male strippers and never went to their shows?"

"I'm just a landlord, not a fan, Grady."

"Then perhaps, you should come to see what I do before you pass judgment on it. The Roman writer, Publilius Syrus, said, 'A hasty judgment is the first step to recantation.'"

"Where do you come up with these quotes? And I wasn't passing judgment, I was stating a fact," she argued, the tone of her voice steadily rising.

"How can it be a fact when you have never even seen what I do?" Grady proposed, grinning. "I would think someone as educated as yourself would at least consider seeing what goes on at 'my kind of club' before they start making blanket statements about what audience members will or will not notice. You have no idea how discerning my audience can be."

"'Discerning?'" she snickered. "Really, Grady, it's not fine dining. It's a bunch of drunk women watching a man take off his clothes. How discerning do you have to be?"

"Why don't you come tonight and find out?"

She adamantly shook her head. "I have my dinner meeting."

"What about after your meeting? I have an eleven o'clock show you can make."

She gave him an apprehensive side-glance. "I don't think so."

His grin widened, knowing he was breaking down her defenses. "Are you embarrassed to be seen at my club?"

"I'm not a snob, Grady."

"So what's stopping you?"

"Are you going to let this go or pester me until I give in?"

He tilted a little closer to her, still grinning with delight. "I am a great pester…er."

She lightly chuckled and Grady was momentarily swept away by her laugh. Al may have looked like a little girl, but her tinkling, feminine laugh hinted at the sexy and insightful woman hidden underneath.

Her laugh abated and she nodded. "All right. I'll stop by after my dinner meeting. Then I'll pass judgment on your club."

The thrill of victory rippled through him. "After, we can come back here and you can change my bandage for me."

She playfully shoved him away. "You're impossible."

"Not impossible, incorrigible."

"That, too."

At that moment, the buzzer for the front gate resonated throughout the foyer. Al went to the intercom box by the front doors and pressed the speaker button.

"Can I help you?"

"Hi," an exuberant female voice said over the intercom. "I'm Cathy, here to see Grady in apartment C."

Al lifted her finger from the button while swerving her gray eyes to Grady. "Is this the same Cathy I met the other night?"

Grady's blue eyes darted about in panic. "Shit!"

"Obviously you're not excited about seeing your obtuse little friend again."

Perfect timing! He could not believe his bad luck. "She thinks we have a date tonight, or I think it's tonight … I'm not sure."

"Did you plan a date with her or not, Grady?"

"I wasn't really paying attention when she mentioned it. I was thinking about … something else."

Grady had been thinking of Al, but he could not tell her that.

He glimpsed the long hallway to his left. "Tell her I'm not here. I'll sneak out the back door."

"You're not that cruel. You have to tell her you can't make it tonight, not stand her up," Al insisted.

"I am that cruel with crazy women. And she is crazy."

Al furrowed her brow, momentarily lost in thought. "Okay, I have an idea," she eventually asserted. "We'll go out together, have a little chat with her, and then walk to my car."

"What are you going to do?"

"Do you want to see her again?"

He emphatically sliced his hand through the air. "Hell no!"

"Then, we have to give her a reason not to keep coming back. I know her type, Grady. She'll keep stopping by until she is scared off." Al went to the front doors. "Come on."

Grady rushed to her side. "What do you mean by 'scared off'?"

She put her hand on the ornate brass door handle. "Just keep your mouth shut and let me do the talking."

"I don't think I like the sound of that," Grady muttered.

Al pulled one of the heavy doors open and the late afternoon sun blanketed the front steps with its vibrant, yellow glow. Beyond the short walkway, standing behind the high black gate and smiling eagerly, was Cathy.

Seeing her very snug jeans and tight pink tank top, made Grady want to run back inside. Al pushed him out the door, snickering with amusement.

"Please tell me what you are going to do," he whispered out of the side of his mouth.

"No," Al softly returned. "I'm enjoying watching you squirm."

"You're heartless."

"You have no idea," she added, heading down the steps.

When they reached the gate, Al turned the brass handle and allowed Cathy to come bounding up to Grady. After planting a kiss on his unsuspecting lips, Al spoke up beside them.

"Did you come to see Grady off?"

"See him off?" Cathy spun around to Al, appearing surprised. "Where is he going?" Her eyes flew back to Grady, and then she saw the bags he was carrying.

"I was just taking him to the airport for his flight to Atlanta."

Grady's eyes warily veered to Al.

"Atlanta?" Cathy repeated. "What's in Atlanta? Another software job?"

Al smiled, looking like a cat that had just swallowed the pet canary. Grady had a sickening feeling that this was going to go in a direction he was never going to be able live down.

"No, his doctors are in Atlanta," Al pronounced.

Grady could feel the groan rising up his throat.

Cathy's green eyes shot to Grady's face. "What doctors? Are you all right? Is something wrong?"

"I, ah, just found out about it," he told her.

"Yes, he's still getting over the shock of learning about his diagnosis." Al patted his shoulder. "This has been very difficult for him. It's not every day you get exposed to such an uncomfortable disease."

"What disease?" Cathy pleaded, gaping from Al to Grady.

Grady stared at Al, anxious to hear what she had to say.

"You have to respect Grady's medical confidentiality, Cathy. I am not at liberty to say."

"Please, I have to know," Cathy implored. "I mean, have I been exposed, since we …?"

Al frowned at Grady. "We should tell her."

At this point, Grady was so caught up in the theatrics that he was even curious to see what Al came up with. "Fine, I have nothing to hide from Cathy."

"All right." Al faced Cathy. "It's tinea cruris."

The look of horror Cathy gave them was quickly replaced by bewilderment. "What is that? Can I get it?" She backed away from Grady.

Al sighed dramatically for effect. Grady ran his hand over his forehead, trying to hide his amusement. This was too much.

"No, you are safe as long as you used condoms." Al placed her hand on her chest. "I hope you can be discreet, Cathy. Once he gets treatment, he will be fine. I promise."

"He doesn't look sick," Cathy argued.

Al leaned toward her, dropping her voice. "Patients with this disease never look sick, unless it goes untreated, and then … well, things tend to fall off."

Cathy gasped and her eyes immediately went to Grady's crotch.

Grady wasn't sure if he would ever live this down. Next to being found naked at sixteen with Linda Tipton in the back of her father's car, this was the most embarrassing moment he had ever experienced.

Cathy pressed her lips tightly together, as if deciding if she could believe what she was hearing. "I promise your secret is safe with me," she finally said to Grady.

Out of the corner of his eye, Grady saw Al taking in every moment of the mini-drama with an enthusiastic smirk. He cleared his throat.

"That's why I'm getting treatment right away. Once I get back from Atlanta, we can get together again."

Cathy raised her blonde brows. "Ah, I don't know if I will be able to." She took another step back. "School is getting real busy, and I have …. Why don't I call you when I'm free?"

Grady nodded and lowered his eyes to the cracked sidewalk, fighting to keep his smile from getting the better of him. "Thank you for coming to see me off, Cathy."

She nodded her head, gave him one last going over with her green eyes, and sighed. She thumbed the French Quarter behind her. "I should go. Good luck, Grady." She spun around and began walking away.

As Cathy's figure grew smaller in the distance, Grady turned to Al. "Jock itch? Are you kidding me?"

Al shrugged. "It was all I could think of. Anyway, I figured she would buy it. I told you she wasn't too bright."

"She could go home and Google it, then what?"

Al gave him one of her playful smirks. "I seriously doubt she even knows how to spell Google."

"So was that your idea of rescuing me or humiliating me?"

She smacked the gate closed. "A little of both, I think."

"Might I ask why you did that?"

"Because you didn't care for the girl, but still you had your fun with her the other night. Then you act all shocked when she shows up here, expecting you to be her boyfriend. You needed to suffer a little."

"Suffer for what? And I never said I was her boyfriend," he defended.

Al turned to the right and headed along the sidewalk. "Yes, but you slept with her and she thought that meant something to you."

"It was just sex; it wasn't a lifetime commitment," Grady countered, walking alongside her.

She paused at the paved driveway. "I always find it amazing how men see sex as just a rudimentary function, like eating or going to the bathroom, but for women there is an emotional element to it."

"I know that," Grady assured her. "Don't categorize all men in the same bastard class, Allison. Some of us give a damn about relationships."

"How many other girls, like Cathy, have you left in all the towns you have passed through over the years?"

He threw his garment bag to the ground. "Jesus, what in the hell is the matter with you? Why are you turning some twisted girl's fantasy about me into my fault? She hit on me the other night at a bar. She is the one who wanted to come back to my room and …." He stopped and shook his head. "I don't lead women on, Allison. I don't tell them things they need to hear so I can get them into bed. If anything, they're the ones sneaking out of my room before sunrise so they don't have to wake up with me. Being a male stripper makes you an intriguing one-night stand, not dating material. Once a woman finds out what I am, she treats me like a meaningless fuck. I'm the one considered not worthy enough to have a relationship with, and I'm sick of feeling worthless."

Al stared into his blue eyes, weighing his words. "That's why you don't tell anyone what you do, isn't it?"

Furious that he had shared such intimate feelings with her, Grady snatched up his bag and marched toward the neutral ground that divided Esplanade Avenue. He was heading for the French Quarter when Al came running up to him.

"Wait, Grady. Don't walk away angry. I didn't mean to—"

"To what? Judge me?" He turned to her. "Do you know how it feels for people to judge you before you even open your mouth?" He waved his hand down her body. "When people find out what you do, you earn their respect. When they find out what I do, I earn their disgust. Thanks for all of your help."

He was about to storm off when Al placed her hand on his arm. "I'm sorry. You're right. I was judging you. I shouldn't have done that."

He studied the traffic on the busy street. "Don't worry about it."

"I will worry about it. I don't want you to think … that show of yours starts at eleven, right?"

He nodded, but did not look at her.

"You'd better make it real damn good, if you plan on changing my mind."

Grady's resentment eased, and he faced her. "Are you sure?"

She let go of his arm. "I'll be there. I promise."

He blew out a breath, letting go of his frustration. "All right, Allison. I'll be watching for you."

He admired the contours of her face and the attraction that had plagued him, since he had first set eyes on Al, turned from a spark into a full on bonfire. In a matter of seconds, he had gone from wanting her to caring for her. The shift in his feelings worried, more than excited, Grady.

How could such an amazing woman ever care for a man like me?

As he mulled over the expression in her gray eyes, he noticed a slight change in them. No longer did he see the glare of cold contempt in her unsettling orbs; now there was a glint of genuine warmth. It was the first time he could remember sensing anything like that from her. Until he had seen the change in her, he would never have thought he stood a chance. Grady believed the winds of fate had shifted his way, and that the recalcitrant Allison Wagner was beginning to see the man and not the G-string.

Chapter 7

For the third time in an hour, Grady made the trek from his dressing room to the side stage door to check the pit for Al. He had cracked the door and was scanning the crowd for her head of long, blonde hair. Even so, the dim lights set over the pit area made it impossible to see much of anything. Dressed in his tuxedo, he had less than ten minutes to go before his act was due on stage. He was dabbing his forehead with a towel and trying not to soak his costume in sweat before he went out under the bright lights.

"Who you are looking for?" Lewis asked, coming up to him. "Have you got another club owner coming to check you out?"

Lewis had donned his second costume for the night: a black biker outfit with black leather pants, a black leather jacket, red bandana, and dark sunglasses.

Grady tossed the towel to a backstage chair. "No, a friend is coming."

"A friend that makes you sweat like that?" He peered over Grady's shoulder into the crowd of women. "Who is she?"

"Damn, I can't find her," Grady admitted.

"Give me a description and a name," Lewis demanded.

Grady glanced back at him. "Why?"

"I'll tell Teddy, the bouncer, to let your girlfriend in for free."

"Friend, not girlfriend. Actually … she's my landlord."

Lewis chuckled and slapped Grady's back. "You're kidding? You invited your landlord here? Does she know what you do?"

"Yeah, she knows."

"What does the hag look like?" Lewis joked.

"Al's not a hag. She's petite with long, blonde hair, deep gray eyes that always look like they don't approve of me, round face, pale, creamy skin, high cheekbones, and a toned body. She was wearing a pair of black slacks and a light blue silk blouse when she left the house."

Lewis stared at him, his deep brown eyes looking thoroughly amused. "That's a rather detailed description for someone who is just a friend."

"Let's just say she's a friend, for now. I'm hoping for more."

Lewis pointed to Grady's face. "I guess that explains the sweat." He pushed the stage door open. "I'll go and give Teddy your detailed description. He used to be a PI before he became a bouncer, so if she's here, he'll know."

Lewis slipped through the stage door. He stayed in the shadows along the bar and made his way around the pillars in front to the entrance.

Grady closed the door and felt another trickle of sweat on his face. "I feel like I'm sixteen again, going to my first prom," he mumbled.

He retrieved the towel he had tossed to a nearby chair and quickly wiped his face. "Shit, I've got to get it together."

"Paulson," a deep, stormy voice called from the off stage area behind him. "You need to get ready."

Grady threw the towel back on the chair and went to the entrance that led to the stage. As he approached, Colin blocked his way. "You should've been up ready to go when I came off stage five minutes ago. Don't make me come looking for you again."

Grady nodded, attempting to go around the man's thick body. "Won't happen again, Colin."

Colin did not budge. "See that it doesn't, Paulson." He pulled at the black bow tie around his neck, snapping it off. "You traveling geeks always think you own the show."

"No, Colin, we leave that to you headliners." Grady scrambled around him.

Suddenly, a mammoth hand reached for Grady's shoulder. "Do we have a problem?"

Grady turned and shoved the man's hand away. "Don't push me, Colin, or we might just have a real big problem."

The man's dark eyes carefully calculated Grady's angry scowl, and then he took a step back. "Get out there. The women are waiting."

Heading to his mark right behind the red velvet curtains that led to the stage, Grady looked back at Colin waiting to the side and still wearing his red G-string. He had no intention of getting into a fight, but the man was pushing him, hard. Grady never let anyone get to him, especially not in a club, but if he had to, he would fight back. He had learned a long time ago that he had to stand up for himself on the circuit; otherwise, he would be cut to shreds by the other dancers.

Forget about that asshole, his voice of reason scolded. *She is out there.*

Grady heard his music start overhead. Blowing out a few deep breaths, he gripped the red velvet curtains. He counted off the beats to the peppy dance music in his head, and when he heard his cue, he rushed onto the stage.

First, the screaming pierced his ears as the hot lights hit his tuxedo and face. Then the repetition of the dance he had performed a thousand times—in a hundred different clubs—took over. As he seductively shook his hips, the shrill cries of women drowned out sections of his music. Unfazed, he danced on. He could dance his entire routine without a scrap of music and it would still be the same every time. Some dancers frequently changed their choreography and music to keep it fresh, but Grady had brushed off such updating, just like he had refused to make new costumes. To make any changes had simply meant this was a career, and not a temporary way to make ends meet.

As he stretched, swiveled, and strutted across the stage, his eyes kept searching the audience for Al. Unfortunately, he could not find her, so he made an extra effort with his performance in the hope that she was watching.

With every article of clothing he removed, the screaming grew louder. When he had only his tuxedo pants to pull away, his eyes traveled the audience in front of the stage for that unwilling victim to be his orgasm girl. Just when he was sizing up a likely candidate in the crowd, off to stage right, he spotted Al.

Sitting at a table at the far edge of the stage, she was nursing a drink in her hand and taking in the show. She appeared to be having a good time and was smiling up at him. Determined to get a little payback for what she did with Cathy, he slowly made his way across the stage to her table. When he hopped from the stage and landed next to her table, he saw Al's eyes widen with surprise. He took her hand and urged her to the stage, but she refused to budge.

"What are you doing?" she shouted above the music and screaming.

"Showing you what I do."

With a firm tug, he pulled her from her chair and practically lifted her onto the stage. He was amazed at her light weight in his arms, and when he placed her feet on the boards of the stage, he hated to let her go. She seemed uncomfortable when he approached, swinging his hips and keeping his eyes locked on hers. Unlike the other women he had brought on stage, she was not covering her face, turning red, giddily laughing, or trying to rip off his clothes. Al just stood there, her eyes riveted on his. She did not flinch when he rubbed up against her; Al simply put her hand on his bare chest and gave him the most seductive grin he had ever seen.

The noise around them drifted away, and Grady discovered he was not dancing for the audience anymore; he was dancing for her. Swaying next to her, he placed his hand behind her back and pulled her to him. Instead of moving in and then out, and trying to tease his orgasm victim with exaggerated thrusts, he stayed close to Al, holding on to her and gently rubbing up and down her sides with his hands. God, she felt so good. He lingered over her hips, and licked his lips when his hands rose up her waist to her breasts.

Al's body swayed in time with his, and Grady reached for her leg, wrapping it around him, placing her crotch right over his cock.

Al fell against him and he caught her in his arms. Then her eyes changed. They weren't taunting him anymore. They were on fire with a tormenting desire that reached down to his very core and shattered his confidence. In that instant, he knew he would do anything to have her.

The tone of their dance changed. What had started out as playful turned intensely erotic. His hands caressed her back and round ass, becoming much more intimate than he had ever been with any other victim up on the stage. Al explored his thick chest and shoulders. When her hands reached around and clutched his butt, Grady closed his eyes and eased forward, reveling in the hint of perfume along her neck. His lips grazed her flesh, and Al responded by bending backward like a tree in an unforgiving wind. He was on fire for her. His hands ached to rip the clothes from her body and feel every inch of her soft skin.

"Woohoo! Go for it baby!" a woman's voice screamed from the audience, snapping Grady from his daydream. Out of the corner of his eye, he caught the hungry glare of the audience eating up their performance.

He gazed into her face, and whispered, "You are the most fascinating woman I've ever known."

She raised her lips to his, stopping inches away from kissing him. "You don't know me yet, Grady."

He thrust his hips hard into her crotch. "I don't, huh?"

She removed her leg from around his hip and stood back from him. "Not even close."

When she turned from the stage and went back to her seat, the audience broke out in an exuberant applause.

Fighting to stay focused, Grady returned to his performance, ripping off his tuxedo pants and parading around in his G-string. The last few minutes he spent up on the stage, doing his sexy strut, he never took his eyes off Al. She had returned to her chair and was calmly sipping her drink, taking in the final moments of his show.

When the last notes from his music boomed from the speakers overhead, he quickly grabbed his clothes from the floor and hustled off stage, omitting his customary final bow. The second Grady walked off stage, he ran right into Matt Harrison.

"Now that was some hot shit!" Matt exclaimed, slapping his hand over Grady's back. "The women out there went crazy watching the two of you. We should get that broad a job here."

Grady refrained from telling Matt what he thought of his idea. Instead, he just put on his stage smile. "Glad you liked it." He went around the club owner and was heading to the door that led to the dressing rooms when Matt called to him.

"Who was she? She looked familiar."

Grady turned to face his boss. Keeping the anger from his voice, he said, "She was just a woman in the audience, Matt. I can do the same thing tomorrow night with someone else."

Matt walked up to him. "Sure, kid. You do that."

Grady ignored him and opened the hallway door to the dressing rooms. As he marched down the hall, Lewis passed him, ready to go on.

"I caught your show. Was that her?"

Grady fumbled with the clothes in his hands. "Yeah, that was her."

"Nice looking lady," Lewis told him. "Better hurry up and change before she leaves."

Tightening his grip on his clothes, Grady went around him. "Thanks for the advice."

"The answer to your question is, yes. She's interested, Grady."

Grady turned to him. "Interested … perhaps? Just not sure about me yet."

Lewis shook his head, snickering. "It sucks, doesn't it?"

Grady gave him a quizzical look. "What does?"

"Opening up to someone. The problem is that until you open up to her, she will never open up to you. It's a hell of a dilemma, but I think you already know what you're going to do about it." Lewis headed toward the stage door at the end of the hallway, his white wings flapping behind him.

When Grady reached his dressing room, he hurriedly grabbed at his jeans and slid them on over his G-string. Forgoing his customary routine of reassembling his costume for the next night and wiping the oil from his body, he stuffed his outfits into his garment bag. Tossing the black dress shoes for his tuxedo and the silver boots from his other costume into the duffel bag, he grabbed for his blue T-shirt. With the T-shirt clinging to his sweaty, oily chest, he raced out of the dressing room and down the hall.

When he stepped from the backstage door, he searched the pit for Al, but she wasn't at her table. He went to the bar and scanned the room, but he could not stay in one place for long before the eyes of the women in the pit began to notice him.

"She left," one of the bartenders announced.

Grady edged closer to the bar. "Who left?"

A young man with thick, brown, wavy hair motioned to the entrance. "The woman you danced with, she left about five minutes ago," he explained.

Without looking back, Grady bolted for the entrance. He gave a curt wave to Teddy, the burly bouncer, and bolted out the front doors. When his feet hit the sidewalk, his eyes frantically scoured up and down Bourbon Street for any trace of Al.

"Are you looking for me?" Al emerged from the shadows next to the entrance. "I thought I would wait out here for you. The noise and smoke in there was getting to me."

He strolled up to her. "I thought you had left."

She stood before him, taking in his handsome face. "Why would I leave?"

He pulled at the strap of the duffel bag. "Maybe you're mad at me for pulling you up on stage like that."

"If I was mad at you, I would have left already, Grady." She grinned. "I'm still here."

He sucked in a relieved breath. "Yes, you are."

Al gestured to the brightly lit entrance of The Flesh Factory "You were pretty good in there. I was impressed. Where did you learn to dance like that?"

He sheepishly smiled. "Ten years of tap and jazz at Mrs. Armstrong's School of Dance."

"What made you want to study dance?"

"I saw *West Side Story* on TV when I was six. I thought dancing would make me cool," he disclosed with a casual shrug.

They stood beneath the lights of the club, staring into each other's eyes. Grady wanted so much to pull her into his arms, but this wasn't a stage, it was real life. In such a world, relationships took time to foster, and those awkward, unrehearsed moments between two people were the true showstoppers.

"Can I give you a lift home?" Al finally asked.

"You sure it's not out of your way?"

"I think I might be heading in your direction."

Grady held out his right arm to her. Al took it and spied the swollen pinkie on his hand.

"That didn't seem to bother you tonight."

Grady glimpsed his finger, and instantly the throbbing started up again. He thought it odd how he had been so preoccupied, waiting for her and then dancing with her on stage, that he had forgotten all about his finger.

"It's fine," he told her, escorting her along the street.

"It still needs to be taped."

"Are you volunteering?"

She tightened her grip on his arm. "You could come back to my place, and I might even be able to offer you some pain reliever."

"What do you suggest?"

She surveyed the people milling about Bourbon Street. "I have a beer and a bottle of vodka chilling in my fridge."

"Sounds enticing. Maybe you could even show me your cupola."

She laughed, and the light, airy sound made Grady's insides smolder.

"You're obsessed with my cupola."

He adored the feel of her arm around his, and his thoughts drifted back to their dance on the stage. Silently chastising his runaway libido, he tried to think of something to say.

"How was your meeting?"

"Uneventful, like most of our meetings. When a bunch of medical people get in a room, there are usually three topics of conversation: what a patient had wrong with them, what the doctor diagnosed, and the outcome of the case."

"Sounds pretty boring," he reflected, while they maneuvered through the crowded sidewalks.

"Vodka helps."

"How many vodkas did it take for you to work up the courage to come to my club tonight?"

"Two." She removed her arm from his. "I didn't want to come, but I'm glad I did. It was interesting to see you working, and also very enlightening." She lowered her gaze to the sidewalk. "About that dance of ours, I don't want you to think that—"

"It was just a dance, Allison. It doesn't change anything between us."

"Are you sure about that?" She started down the sidewalk again.

He took a few quick steps and caught up to her.

"Is that customary, to dance with women on the stage like that?" she questioned, keeping her eyes directed ahead of them.

"No, not quite like what we did tonight. Usually, it's more tongue in cheek. I dance to entertain the audience, but with you it was …." His voice failed him.

"Was what?"

"Personal. Like it was just you and me up there."

Al curled her hands about his right arm. "Do you like dancing?"

He swung the garment bag beside him, feeling invigorated by her presence. "It pays the bills, the hours aren't all bad, and I'm not tied to a desk. That was the one thing I hated about my job at Lehman Brothers; sitting all day at a desk. I swear I must have gained ten pounds when I worked on Wall Street."

"What if you could do something else? Something you really loved doing, what would it be?"

"Working with kids," he quickly responded. "I always wanted to be a teacher, but didn't think there would be enough money in it to support a family."

She studied him with an engaging gleam in her gray eyes. "Kids? I never figured you for the type who would be interested in kids."

"Before I started dancing in college, I worked as a little league baseball coach. Best job I ever had. I loved working with kids, watching them gain confidence in their skills. Knowing I had a small part in shaping their future made me feel like I was doing something worthwhile with my life."

"You're a good man, Grady Paulson." She let go of his arm. "I think if you want to work with kids, you should find a way to make that dream come true."

"One day, I'll get what I want." He inched closer to her. "Maybe one day real soon."

She abruptly moved back from him. "I'm parked right ahead." Al took off in the direction of her car.

Grady happily grinned as he followed her. He was convinced he was beginning to make some headway with the captivating woman. Soon, he hoped, he would have her right where he wanted. Then, the image of her slender, naked body beneath him made his blood surge.

"Doug was right, I've got it bad," he mumbled, spotting her red BMW parked a few feet away.

Careful, Grady, his inner voice cautioned. *This one could break your heart.*

Chapter 8

Al maneuvered her red BMW along the driveway next to her imposing, three-story mansion. As the shadows from the house engulfed her car, Grady took in her silhouette.

He wondered what it was about her that he found so damned alluring. Like most mysteries in life, he decided that there was no easy answer. He knew her looks turned him on. Nevertheless, he had been with many really beautiful women that had never made him feel quite this undone. It was as if there was something behind her disapproving glances and condescending smirks that ate away at him. Like a difficult teacher a student struggles to win over, Al was someone whose approval mattered to him. That realization hit Grady hard.

Ever since his divorce, he had made a point to never open up to a woman. The lies he had told helped to keep the one-night stands from growing into relationships. However, here was someone with whom he wanted to share all of those sordid details. For a man who had made a living out of selling his looks and moves to a room full of strangers, it was more than a little disconcerting to discover that he actually wanted to share his thoughts and feelings with another.

Al switched off the engine, sat back in her seat, and lovingly peered up at her home. "I adore this old house. When I was a kid, I used to sneak around at night, when everyone was asleep, and pretend it was my castle. A lot of other kids would be afraid of all the shadows and creepy noises, but not me. I think this place is comforting in the dark."

"Or maybe you felt more comfortable with the dark. You ever think of it that way?"

She ran her small hand over the black leather steering wheel. "Maybe in some way that's true. I was rather a shy kid who spent most of my time with my nose in a book. I read to get away from my sister and mother continually screaming at each other."

Grady folded his arms over his chest. "They fought a lot?"

Al's hand fell from the steering wheel. "Cassie was … not the easiest person to get along with. My mother used to call it her wild streak and always claimed she was just like our father. Cassie was never happy in one place. She went through dance school, horseback riding lessons, ice skating lessons, gymnastics, tennis lessons … you name it. She could never stay interested in anything for long, including boys. She had a line of guys chasing after her, and I think that, more than her bad grades and restlessness, really worried my mother."

"Well, she must have gotten it together after your mother died. You said she took care of you."

Al shook her head. "I don't know if she took care of me or I took care of her. With Cassie, it was hard to tell."

"What does she do in L.A.?"

She glared at him. "I never said she went there."

Grady was slightly confused. "You said she went west and when I—"

"I know what I said, Grady," she snapped.

An uncomfortable silence permeated the car, and Grady decided to let the seconds tick by instead of trying to soothe her anger. Two years of marriage had taught him that silence had its own way of smoothing out those rough moments between two people.

"I'm sorry. I don't like to talk about my sister," she finally confided.

He gazed out his passenger window. "That's all right. I don't like talking about my brother."

"Why don't you like talking about your brother?"

Grady faced her. "Because he's an asshole. I was on the road when our parents died in a car accident. Dalton decided to handle all the details of the funeral and settle their estate without me. He didn't even tell me about their deaths until three months later. He claimed he could not get ahold of me, even though my cell phone worked just fine for my agent and anyone else wanting to contact me."

Al edged back in her seat. "That must have been rough."

"That's when I went to Denver to confront him. His wife, Lizzie, didn't want me around. She's never approved of what I do."

"Why not?"

He slapped his hand against his thigh, stirring the anger in his belly. "She comes from a wealthy family in Denver. She and Dalton met at the University of Colorado, and he chased after her like a son of a bitch." Grady paused as memories of his brother clogged his thoughts. "Dalton was always enamored with money. He studied medicine in school, hoping to become a rich doctor, but he had to switch to accounting in his sophomore year because he couldn't hack the science. That's when he met Lizzie. I always figured if he couldn't make money, he'd marry it."

"Sounds like a real asshole," Al insisted with a frown.

He snickered. "Yeah, big time."

She reached for her car door.

"What about your sister?" he pursued before she opened the door. "Is she married?"

Al kept her eyes on the handle of her car door. "Cassie died seventeen years ago." Her shoulders sagged forward, pushed down by some invisible weight. "The ancient Egyptians used to say when someone died they 'went west.' I always found that a little more palatable when telling people about Cassie. Saves me having to explain what really happened to her."

Grady suddenly felt like shit. He shouldn't have pressed about her sister. He had just wanted to get to know her better, and in the process had opened an old wound.

"I'm sorry," he said, gripping her forearm.

"So am I." She attempted to climb from the car, but Grady's hand tightened, holding her in her seat.

"You have an aggravating habit of walking out on a conversation just when it's about to get interesting," he softly complained.

She raised her eyes to him. "No, I don't."

Grady leaned across the car, stopping inches away from her delectable mouth. "Yes, you do, Allison."

Her eyes flashed with annoyance. "Do you think you could please stop calling me Allison?"

"No," he replied, amused at her response.

Egged on by the caustic luster in her eyes and the delicate pinkness of her lips, Grady eased forward and kissed her.

When their lips touched, a heavenly warmth pervaded his body. It was a reassuring sensation, as if she were the long-awaited sanctuary from his world of troubles. Encouraged by his feelings, Grady embraced her. Her mouth slowly yielded to him. Her rigid body relaxed, and then her hands tentatively moved up his chest. When her arms slowly slipped behind his neck, her lips parted. Incensed by the gathering heat in his groin, Grady's strong left arm pulled her to him as his tongue caressed the tip of hers.

Al moaned, and her body curled into his chest, begging for more. She was giving in to him, her hands combing through his hair. Her breath was coming in short, rapid gasps. Then, without warning, Al pulled away.

"I shouldn't have done that." Blushing, she retreated to her seat, her hand covering her mouth. "We can't get involved."

Grady grinned, thrilled that she had responded to his kiss. "Why, because it's one of your silly ground rules?"

She slapped her hand on the steering wheel. "Yes!"

Still grinning, his hand went to her thigh, rubbing it gently. "It's a stupid rule, Allison."

She batted his hand away. "You just don't get it, Grady." Al hurriedly climbed out of the car.

He shoved his car door open and jumped out. "Get what? That you like me? That we would be good together?" he declared, looking over the roof of the car at her.

"You're a tenant, Grady. In four months you'll be moving on, and then what am I supposed to do? Wait for you? Chase after you?" She reached inside the car and grabbed her purse.

He bent down and pulled his duffel and garment bags from the back seat. "It was a kiss, Allison, just a kiss. If we were to get involved, who's to say how long it would last?"

She stood from the car. "Do you usually go into relationships expecting them to fail?"

He stood from the car holding his bags. "What are you talking about?"

She slammed her door. "You sound like you fully expect whatever would happen between us to be over by the time you are ready to move on to your next gig."

He kicked his car door closed with his foot. "I never said that!"

"You implied it!"

Tightly clutching the garment bag, he threw the duffel bag over his left shoulder. "I never did anything of the kind. I simply meant that there are no guarantees. You're getting all bent out of shape about a relationship when we haven't even gone on a date."

Annoyed, she slung her handbag over her shoulder and headed to the back door of the house. "You know, you really don't have to tell anyone you're not interested in a real relationship, Grady."

"I never said I wasn't interested," he called to her back.

She yanked her keys from her purse. "I will not end up like Cathy. I don't want a one-night stand with you. When I get involved with a man, I want a relationship. I want someone to stick around for a while. I want—"

"What you have with Geoff?" he cut in.

She placed the key in the lock. "I don't have anything with Geoff." Al forced her shoulder into the back door to get it to open, without success.

Grady pushed the door open for her. "Then what do you have with the man?"

"We have sex, that's it. Satisfied?" Al blew past him and entered the house.

He followed her down the dimly lit hallway to the stairs. "Why do you waste your time in a relationship you know won't go anywhere?"

She halted in the hallway and spun around to face him. "At least I know he will stay in the same city after I sleep with him. Can you give me that kind of assurance?"

Grady inched closer to her, not sure of how to convince her of his sincerity, but determined to try. "Look, all I know is that I want to be with you. I wish I could give you assurances that I will give up everything for you, always be there for you, but that would be a lie. I haven't been that guy in a real long time."

"That's the guy I want to get to know, Grady. Not the asshole that slept with Cathy and then was afraid to confront her." She moved away from him. "What you do isn't who you are; I know that. Do you?"

Her words cut through Grady like a machete through butter. No one had ever told him that. He had never met anyone who had held up that mirror of self-reflection before him and forced him to confront the ugly reality of his life. All the women he had known wanted the dancer on the stage in their bed. For the first time since his marriage, he had met a woman who wanted the man at her side.

Giving a small snort of dismay at his silence, Al shook her head. "That's what I thought you would say."

As her tiny figure bolted for the stairs, an unknown voice in Grady's head screamed for him to pursue her. Coming out of his daze, he took off after her, determined to take a chance and open his heart to another. When he rounded the end of the hall to the staircase, he came to a grinding halt.

Standing at the top of the steps was Al and a very tall gentleman dressed in a tailored, double-breasted blue suit and yellow silk tie. He had salt and pepper hair, a long face, pointy nose, round chin, and when he looked down the steps to Grady, his dark brown eyes had the same condescending gaze of indifference he had seen before with Al.

"Grady," Al called down the stairs, her voice wavering slightly. "I would like you to meet Geoff Handler. Geoff, this is one of my tenants, Grady Paulson."

So this is Geoff.

Grady climbed the steps, studying the man's hard eyes. He instantly hated Geoff, not because of his relationship with Al, but for his air of self-importance.

"You must be the new guy," Geoff remarked in an unusually deep voice. "Allison gets so many tenants, I swear I have a hard time keeping track."

"Allison?" Grady veered his blue eyes to her. "I thought you hated being called by that name."

"She does," Geoff confirmed, smiling at her. "I like to tease her about it."

Grady gritted his teeth while approaching the top of the steps, fighting a growing impulse to punch the haughty Geoff right in the nose.

"Are you another stripper?" Geoff inquired, with a heavy lilt of arrogance in his voice.

Grady put on his stage smile. "Yes. I just started dancing at The Flesh Factory."

"You're in very good shape. I know all you guys have to be to keep the women interested." Geoff chuckled. His fake laugh came across as insincere as his smile. "You must get all kinds of offers."

Al turned to Geoff. "Stop it. Grady actually went to Yale and worked at Lehman Brothers until the economy fell apart."

"Yale?" Geoff sounded impressed. "Who would have thought? I guess all you financial guys got into trouble after the market collapsed. Makes me glad I went into a business resilient against all of that."

Grady put his garment bag down on the steps. "What is it you do, Geoff?"

Geoff appeared surprised by the question. "I'm a plastic surgeon. Al works for me."

Grady sucked in a sudden breath, feeling as if he had been punched in the gut. So, Geoff was a doctor. No wonder she had not been willing to get rid of him.

"Al never mentioned she worked for a plastic surgeon," Grady admitted.

Geoff casually shrugged. "Nothing much to tell. We do a lot of pretty routine cases. Nose jobs, liposuction, breast augmentation … the usual. She probably didn't think it would interest you."

Grady picked up his garment bag with his left hand, and a nagging feeling that something was not right with this picture pricked at him. For a man who was supposedly seeing Al, he seemed awfully tight-lipped about their relationship.

Grady climbed the steps, and when he was about to move past Geoff, the man's long arm reached out and held his shoulder.

"What happened to your finger?" Geoff examined the red and swollen pinkie.

"I got it caught in a door."

Geoff reached for his right hand. "The pinkie looks broken." He pressed his fingers along the joint. "You need to splint this."

Grady mashed his lips together; not wanting to show just how much Geoff's probing was hurting him. "I had it taped up, but had to take it off for my show." Grady jerked back his hand. "I haven't had a chance to re-tape it yet."

Geoff dipped into the inner pocket of his suit jacket and pulled out a white card. "Come by my office tomorrow. You need a pre-made splint for that. Something you can take on and off, but keep the proper placement to make sure the bone heals correctly. You should probably have an x-ray, too."

Grady took the card and read the fancy gold lettering.

Geoffrey Handler, MD, FACS

When he returned his eyes back to Geoff, he nonchalantly shrugged. "Thanks, but I don't have any insurance to pay for a doctor's visit."

"Don't worry about that." Geoff waved off Grady's concern with his long hand. "I often take care of Allison's tenants. I've even done some work on a few of them." He pivoted to Al standing next to him. "Who was that blonde I did the breast augmentation on a few weeks back?"

"Suzie," Al reminded him.

Geoff turned back to Grady. "Yeah, Suzie. She was a handful." He motioned to the card. "Come by tomorrow morning … I can fit you in between cases. I'll tell my girls in reception to watch out for you."

Grady held up the card in his hand. "Thanks, I'll try and stop by." He slipped the card in the front pocket of his jeans.

Geoff tapped the stainless Rolex on his wrist. "Ah, I'm going to need to pick up those papers tonight."

She clasped her hands together. "They're in my office."

Purposefully avoiding Grady's determined stare, Al headed across the landing to the stairs leading to her third-floor apartment.

Geoff gave Grady one last nod. "Make sure you come and see me about that finger," he added, and then followed Al to the dark oak staircase.

While Grady watched them slowly ascend the steps, a sickening feeling came over him. He fought against an overwhelming urge to rip her away from Geoff's side, pull her into his apartment, and beg her to tell him what was in her heart. Did she really want to be with a man like Geoff Handler?

Instead of acting on his impulse, he went to his door. He put his garment bag down and used his left hand to wrestle his keys from the pocket of his jeans. Just as he was about to open his apartment door, he heard a woman's giggle come from the third floor.

His heart sank at the sound of that flirtatious laugh. He knew it was Al, and he suddenly wondered if he had been wrong about her. Maybe she was the kind of woman who would only give herself to a wealthy and successful man. Such a woman would never waste her time with a male stripper, who only possessed a beat-up car and the clothes on his back.

Angrily kicking his front door open, Grady fought back those self-deprecating feelings that often engulfed him. At first, he had attributed his sadness to his divorce, but with time he realized it had not been his wife that had brought on his forlorn moods, but his heart. No matter how much he tried to convince himself that Allison Wagner was just another gold digger, he knew he was steadily losing the battle against his desires. The woman was doing something he had never experienced during his four years on the road; she was leaving a lasting impression. Cities and women could all look the same to a man without a direction. However, when one, or both, began to eat away at your soul, you might either end up staying, or forever regret leaving them behind.

Grady dumped his bags on the floor. After quietly shutting his door, he went to his brown sofa and placed his head in his hands. Just as his hand touched his head, his right pinkie shot a painful zing up his arm.

"Goddamn it!" he roared, holding out his right hand.

He remembered Geoff's card and reached into the front pocket of his jeans. While holding the white card in his left hand, Grady wondered if perhaps he should pay a visit to the pretentious doctor. He could get his finger some relief and try to learn a little more about the man. After all, years of playing competitive sports had taught him that to win against an opponent one must first discover their weaknesses. Grady was suddenly keen to find a crack in the perfect picture Dr. Geoffrey Handler presented.

Yeah, time to see if the cocky doctor has anything to hide.

Chapter 9

The next morning, Grady was up early and driving to the address on the business card Geoff had given him. While his gray Honda maneuvered through the traffic on St. Charles Avenue, he caught sight of a green trolley riding down the tracks beside him in the center of the street. The elegant homes that began cropping up, right past Jackson Avenue, reminded Grady of all the pictures he had seen of the old South. Shaded porches with white rockers, massive oak trees in the front gardens, inviting balconies, wide stained-glass inlaid front doors, and intricately detailed woodwork complemented many of the grand homes he passed along the way. Once he came to Louisiana Avenue, the GPS in his car began to beep, alerting him to the proximity of his final destination, 3700 St. Charles Avenue.

When he pulled in front of the modern, light beige building, Grady thought the mammoth ten-story structure appeared out of place amid the grand homes surrounding it.

After entering the adjoining garage, it took him ten minutes to find a parking spot, but when he was finally standing before the brightly polished oak door of Suite 310, he began to think coming to see Dr. Handler might have been a really bad idea. The hallway outside of the office reeked of that antiseptic smell he had always hated as a kid. Doctors and hospitals meant needles, and for a boy who had seemed to constantly need stitches, being back in that environment made him very uncomfortable.

He put his hand on the doorknob and reprimanded his childish fears. If he wanted to find a way to be with Al, he needed to spend a little time with the asshole doctor.

Once inside, Grady inspected the deep burgundy leather chairs, profusely paneled dark wood walls, dark moldings, and rustic paintings of the English countryside. At the far end of the room, seated behind a Queen Anne desk, was a pretty young woman with very short brown hair. When she saw Grady enter the room, her blue eyes explored his body with a keen interest.

"You must be the man Dr. Handler told me to watch out for." She pointed the pencil in her hand at Grady's bandaged finger. "Broken finger, right?"

Grady approached her desk and glimpsed the two other people flicking through magazines in the waiting area.

"How did you know?" he asked, holding up his bandaged fingers.

"Dr. Handler said you were a friend of Al's." She momentarily ogled his broad chest. "I'll take you back to x-ray."

Grady waved at her desk. "Do you need me to fill out any forms?"

She stood from her chair. "Nah, Dr. Handler told me to bring you in the back, as soon as you got here." She smiled for him. "I'm Jessica, by the way."

"I'm Grady, Grady Paulson."

"Come with me, Mr. Paulson." Jessica went to a dark door to her right and opened it for him. "You live at Al's place?"

Grady came up to the door, smiling. "Yeah. Do you know Al well?"

Jessica shrugged and walked through the door. "Not really. She works back in the OR, and I work the front desk. We just see each other in the break room, from time to time, but she seems real nice." She gestured down a white-tiled hall with doors on either side. "We're going all the way down this hall and to the left."

Grady followed as Jessica moved ahead of him. "I met Dr. Handler at Al's place last night. They seem to be good friends."

"Al has been putting up with Dr. Handler for over ten years in our OR. She has a way with him that the other OR staff don't."

"I don't understand." He came to the end of the hall. "She has a way with him?"

"She can talk to him when he is in a bad mood. Everyone else in the office steers clear of him, but Al can calm him down. He listens to her, more than anyone else here." She waved to a pair of dark double doors on her right. "Through there," she added.

Grady ambled toward the doors and noticed that the antiseptic smell he had detected outside of the office was getting stronger. When he pushed the double doors open, the bright light of the large room beyond briefly startled him.

It was a stark white area with four stalls filled with hospital beds, along with an array of IV poles, heart monitors mounted on the walls beside the beds, oxygen taps in the walls, and rolling plastic cabinets made up of red drawers located next to each of the beds.

"Our recovery area," Jessica informed him.

"Is Al around?" Grady inquired.

"She's in the OR, working on a case with Dr. Handler."

"Will she be free any time soon?"

"No. They've got a full morning of surgeries." She passed the four stalls until she came to a heavy metal door. "This is x-ray."

Jessica opened the door and stuck her head inside. "Ed, that broken finger Doc Handler told you about is here."

Jessica turned back to Grady while holding the heavy door open for him. "Ed is the x-ray tech who is going to take your films."

Grady stepped through the door. "Thanks, Jessica."

"No problem." She let the door close behind him.

Grady stood in the stark, gray room as an uncomfortable shiver passed through him. When his eyes landed on the metal table and the tall x-ray machine in the middle of the room, his childhood fears returned.

"Hey, you're the broken finger?" a man's voice said behind Grady.

Grady spun around to see a bald man, dressed in green scrubs and wearing square-framed glasses, stepping out from behind a thick metal partition in the corner of the room.

Grady held up his bandaged fingers to the man. “That’s me.”

* * *

After getting his hand x-rayed, Grady was taken to an exam room, where a pretty nurse with green eyes gave him a metal splint and showed him how to place it on his finger. When she was done, Grady was promptly deposited on a chair in front of Dr. Handler’s monstrous desk.

The man’s office reminded Grady of the overbearing surgeon he had met the night before. His desk was a heavy, cherry-stained Napoleon era piece with gold-tipped corners, exquisite carvings of intertwined grape vines bursting with grapes, and a gold-plated desk set. On the walls hung numerous framed degrees, accommodations from the city of New Orleans, recognitions from a variety of medical associations, plus an assortment of magazine articles touting the good doctor’s talents. However, it was the framed family portraits on a bookcase behind Geoff’s desk that interested Grady more than the accolades on the wall.

In one photograph were two brown-haired girls with round brown eyes, holding on to stuffed bunnies. In another, the same two girls appeared older, perhaps their early teens, and were holding on to golden puppies. Situated between the portraits was a single picture of a beautiful woman with long brown hair, round, brown eyes, and wrapped in the arms of Dr. Geoffrey Handler.

“I got your x-rays,” Geoff Handler’s very deep voice called as he entered the office.

Grady lowered his gaze from the photographs and waited as Geoff closed his office door and went behind his desk. He was wearing a starched long white coat with his name and credentials stitched on to the right breast. Beneath his white coat, wrinkled dark green scrubs peeked out. A hint of citrusy sandalwood cologne followed him across the room, and Grady thought it prideful to reek of something so potent at ten in the morning. As Geoff had a seat in the black leather chair, he held up an x-ray image of a hand to the fluorescent lights, pretending to exam the puzzle of bones pictured on it.

"Well, you definitely broke your finger." Geoff then tossed the film to his desk.

"Was there any doubt about that, Dr. Handler?"

Geoff sat back in his chair and folded his hands in front of him. His cautious brown eyes seemed to study Grady for a moment before he spoke. "I wanted to talk to you about last night. After we left you on the stairs, Allison told me that you knew about our relationship."

Grady nodded and then directed his eyes to the portraits behind his desk. "How long have you been married?"

"Eighteen years."

"How long have you been sleeping with Allison?"

Blowing out a long breath, Geoff put his hands on the desktop. "Allison may have a lot of faith in you, but I don't. My wife already knows about Allison, and is happy with the arrangement. I take care of her financially, and we stay together for our daughters." He glowered at Grady. "So don't think you can blackmail me or Allison with any of this."

"Blackmail?" Grady challenged, raising his voice. "Is that what you think I'm here for?"

"I've been dealing with Allison's vagabond tenants for years, and you wouldn't be the first to try to blackmail either one of us. I don't like the element she keeps at that house. I have tried, in vain, to get her to stop letting rooms to people like you. I will not have you hurt Allison, me, or my family."

Grady tilted forward in his chair. "I didn't come here to blackmail you, and I would certainly never want to harm Allison." He held up his injured hand. "I came to take you up on your offer to help me with my finger."

Geoff gave him an audacious grin. "We both know that's not true."

Grady analyzed the man's cool, pretentious looks. "The truth? I came here to find out what kind of man you are."

"What do you think you've learned?"

"That you're not worthy of her."

"Worthy?" Geoff snickered. "I don't know what your game is, Grady, but a woman like Allison is way out of your league. You're a stripper. You parade around naked in front of women for money. If anybody is not worthy of her, it's you."

"Do you love her?"

"That is none of your business," Geoff snarled.

"I think that pretty much answers my question." Grady stood from his chair.

Geoff slapped his hand on his desk. "She doesn't want anything more than what we have. If you knew her like I do, you would see that this is her choice. She wants it this way."

"If you loved her, you would never have allowed her to make that choice." Grady turned for the door and then paused. "Thank you for the medical help," he added, holding up his right hand.

"You know, she asked me not to see you last night. She said explaining how things are between us would not change anything, because in four months you would be gone," Geoff asserted from his chair.

Grady went to the door and placed his hand on the knob. "She's right. It doesn't change anything, but I needed to hear it from you." He opened the door and stepped into the hall.

Keeping his eyes to the ground, Grady walked directly out of the office, and did not look up until he reached his car. When he finally viewed St. Charles Avenue from his fourth floor parking spot, he let go of his anger.

"Fuck!"

How could she be with such an empty shell of a man … and a married one at that? Grady could not accept the fact that Al had turned out to be like all the other women he had known. He had believed her to be kindred spirit. Like Grady, her life had fallen short of her dreams. Perhaps thinking herself unworthy, she had settled for a married man, but Grady knew in his heart she wanted more. He had tasted it in her kiss.

Turning over the engine of his car, Grady concluded he was not ready to give up on her. Despite his disappointment in her choice of men, he still ached to be with her. If anything, his confrontation with the pompous doctor had made him more attracted to her than ever.

"I just need to show her that she is worth so much more than being another man's mistress." He angrily shifted the car into reverse. "Then, she'll be mine."

* * *

It was early afternoon when Grady returned to the house on Esplanade Avenue, but he was too restless to sit around and wait to go to the club. After everything he had discovered about Geoff, his whirlwind of emotions needed to be stilled. Grady knew of only one way to dull his senses. Maybe it was prophetic that he was suffering through such upheaval in a city renowned for its alcoholic delights. The only question was where, among the thousands of drinking establishments, could he go and get comfortably drunk? He chuckled at his predicament. Usually it was the other way around. Only in New Orleans could one be confounded by too many bars instead of too few.

Once he had packed up his costumes, Grady headed out the door of his apartment, determined to find a nice quiet barstool and drink until it was time for him to dance. He wasn't concerned about dancing drunk—he had done it many times before—and knew the audience would never be able to tell the difference. Whether he gave a hundred percent or fifty, the hoots, screams, catcalls, and applause were always the same, reinforcing his belief in the emptiness of what he did.

Darting down the stairs, he was relieved when he finally stepped outside of the old home. Being within the confines of the mansion was suffocating, especially after all that he had learned. Heading across the wide neutral ground that divided Esplanade Avenue, Grady sucked in the dingy city air and was comforted by the warm spring sun on his face. He tugged at the garment bag he had purposefully put in his right hand, and winced as a pain shot up his arm.

This was good. He wanted the pain. He remembered the splint Geoff's nurse had given him and knew he would never wear it.

The pain would help him to forget about how much he wanted Al. He had to stop thinking about their kiss, the way she had felt in his arms, and the smell of lavender in her hair. The pain would also help him to stay angry. When he was angry, he could think clearly, and try to figure out some way to win her away from that asshole, Geoff.

As he walked along the battered sidewalks of the French Quarter, Grady distracted his weary mind with the tourists surrounding him. Young and old wandered the streets, carrying drinks or maps of the city in their hands. Their faces were filled with enthusiasm for the eclectic Creole cottages, and Grady found some reassurance in their presence. Thankfully, the entire world was not as shady as the one in which he existed. It was good to know that decency still thrived, even if it was tainted with a touch of sin.

Not really heading in any particular direction, Grady soon found his trek taking him right past the front of his club. Looking up at the faded posters of men in come-hither poses, Grady figured this was as good a place as any to drink. At least he would not have to stumble too far to get ready for his show.

Inside, the club was empty. The tables were still stacked with chairs and bright lights shone down on the usually darkened pit area. Grady carried his bags to the bar and had a seat on a worn wooden stool.

Nick Davies was stocking glasses on a rack behind the bar when he saw Grady enter the club. His tall, agile figure strolled up to him.

"You're early," Nick said, looking over Grady with weary eyes.

Grady dropped his bags on the floor beside his stool. "Too early for a drink?"

"Matt would shit if he knew you were here to drink his booze."

Grady rubbed his face with his left hand. "I just need a quiet place to drink."

Nick nodded. "One of those days, huh?" After setting an empty glass on the bar before Grady, he inquired, "What'll ya have?"

"Bourbon. Neat, no ice … and keep 'em coming."

Nick turned to the bottle display behind him and selected a bottle of Jim Beam. "Here, this one hasn't been watered down yet." He plunked the bottle on the bar beside the empty glass.

"Thanks, Nick." Grady reached for the bottle and unscrewed the cap.

The bartender picked up an empty crate that had held clean glasses and nodded to Grady. "Just put it back behind the bar when you're done. I've got to go in the back and check the inventory."

"Sure thing," Grady assured him, pouring the light amber liquid into his glass.

Nick shook his head as Grady filled the glass to the rim. "Man, you're gonna be a lot of fun on stage tonight. Just don't tell Matt where you got the booze. I need my job." He then headed to the door in the wall at the end of the bar.

Grady slapped the bottle down on the bar when he heard the door behind the bar close. Lifting his glass to his lips, he reveled in the quiet around him. The first sip of the warm liquid burned his throat, but Grady ignored the discomfort and quickly shot back three long, deep gulps of bourbon. As the warmth of the alcohol hit his belly, he sighed with pleasure and put the glass down on the bar with a dull thud.

Not two minutes later, he heard the entrance door of the establishment bang closed. Grady careened his head around to see who would be coming in at this early hour. His gut twisted when he saw the imposing figure of a man with black, short-cropped hair, and a lean, muscular body. He confidently strode up to the bar, and it was then that Grady saw the gun tucked into the waistband of his jeans.

"Doug?" Grady stood from his bar stool. "What in the hell are you doing here?" He pointed at the gun. "What is that for?"

Doug's frantic black eyes stared into Grady's face. "Where is that son of a bitch? I'm going to kill him."

Grady stood before Doug and grabbed his arms, holding him in place by the bar. "What's going on? Who are you going to kill?"

"Matt," Doug growled. "He beat the shit out of Beverly last night. She just called me from the hospital. She told him she wanted out of the marriage, and Matt went ballistic." Doug's panic-stricken eyes ripped into Grady. "I can't let him get away with this. He can't keep her."

The alcohol in Grady's stomach churned. He needed to get Doug out of the bar before Matt found him and the situation got out of hand.

"Come on." Grady let go of Doug. He picked up the bottle of Jim Beam and shoved it into Doug's chest. "Take this. We need to get you the hell out of here."

"I need to settle this with him," Doug bellowed, gripping the bottle.

"Bullshit." Grady picked up his bags from the floor. "What in the hell do you think is going to happen to you if you shoot Matt? You think you're going to be able to help Beverly from prison?" He slung his duffel bag over his shoulder and picked up the garment bag with his left hand. Turning Doug back toward the entrance, he shoved him forward.

"Where are we going, Grady?"

"To get you good and drunk. You'll be less likely to kill anyone then, and if you did get a chance to fire that damn gun, you'd probably miss."

"I need to go to the hospital and see Beverly," Doug argued.

"Right after you calm down and think about the situation." Grady kept pushing him toward the club door. "You need to let the police handle things with Beverly. She can file charges against Matt and—"

Doug abruptly faced him. "She's not filing charges. She told the staff in the emergency room that she fell down the stairs."

"Why?" Grady asked, confused.

"She's afraid. Matt's been in bed with the local Mafia for years. How do you think he got the money to open this place and all of his other clubs?"

"What do you have … a death wish? How could you be stupid enough to get involved with his wife?" Grady shouted and wrenched the gun from Doug's waistband. Grady checked the safety on the revolver, a .38 lightweight Ruger. "You're lucky all he did was blackball you when he found out you were sleeping with her." He dropped the garment bag to the floor and slipped the duffel bag from his shoulder.

"How did you know about that?" Doug demanded.

Grady shoved the gun into his duffel bag. "Everyone knows about it, Doug. I heard it from a guy in this club." Grady picked up his bags and pushed Doug back toward the door. "When I met Beverly the other day, I guessed your Beverly and Matt's wife were one and the same." He slung the duffel bag over his shoulder.

When they reached the entrance to the club, Doug slapped the heavy door open and bolted outside. Once they were on the sidewalk, Doug said, "She never told me she met you."

Grady recalled the way Beverly had made her intentions known that night in his dressing room. He reasoned Doug was just another in a long line of men she had lined up to use against her husband. Beverly had no intention of leaving the life of luxury she had with Matt Harrison.

"Yeah, well, it must have slipped her mind." Grady motioned in the direction of Esplanade Avenue. "Let's get you back to the house and then we can both put a dent in that bottle." He nodded to the bottle of Jim Beam in Doug's hands.

Doug thumbed the club entrance behind him. "What about your show?"

"Fuck it," Grady growled. "I'd rather get drunk."

Chapter 10

The light from the streetlamps was shining in through the french windows facing Esplanade Avenue, as Grady and Doug sat at opposite ends of Grady's brown sofa. On the coffee table was a nearly empty bottle of Jim Beam and two old-fashioned glasses, each with a sliver of bourbon left in them.

"Shit," Doug mumbled, leaning over and grabbing his head. "The room won't stop spinning."

"Serves you right, you dumb son of a bitch. Where on earth did you get a gun?"

Doug sat back and rubbed his hands over his rugged features. "Bev got it for me about a year ago. She was afraid for me coming home late at night from Pat O's."

"I heard Matt walked in on the two of you and that was when he had you blackballed."

Doug slapped his hands down on his thighs. "Yeah, fucker was supposed to be at his club, but came home early. We almost killed each other then, except Bev broke it up by putting a gun in Matt's face. She told him if he ever touched me, she would kill him."

"The lady's got balls," Grady conceded.

"I should have walked away then … hell, I did walk away because I knew I didn't need that kind of shit in my life. After that, she came to Pat O's and found me. We started finding places to meet, trying to keep it real quiet." Doug let out a long, frustrated breath. "I've walked away so many times from that woman, but I'll be damned if I don't keep going back. There's just something about her I can't get out of my system."

Grady sat back and combed his hand through his short-cropped, hair. "You do realize you need to end it. She's married and she won't leave him for you."

"I used to think that, but lately things have changed. She's been talking about the two of us being together. She's tired of putting up with Matt's affairs."

"He gets his but doesn't want his wife to get hers, is that it?"

"Not quite." Doug shook his head. "Matt's affairs aren't with other women, they're with men. That's why he has gone over to the male clubs … easier to meet men that way."

A wave of revulsion shrunk Grady's stomach. "I got the impression he didn't like gay dancers."

"Matt Harrison doesn't want anyone to know about his preference for boys. Bev told me she discovered the marriage was a sham right from the honeymoon."

"What about the kids?"

"Dumb luck," Doug reasoned. "Bev told me the kids were the result of the few times they did have sex."

"So why is he fighting to keep her?"

Doug reached across to the coffee table and picked up his nearly empty glass. He lifted the glass to his lips and drained the last dregs of bourbon from it. "Matt Harrison is a very proud man, who doesn't let people walk away from him. He would kill Bev before he let her go." He gently replaced the glass on the coffee table. "She knows that, but I think she's ready to call his bluff."

"Do you think he's bluffing?"

Doug rested his head against the back of the sofa. "I wish I knew." He folded his arms across his chest, closed his eyes, and a few seconds later, he began snoring.

Grady listened to the rhythmic, hoarse noises coming from Doug. Convinced the man was safe where he was until dawn, Grady stood from the sofa. When he rose to his feet he wobbled slightly. The numerous glasses of Jim Beam he had downed to keep up with Doug quickly hit him. Remembering the gun, he went to his duffel bag by the door. After checking to make sure the gun was still there, he pulled out his black iPhone. There were four messages on his phone from the club, probably wondering where he was. The last voice mail sounded like it was from an angry Matt Harrison, threatening to fire his ass unless he showed up.

Shrugging off the threat, he dropped the phone on top of the duffel bag. "Let him fire me. What do I care?"

Grady was surprised by his reaction. This was a new experience for him, not caring about his job. For four years he had shown up for every performance, despite flu, hangovers, or no sleep. In a matter of days, he had lost interest in all the things he had once thought important. Grady knew why he had lost his motivation; or more to the point, he knew who had taken it away from him.

Furious that he had let another woman put a stranglehold on his life, Grady stumbled toward the front door of his apartment. He wanted to yell at her, tell her what she had done to him, or at least make her feel guilty for screwing up his livelihood. Driven on more by Jim Beam than sense, he somehow found his way up the dark oak stairs to her apartment door.

At first, he lightly tapped on the heavy cypress door, secretly hoping that she would not answer. With every knock of his fist against the wood, his determination to see her escalated. He was still pounding against the door when it finally flew open.

Al was standing in the doorway, wearing only a short T-shirt and lit from behind by the streetlamps beyond her living room windows. As the silhouette of her figure shone through her flimsy nightshirt, Grady wanted to groan out loud with longing.

"What in the hell are you doing?" she shouted.

"I just wanted to tell you …." His eyes swept over her body, and he lost his train of thought.

"Are you drunk?"

He nodded. "Absolutely."

"Grady, it's one o'clock in the morning, and I have got an early case. Do you want to tell me why you're banging on my door in the middle of the goddamned night?"

He smirked. "Did I break one of your rules?"

"Go to bed and sleep it off."

She was about to slam the door on him when Grady placed his foot in the threshold.

She glared down at his foot. "What is your problem?"

"My problem? You want to know what my problem is … it's you." He pointed at her. "You, with all your rules, your lofty values, and your condescending eyes. I actually thought you were better than me, you know that? I thought there was no way a woman like that would ever want me. Then I met your boyfriend … the illustrious—and very married—Doctor Geoff, and I realized you're just like me. You're afraid of letting someone into your life. You'd rather stay with that pompous peacock—who will never love you—and avoid getting involved with someone who could give you everything you ever wanted, if you would only give him a chance. I know. I'm just like you. I was fine until I came here and met you."

Al leaned against her door. "Grady, you're drunk and you don't know what you're saying."

"Yes, I do. If I was sober, I couldn't say any of this shit."

She smiled at him, and Grady's heart stilled. "Perhaps we should have this conversation when you're sober."

Seeing the doorway spinning before him, he reached for the frame. "Good idea." He then stumbled backward.

Al giggled at him. "You're cute when you're drunk."

Grady tried like hell to stay upright. "I'm glad you think so."

"Don't fall down stairs on the way back to your apartment," she suggested.

"We're gonna talk about this tomorrow, right?"

"If you can remember that we even had this conversation, then yes, we can talk about it tomorrow."

"Good." Grady removed his foot from the doorway. "Because you and me … we would be good together. I think we should go out on a date. Anywhere you want."

"Good night, Grady." She quietly shut the front door.

When he finally made it back into his apartment, Grady made sure Doug was still asleep on the sofa. Retreating to his bedroom, he sat down on his bed and attempted to undress. He had only pulled off his right tennis shoe when everything began to spin. Before he could reach for his left shoe, Grady passed out.

* * *

He was dreaming of sinking beneath a wave of hot, dry sand in the desert when the sound of his own snoring startled Grady awake. He opened his eyes. The light filtering through the window next to his bed caused an intense pain in his eyeballs. Slapping his right hand over his eyes, Grady yelped as a shooting pain came from his broken pinkie. He rolled over to his side just as a coughing fit overtook him. When the painful pounding in his head began, Grady silently vowed to never drink again.

Soon, pictures from the night before began to appear in his fuzzy mind. He saw Doug and a bottle of Jim Beam, and recalled something about messages on his phone about missing his performance at the club. An image of Al in a flimsy T-shirt standing in her doorway made him bolt upright in the bed.

"Shit," he moaned, grabbing his head.

Stumbling out of bed, Grady realized he still had on his clothes and one tennis shoe on his left foot. He made his way to the bathroom and immediately gulped back some water to relieve the horrible dryness in his mouth. He ran his hand over his five o'clock shadow, gazed in the mirror above the vanity, and instantly regretted taking in his reflection. He looked as bad as he felt.

Remembering Doug on his sofa, Grady went to his open bedroom door and peered into the living room. Thankfully, Doug was still there, in almost the same position he had left him in the night before. Satisfied that Doug was not going anywhere for a while, Grady went back to his bed and sat down. He carefully pulled off his left tennis shoe and T-shirt, while trying to keep from using his swollen pinkie. When he stood from the bed, a brief wave of nausea hit him and then he staggered toward the bathroom.

"First, a shower, and then I'll deal with Doug."

* * *

Twenty minutes later he was dressed in a clean T-shirt and jeans. Pushing back his damp blond hair, he kicked the sofa.

"Hey, Doug, get up."

Doug's dark eyes opened and then he cried out when he saw the sunlight streaming in through the french windows.

"Are you kidding me?" Doug covered his eyes. Then he cradled his head. "Aww, shit," he groaned.

Grady trudged into the kitchen. "I'll make us some coffee."

Doug sat up and rubbed his hands over his face. "Remind me never to get drunk on bourbon again."

Grady went to the cabinet above the oven and reached for the jar of instant coffee he had purchased the day before at the convenience store down the street.

Doug got up from the sofa and wobbled toward the kitchen. "Instant? Is that the best you've got?" he asked, propping his body up against the counter.

"What's wrong with instant?"

Doug pointed to the coffee jar. "That will only make things worse, trust me. I'm going to go to my apartment, throw up, and take a shower. Then we'll go to Café Du Monde and get some real coffee."

Grady put the jar of instant coffee down on the countertop. "I'll drive us there. I don't think we're in any shape to walk."

"Good idea. While I'm gone, you can be looking for my gun."

Grady was momentarily entertained by the way Doug weaved his way toward the apartment door. "I'll hold on to the gun for a while … at least until you sober up."

At the door, Doug faced Grady. "I still want to kill the son of a bitch, you know that?"

"I know, but after we have our coffee, let's try to think of another way you can settle the situation … without bloodshed."

After a few seconds of struggling with the doorknob, Doug opened the heavy cypress door. "Lucky for you, I'm too hung over to argue." He stepped into the hall and quietly shut the door behind him.

Grady tried to prop up his aching body against the kitchen counter. He hoped a couple of cups of coffee and a long talk would help Doug get over his bloodlust.

Spotting his garment and duffel bags on the floor by his door, he remembered the gun. He rummaged through his duffel bag until he found the revolver. Flipping open the chamber, Grady removed the bullets. At least if Doug did find it, he could not use it without bullets. Tossing the bullets and gun back into his duffel bag, Grady then carried his bags to his bed.

After removing his costumes from the garment bag and hanging them in his closet, Grady questioned whether he still had a job after missing his show the night before. Thoughts of unemployment filled his head, but he didn't care anymore if he lost his only source of income. He had saved a good portion of what he made and figured he had a year before things got bad. Perhaps it was time to start looking for a new career. Grady thought it odd how much his mindset had changed. Prior to coming to New Orleans, he had never seriously considered getting out of the business. After meeting Al, he wanted nothing more than a fresh start.

But does she want a fresh start with you? After the shit you pulled last night?

He labored to remember bits and pieces of what he had said to her during his drunken tirade. Grady felt foolish, but then again, he was relieved. Under the influence of alcohol, he had finally disclosed some of the things he had never found the courage to say sober. Al's reaction to him the next time they saw each other would let him know where he stood. He just hoped that he still had a chance, because kissing her was the only good thing that had happened to him in a really long time.

Chapter 11

The green and white awning of Café Du Monde helped keep the sun out of the bloodshot eyes of Grady and Doug. They sat at their table along the edge of the black railing, enclosing the famous landmark's patio, with thick morning stubble on their foggy faces. Perched over their respective white mugs of coffee, the two men waited for their caffeine boost to kick in.

"Did I pass out on your sofa, or did you put me there?" Doug inquired, peering into his black coffee.

"You were sitting there and just fell asleep," Grady reported.

"Was that before or after you went upstairs to Al's apartment?"

"Before … I think."

Doug lifted the mug from the table. "Are you sure you can't remember everything you said to Al?"

"I don't know if I want to remember. I think there was something in there about making fun of her rules … then I attacked her for pretending to be better than me because she was dating a married man. I'm pretty certain I asked her out on a date, too."

Doug took a sip from his coffee. "Never figured Al to be mistress material. She always struck me as a real confident woman who would not put up with that kind of shit from any man."

Grady picked up his mug with his left hand. "Not just any man. Geoff Handler is a rich plastic surgeon with a nice office, two kids, and a very pretty wife."

Doug put his mug down on the black iron table, frowning skeptically. "Geoff Handler? The big plastic surgeon? He works on the city's social set."

Grady put on a perturbed smirk. "Sounds like his crowd."

Doug chuckled at his reaction. "His wife is one of the blue bloods in New Orleans. Her family owned the largest dairy company in the city, Brown's Velvet Dairy. They got a ton of money when a big corporation bought them out in 1993. Her wealthy family could explain why the good doctor is not too eager to leave her."

Mulling over Doug's words, Grady listened to the faint trill of a calliope from atop the riverboat Natchez. "He made it seem like the wife was all right with their arrangement," he finally confided.

Doug picked up his coffee. "That's how it is with their kind. They marry the person with the money, but prefer to sleep with the help." He gulped back a deep swig from his mug.

"Al is hardly the help," Grady argued.

Doug slapped his mug on the glass-covered table. "She works for him. She is dependent on him. Staying in his good graces, keeps her gainfully employed."

"I'm sure, if she wanted, she could get another job."

"But does she want to give up what she has for you?"

Grady set his eyes on an older couple not far from their table. They were laughing and enjoying each other's company, and he speculated if he and Al could achieve that. Then, he remembered the kiss they shared in the car, and his certainty about wanting to have a chance with her returned.

"She doesn't love Geoff," Grady affirmed, turning back to Doug.

Doug rested his arms on the tabletop. "Look, Grady, I love Al to death, but she is in the same boat as you and me. We've had to kiss a lot of ass to get ahead, and give up a lot to keep it." He patted his chest. "I danced for seven years in some of the top clubs across the country. I knew when I got involved with Bev that it could ruin me, but I didn't care. I was ready to give it up for her. I have a feeling that if you want Al—I mean really want her—

you're both going to have to give up a lot to be together. That includes your dancing. Christ, it's hard enough holding on to someone when you have a normal life, but when you do what you do, it's practically impossible."

Grady drummed his fingers against his white mug. "Maybe it's time I get out of the game."

Doug reached for his coffee. "What will you do instead?"

"I could go back to finance. I still have a degree, and with time I could find something."

"Do you even own a suit?" Doug teased.

Grady observed the tourists milling about the sidewalk by their table. "I might have to buy some new ones."

Doug drained his coffee mug. "My hat's off to you, but I know how you feel. I don't miss working out all the time to keep bulked up, watching everything I ate, staying tanned, or waking up with another nameless face beside me." He put his mug on the table and waved down a passing server.

"Have you talked to Bev? How is she?"

He returned his gaze to Grady. "I called her when I got back to my place. She's got a busted lip, a black eye, and some stitches in her chin. They kept her overnight for observation in the hospital and then sent her home."

"Does she know you showed up at the club ready to kill Matt yesterday?"

He slowly nodded. "Bev made me promise not to do anything to Matt. She swears she's going to call some hotshot divorce attorney and get the ball rolling."

Grady ran his fingers across the glass top of the black iron table. "That could get ugly and be very dangerous for both of you."

"Possibly, but at least we can be together."

"Are you eventually going to make it permanent between you two?"

Doug smiled for him, adding a bit of warmth to his black eyes. "All your life you grow up knowing what you want: a career, a wife, a house, and kids. You're just never quite sure how you will accomplish that dream." He paused as a small woman with long black hair and deep, almond-shaped eyes came up to the table carrying a fresh cup of coffee on a black tray. She put the coffee down and turned away. "I didn't go to college, like you," he continued. "I started out as a bartender, got into dancing, and figured sooner or later I would get my act together and have a normal life. Suddenly, here is my chance at normal. The wife, kids, white-picket fence … so yeah, I'm ready to make it permanent with Bev and me."

Grady recalled his encounter with the long-legged woman and her roaming blue eyes. "Are you sure she's the one, Doug?"

"No one else has ever made me feel this way. No one else ever will."

"White-picket fences are expensive, my friend. I know, I had one once. And kids?" Grady shook his head. "That would terrify the crap out of me."

Doug picked up his fresh cup of coffee. "Being scared makes it worthwhile, Grady. Only then do we know it's real."

Taking in the effervescent sounds of a band of street musicians on a nearby corner, Doug eased back and enjoyed his second cup of coffee. As Grady watched him soaking up the lively French Quarter atmosphere, he could not help but admire Doug's choices. He was taking his shot at happiness; even if the outcome was uncertain, Grady believed everyone deserved their moment in the warm sunlight of bliss. When he was going to get his chance?

* * *

Later that night, Grady returned to The Flesh Factory, ready for a confrontation with Matt Harrison about missing the previous night's performance. His conversation with Doug at Café Du Monde had been nagging at him all day. He knew to have any shot at a relationship with Al he had to get out of the skin game, but was she ready for a relationship with him? What about Geoff? Would she walk away from him?

As Grady entered his dressing room, the questions consumed him. He had left dancing before to appease a woman, and look how that had turned out. Yet this time, he was convinced he needed to make a change. He just wished he knew for certain if the woman who was changing him was just as willing to embrace the uncertainty of their future together as he was.

Grady removed his costumes from the garment bag and spent a few minutes attempting to get the wrinkles out of his tuxedo pants. When he heard the door to his dressing room open, he assumed it was Lewis arriving. When Matt's voice rose from the open doorway, his jaw clenched.

"You want to tell me where you were last night? I had to have one of my review dancers fill in for your number, and let me tell you … he sucked."

Grady seethed as he kept his eyes on the man's meticulously tailored black suit and gray silk tie. After Doug's disclosures about what Matt had done to his wife, Grady had a hard time looking him in the face. There were a lot of things Grady hated in life, but a man who raised his fist to a woman was the one thing he had never tolerated.

"I, ah, got called away on an emergency," Grady told him.

"You ever thought of checking your cell phone?" Matt barked. "I called you about four times last night."

"Like I said, it was an emergency, and by the time I checked my phone, it was too late to call."

"I should fire your ass for cutting out on me like that."

Grady squared his shoulders. "I'll save you the trouble. I'm giving you my notice, effective immediately. Take the time you need to find another dancer to replace me, and then I'll be out of your hair for good."

"You've got a contract with me. You're supposed to dance eleven shows a week for four months. I could call Burt and start a whole lot of shit for you, or I could sue."

Grady remembered all he had learned from Doug and he slowly grinned at Matt. "You won't do that."

Matt placed his hands on his skinny hips, staring Grady down. "You smug son of a bitch. Don't think I won't go after you for the money you—"

"How's your wife?" Grady interrupted.

Matt was stunned into silence. "What do you know about my wife?"

"I know she spent the night in the hospital because she told everyone she fell down the stairs, but we both know what really happened."

Matt came into the dressing room and closed the door. "You mind telling me how you know about that?"

Grady folded his arms over his chest. "A mutual friend."

Matt dissected Grady with his black eyes, and then he slowly nodded. "What else did Doug Larson tell you?"

Grady fought to keep control of his emotions. He had to play it cool and not incense the man into a fury. He had dealt enough with shady club owners to know how to talk to them. They respected smarts, strength, and guys who knew how to play the game. Grady took a moment, finding a way to show his hand to Matt.

"Doug told me some interesting things about you. Things you don't want other people to know."

Matt's mouth pulled back into a tight-lipped grimace. "You've got a lot of nerve, kid. You might want to think long and hard about threatening me."

"I'm not threatening, Matt. I would never threaten, that could be constituted as blackmail. I'm just stating a fact that will hopefully allow me to get out of my contract without any fear of legal repercussions."

Matt's face relaxed and he squinted at Grady. "Are you a lawyer or something?"

"No, but I have quite a few very good friends who are lawyers. I frequently consult with them for advice … and tell them of my current business dealings. You know, where I am, and what I am into. They keep me out of trouble and hold on to all of my vital papers. In case anything happens to me, they know exactly how to proceed." Grady silently prayed Matt bought his lie. It was the only bargaining chip he could think of to keep his ass from getting killed.

Matt's coal black eyes carefully weighed Grady's proposition. "So you know lawyers. So what?" he eventually commented.

Grady fought to stay relaxed, while a swell of nerves knotted up his stomach. "We both know you don't want the legal headache involved in suing me for breach of contract. There would be lawyers involved, depositions, and think of all the nasty details that could come out in a trial. I have a much easier solution in mind."

Matt shook his head, chuckling. "You're good. All right. What do you want?"

"Out of my contract. I'll stay until you find a suitable replacement. If anyone asks, including my agent, I'll just say I wanted to take some time off and we ended everything amicably. Once we're done, you will never hear from me again."

Matt analyzed Grady's chiseled features while he considered his offer. "Fine," Matt finally agreed. "I'll toss out the contract, but let's hold off on finding a replacement. I might want to keep you around, let's say as a permanent dancer. Give you a raise, even pay for some of your expenses."

It was Grady's turn to be surprised. He had to wonder what the disreputable man was hoping to accomplish by buying him off.

"Generous of you." Grady reflected on Matt's offer. "May I ask why the sudden change of heart?"

Matt eased into the dressing room. "The women like you, a lot. Making you a headliner will pull in more business. Plus, keeping you under my roof will guarantee your silence. I find it best to keep my enemies close, like that Chinese general guy said."

Grady placed his hands behind his back. "Actually Sun-tzu did not say precisely that. The origin of the quote comes from Machiavelli in *The Prince,* which is the definitive reference for how to be a dictator, not a military commander."

Matt clapped his hands together. "Now you see … that's why I want to keep you around. You're a smart guy. Where did you learn that shit?"

"Yale."

Matt's craggy laughter reverberated throughout the room. "You have to stick around. Who would believe a stripper from Yale? Maybe you should change your act. Put on that cap and gown stuff, be an Ivy League stripper." He laughed once more. "That would turn the women on. Brains and brawn."

Grady thought of some pithy reply, but decided against it. He had enough sense to know not to push Matt Harrison, unless he wanted to end up hurt … or dead.

"Can I have some time to consider your offer?" Grady requested.

"Sure." Matt's face sobered and his dark eyes focused on Grady. "You know, I don't let people get the better of me, and I sure as hell would never have figured you to be the type to challenge me, but I like your style, Grady. If you can keep your mouth shut, and prove you're trustworthy, I might just be able to use a guy like you."

"Use me how?" Grady apprehensively pressed.

"Let's just say, when your dancing career is over, I might want to keep you in my employ. I got some good friends who are always looking for a smart guy to help out."

Grady was dumbfounded. He had never expected Matt to make such an offer. A few minutes before he had been frightened the man was going to kill him.

Grady relaxed the tension in his shoulders. "I'll think about that, too."

Matt gave Grady's chest and lean legs a thorough going over with his intrusive eyes. "I'm glad that's settled. You've got a lot of potential, kid. Don't fuck it up." Matt opened the dressing room door and stepped into the hall.

Listening to his boss's footfalls growing fainter, Grady's rage boiled over. He thought of the man ogling his body and knew why Matt wanted to keep him around. It wasn't for the money or his brains. Grady had been propositioned enough by men in the past to recognize that look. He concluded he had to get out of that club, before Matt Harrison tried to take something Grady was not willing to give.

Chapter 12

It was after midnight when Grady arrived, sweating and panting for breath, at the black gate of the house on Esplanade Avenue. He had just left the club after his last performance when an overzealous fan followed him outside, asking to kiss his G-string. He had run the few blocks to the house, wanting to get away from her. Exhausted from his two acts and his sprint from the French Quarter carrying his duffel and garment bags, he wearily made his way through the gate.

Hell of a night!

Safely inside his apartment, he was resting against the door when he spied a pink envelope on his living room floor. After depositing his bags on his bed, he opened the sealed envelope and smiled when he saw the distinct flowing script of a woman's handwriting. As he read the brief message, he realized the pink note was not from Al, but from Suzie. She had wanted to extend him an invitation to her apartment for dinner to, as she called it, "get to know each other."

Grady groaned, crumpling the pink paper in his hand.

A gentle knocking on his front door startled him. Guessing it was Suzie coming to follow up her note with a more personal invitation, Grady threw the balled up paper to the floor. Making his way to the door, Grady's irritation grew. After Matt's leering gazes, being chased from the club, and then coming home to find Suzie pursuing him with dinner invitations, he had just about had his fill of unwanted advances.

"Can this night get any worse," he muttered.

Angrily yanking the heavy door open, he expected to see Suzie dressed in some provocative negligee. Instead, Al was standing before him, wearing a white T-shirt, blue jeans, and flip-flops.

"You all right?" she asked, taking in the stunned look on his face.

"What are you doing up? Don't you have cases in the morning?"

"The one case I had got cancelled, so I'm off tomorrow." She peeked into his apartment. "Am I interrupting something?"

"No, come on in."

He smelled the scent of lavender in her hair as she walked in the door, and his insides twitched with that recurrent sense of longing. When she reached the center of his living room, Al turned to him. It was then he noticed the slight frown on her thin, pink lips.

"About last night …."

Grady cringed and shut the door. "Please, don't remind me." He held up his hand. "I made an ass of myself. I shouldn't have knocked on your door in the middle of the night. I completely regret everything I said and did." He moved over to his sofa. "I still have the hangover to prove I was out of my mind at the time." He sank down into the brown sofa cushion.

She shoved her hands in her back pockets and her frown deepened. "Oh, okay."

"What is it?"

She removed her hands from her pockets and dashed to the front door. "Never mind," she mumbled, reaching for the knob.

"No, wait." Grady jumped from the sofa and slapped his thick hand on the door, stopping her. "What were you going to say?"

She nervously appraised his wide, muscular chest and then her eyes rose to his face. "Last night you said you thought I had condescending eyes. Did you mean that? Do you think I look at you that way?"

Grady's body sagged a little, but he kept his hand on the door, never moving away from her. "No, of course not. I was drunk, Allison. I said a lot of stupid things."

"People usually say what they mean when they're drunk."

He studied the creaminess of her skin, and without thinking, gathered up a tendril of her long blonde hair. The silkiness of her hair amazed him. He had never known anything could feel so soft.

"From the moment we met, I have felt like I was never good enough for you. You always seemed so … disappointed when you looked at me. That was until the other day in the car, when I kissed you. It was the first time I knew you wanted me as much as I wanted you."

Her frown was back, and so was the anger in her eyes. "You're a tenant, Grady. We can't get involved."

"Because of those stupid rules of yours?"

She grabbed for the doorknob. "No, because in four months you'll be gone."

He held the door, keeping her from opening it. "I won't be gone."

Al arched one eyebrow at him. "You won't?"

"I've been offered a permanent job dancing at the club, but I think I may give finance another go. See if I can find a job here in New Orleans." He lowered his head to her. "However, that would all depend on …."

Al did not retreat when he inched closer. "On what?" she softly implored.

He smiled, his lips closing in on hers. "You."

She angrily pushed him away. "What about that comment about me being afraid of letting someone in my life? Do you still believe that?"

He shook his head. "No. I was drunk and I was … jealous."

"Of Geoff?" She sucked in an uneasy breath. "He told me you went to his office. He believes you're out to blackmail both of us."

Grady apprehensively searched her features. "You know I would never do that to you."

Al dropped her eyes. "Last night, you said … you said your life was fine until you came here and met me. Is that true?"

Grady had to stop and think for a moment. "Did I say that?"

"Right after you called Geoff a pompous peacock."

He leveled his eyes on her. "He is, you know?"

"I know. I also knew he was married when we started, but I could never ask him to leave his wife and daughters."

"Why not?"

Al sighed and lowered her head. "Because I know how it feels to have your father walk out on you. I didn't want to cause his daughters that kind of pain."

Grady set his hand beneath her chin and lifted her eyes to him. "He should never have put you in that position. If he loved you, he would have left them." He paused. "Do you love him?"

"No." She slapped away his hand.

Grady put his hands on the door behind her, trapping her inside of his arms. "Then why stay with him?"

Her eyes tore into him. "Because he doesn't complicate my life."

Grady smirked, happy to get a rise out of her. "And I do? Is that it?"

Al lightly punched his chest. "Yes."

"Good," Grady whispered, right before he kissed her.

It was the softness of her lips that first shocked him. He had never kissed such soft lips and wondered why she tasted so much better than every other woman he had known. Then, as he wrapped his arms around her, the fragility of her tiny figure inflamed his desire. His kiss became more frenzied as his hands began to roam up and down her back. When his mouth slid down her chin and nipped along her neck, Al tipped her head back.

"This isn't why I came to see you, Grady."

"Why did you come?"

She ran her hands up his wide chest. "I was worried about you. Worried about what you thought of me after seeing Geoff. I didn't want you to think—"

He gripped her small bottom and lifted her from the floor. "You know what I think?"

She slipped her arms around his neck. "I'm afraid to ask."

"I think I really need to show you my bedroom."

"I've seen your bedroom before, Grady."

"Yeah, but have you ever slept in it?"

She peered into his eyes. “If we do this, it can only be for tonight.”

He held her close. “What if I want more?”

Al kicked off her flip-flops and hooked her legs around his hips. “Why don’t we just see how tonight goes?”

He carried her to the open bedroom door. “That’s a lot of pressure to put on a guy.”

“I want to see how you perform under pressure,” she giggled against his neck.

“I like the sound of that.” He hurriedly carried her into the bedroom, and then he fell with her in his arms on the large sleigh bed.

“The sound of what?”

Grady reached for her T-shirt. “The sound of your laugh.” He lifted her shirt over her head and his hands eagerly stroked the soft skin on her stomach and chest. “The first time I heard you giggle like that you were with Geoff, and it infuriated me.”

He kissed her stomach while he unclasped her bra. Just when he was about to slip the bra from her shoulders, his sore pinkie caught in the blue comforter.

“Damn it,” he cried out, yanking his hand back.

She sat up and examined his finger. “You should have it taped.”

He traced the outline of her slender shoulders with his left hand. “Later.” He eased the bra from her body and then tossed it to the floor.

Caressing her right breast, he kissed her nipple and then grazed it with his teeth. Moaning, Al raked her fingers through his hair. Insistently, she tugged at his sweaty T-shirt, and Grady lifted his arms to help her. After wrestling off his shirt, Al threw it over the edge of the bed. Her fingertips glided over his tanned chest and abs, making Grady tremble. She gently worked her way down to the crotch of his jeans. Cupping her hand against his erection, she nipped at his neck.

“Take off those pants. I want to see all of you,” she breathlessly begged.

Standing from the bed, Grady hurriedly wiggled out of his jeans and briefs. After dropping his clothes to the floor, he was about to climb back on the bed when Al stopped him.

"No, let me look at you."

Her eyes slowly traversed every contour of his thick shoulders, carved chest, and washboard abs. When her line of sight settled over his erection, that sly smile he adored curled the edges of her pink lips.

"You are a beautiful man," she professed in a voice just above a whisper.

For all the hours he had spent on the stage, dancing for women, it was the first time he actually felt sexy, and not ashamed of a woman's lustful gaze.

"I like hearing you say that."

He could feel himself getting harder just by looking at that damned smile of hers. Anxious to hold her, he was about to climb back on the bed when he remembered the condoms in his wallet. While he was reaching for his pants, Al sat up.

"What are you doing?"

"Getting condoms." He opened his wallet and selected two foil packets.

Al tilted her head to the side, watching him. "Do you always carry condoms around in your wallet?"

Grady frowned at her, perplexed by the question. "Of course."

"Are you one of those men who has a girl in every town?"

Grady dropped his wallet to the floor and came back to the bed.

He placed the condoms on his bedside table. "After Emma, it was a real long time before I was even with another woman. The few one-night stands I did have only made me want a relationship even more."

She lay back in the bed. "Were they all like Cathy?"

He sat on the bed and ran his fingers along the curve of her slim waist. "In a way. They were all women who wanted me more than I wanted them, but none of them ever intrigued me like you. From the moment I met you, I haven't been able to stop thinking about you."

"Ever since I saw you dancing in that club," she murmured into his chest as his fingers unzipped her jeans, "I haven't been able to stop thinking about you, either."

Grady gripped the sides of her jeans and eased them down her hips. "Did I turn you on, Allison?" He shoved her jeans away, dropping them over the edge of the bed.

"I hate to admit it, but yes."

He reached inside the waistband of her white cotton panties. "Why do you hate to admit that?" He hooked his fingers along the edge of her panties and slowly worked them down her legs. When she was finally naked, he delighted in her creamy white skin, the slender muscles in her thighs, and the curve of her narrow hips.

"I was convinced that wanting a man was wrong. I thought it made me weak."

Grady dipped his hand between her legs. "Still feel you don't want a man?"

"The only man I want right now is you," she breathed.

He tempted her folds, relishing her wet flesh. "After tonight, I promise you'll never want anyone else."

Al gripped his shoulder, bracing against the storm of sensations he was creating with his fingers. She opened her legs wider for him and moaned when he slid inside of her. As he slowly eased in and out, his thumb brushed against her clit.

She bit into his shoulder, arching into his chest. "You're killing me."

She was so sensitive to his touch. Grady found her irresistible like this. Raising her knees, he lowered his head between her legs, anxious to taste her, desperate to make her scream. When his tongue first lapped against her clit, she shuddered in his hands. As he clamped his mouth over her, she bucked against the bed and cried out.

He wanted to please her, wanted to make her come again and again. When he felt her body tensing as his tongue mercilessly circled around her clit, he anxiously waited for her to let go. As she rocked her head back and her delicious scream pierced the air, Grady nipped her clit with his teeth, heightening her climax.

After she fell back against the bed, panting and spent, he began tormenting her all over again. She was begging for him to stop when she screamed again, her wetness spilling out onto him. He eased his fingers into her, massaging that delicious spot inside of her with hard, fast strokes. Her body was quivering uncontrollably, and he knew she was ready for him.

Reaching to the nightstand for a condom package, he kneeled between her legs. Al sat up and took the condom from him.

"It's my turn to torture you."

Ripping the condom package open with her teeth, she smiled at him as she slid the latex condom into her mouth. When she lowered her mouth over his erection, Grady gasped.

Her mouth was better than anything he had known. She sucked him hard, teasing his tip with her tongue and then taking his cock all the way to the back of her throat. When he could feel his orgasm rising, she deftly slid the condom over his erection with her tongue.

Damn, this woman is like no other.

"I can't wait anymore," she whispered, guiding him on top of her. "I need you inside of me."

He kissed her neck. "I like it when you're impatient for me."

"Just fuck me, Grady."

Kissing her lips, he placed her legs around his hips. Grady lifted Al's slim hips to his and spread her folds apart with his left hand. When he pushed into her, Grady moaned as her flesh enveloped him. He pushed deep inside her, and then slowly pulled out.

"Yes. Go deeper," Al cried out.

Grady thrust into her slender hips again, and his body exploded with pleasure. As he moved deeper, Al's grip on his shoulders tightened.

Spurred on by her excitement, he shifted his hips slightly and rammed into her, harder than before. She mewed with pleasure, and he repeated his deep, forceful penetrations.

"Grady," Al screamed, and then she arched backward in his arms.

She bucked against him when her orgasm peaked, but Grady fought to maintain control over his urge to come, wanting to bring her to the heights of ecstasy again. She relaxed, but then he changed his rhythm. He began using short, fast thrusts to excite her. Al's nails dug into his firm, round ass, begging him to go deeper, but Grady ignored her demands. She raised her hips higher, wanting more of him, but he kept up his quick, shallow movements until her body trembled with the anticipation of her climax. When she finally rolled her head back and screamed, Grady finally drove himself all the way into her. The eruption of release that overtook him was unlike anything he had known. He bit into her neck, straining to stay upright until the last vestiges of desire drained from him.

Panting into the recesses of her neck, Grady felt her hand gently caress his cheek.

"I've forgotten what it was like to …." Her voice stilled.

"To what?" Grady insisted.

She sighed and lowered her hand from his cheek. "To enjoy myself with a man."

He nestled against her side, intrigued by her statement. "You don't enjoy being with Geoff?"

"It was never … that great between us. I thought maybe it was me, but now after being with you, I know it was him."

"Of course it was him. You're a beautiful, vibrant woman, who is sexy as hell and needs a man who knows how to please you."

"Sexy?" she giggled. "Hardly. My sexy days are far behind me."

"You make it sound like you're ancient."

"Well, I'm a good bit older than you." She nestled her head into the curve of his neck.

"I could care less how old you are, Allison."

"For now."

He nuzzled against her cheek. "Your age is irrelevant. Now, or twenty years from now."

She did not argue, but quietly settled against him.

Holding her in his arms, Grady felt complete. It was the first time since his marriage that he had been so comfortable with a woman. He knew then that he would never leave New Orleans. Wherever Al was, he would be. He would do whatever it took to stay with her, even continue dancing.

"You're very quiet," he mumbled into her hair.

"I was just wondering," she remarked, as her hand began to stroke his chest.

"Hmm, what is that?"

She eased back on the bed, smiling. "How many more condoms do you have in your wallet?"

* * *

Grady awoke to find Al still sleeping soundly in his arms. They lay beneath the blue comforter of his sleigh bed as the sun streamed through his bedroom window. In the distance, he could just make out the rumblings of the city. He gazed down at her face resting against his shoulder and marveled at the delicate curve of her jaw and the way her nose slightly turned up at the tip. He inspected her long, light brown eyelashes, ran his fingers over her silky blonde hair, and finally stroked the creamy skin on her cheek. All the features he had long admired on many different women were all rolled up in one package with her. Her fragile looks, her slim body, and her sharp mind were everything he had always wanted.

Glimpsing the three empty condom packages on his night table, he reflected on their frenzied lovemaking. Grady found it amazing how she had taken control in bed at times, being the demanding and relentless lover he had fantasized about but never expected to actually meet. Here was a woman with every quality he had wished for. In the depths of his soul, he questioned how in the hell was he going to be able to hold on to her.

Al stirred next to him, and he smiled when her gray eyes opened.

"What time is it?" she mumbled, stretching.

He checked his stainless watch on the night table. "A little after eight."

She rubbed her hand over her eyes and sat up. “How long have you been up?”

He traced his fingers down her back, following the outline of the sleek muscles. “Not long.”

She turned to him and kissed his lips. “I’m hungry.”

“I don’t have much here,” he admitted. “We could go out for breakfast.”

“I’d like that.”

He reached around her shoulders and eased her body back against him. “We could even make a day of it,” he added, kissing her ear. “You and me, having a day on the town. What do you say?”

Her hands held on to his thick arm draped across her chest. “You don’t have to do this, Grady. If last night was all you can give me, then I am okay with that. I never expected—”

“How could you think I’d ever be satisfied after one night with you? You’ll never be free of me, Allison. That’s a promise.” He held her close. “The only question I have is … where would you like to go today?”

She was quiet for a moment as she pondered the question. “You know where I would really like to go with you?”

He held her close. “Where?”

“The zoo,” she announced with a childlike laugh. “I haven’t been there in years. We could just wander around and enjoy the day and the animals.”

“Sounds perfect. I love zoos, and I hear yours is pretty good.”

She cuddled against him. “Audubon Zoo is one of the best in the nation. It wasn’t always that way. When I was a kid, it was a pretty run down place.”

A knock on Grady’s door startled them.

“Who in the hell is that at this hour?” he griped.

Grady climbed from the bed and reached for his jeans on the floor.

“Maybe Cathy has come back to see if you’re fully recovered,” Al taunted from the bed.

He struggled to pull on his jeans and scowled at her. "Very funny."

When he stepped through the bedroom entrance, he gently shut the door behind him. Padding his way across the living room, he prayed that Suzie was not following up on her note from the night before. But when he opened the door, he was relieved to see a freshly shaved and showered Doug staring back at him.

"Hey, sorry to wake you," Doug began. "But I need my gun back."

Grady put his hand up against the doorframe. "Now?"

"Is now a bad time?"

Grady nodded to the bedroom door. "Yeah, it's a bad time."

Doug grinned. "Cathy?"

Grady grimaced. "No, definitely not Cathy."

Doug took a step backwards from the door. "Just get me my gun before tonight. I've got to work late at Pat O's and feel better having it with me when I walk home."

"Sure." Grady paused and furrowed his brow. "How's Bev?"

Doug shook his head. "Now she wants to hold off on contacting the lawyer until things cool down between her and Matt."

"I thought she was hot to get a divorce?"

"That was yesterday," Doug clarified with a roll of his dark eyes. "Today, she wants to wait."

"What do you want to do?"

He shrugged his thick shoulders. "Whatever she wants. I can't help it. I'm in that deep." He waved at Grady. "Come by after your friend leaves and we can have lunch."

"I've got plans," Grady announced.

Doug pointed toward the bedroom, raising his dark brows questioningly.

Grady curtly nodded. "We're going to spend the day together."

"She must be special."

"She is," Grady acknowledged. "Very special."

Doug was about to turn away when his eyes slowly made their way back to Grady's face. "You don't have Al in there? Do you?"

"I'll talk to you later," Grady beamed, while easing the door closed.

Grady heard Doug's deep laugh echoing across the second floor as he returned to the bedroom.

When Grady opened the door, he found Al already dressed and sitting on the edge of the bed.

"Was that Doug's voice I heard?"

"Yeah, he was the reason I was so drunk the other night. He had a problem with his girlfriend and needed a friendly ear. After we finished a bottle of bourbon, he passed out on my sofa. He came by looking for something he had left behind."

"Beverly again?"

Grady went to the bed and sat down next to her. "This has happened before?" He reached for his T-shirt on the floor.

Al's loud sigh filled the bedroom. "Lots of times. We spent four hours sitting on the steps outside of my apartment talking one night. He drank whiskey and I listened. I think everyone in the building has heard about his Beverly saga."

"I didn't realize it was that well-known," he commented after pulling on his T-shirt.

"He keeps hoping she will leave her husband, but she never will. From the first day Beverly set foot in this house, she made it known that she was looking for a rich and powerful husband."

"Beverly was a tenant?"

"Sure was." Al nodded. "She was Beverly Lattimore then."

He raised his eyebrows in amazement. "Small town."

"The French Quarter is a little different from the rest of the city. It's a pretty tight-knit community, and they take care of their own. My father played in damn near every club in the Quarter, so when we first opened the house to tenants, a lot of the club owners who had worked with Dad sent their out of town bookings our way to help Cassie and me pay the bills."

Grady ran his hand along her thigh. "When was this?"

"A year after my mother died. Cassie was the one who came up with the idea. I was in my freshman year at college and the money our mother had left us was almost gone." She placed her hand over his. "Taking in tenants helped us keep the house."

He clasped her hand and held it. "Why do you still do it? Don't you make enough as a nurse anesthetist to take care of the place without having all these strangers coming in and out?"

She contemplated their joined hands. "Keeping this house going costs a lot more than I make. If I want to keep my home, I need tenants. There have been times, even with the tenants, that it has been tough to cover the bills. These old mansions are huge money pits, but I could never give it up. It's my home."

Al's stomach growled loudly and she let go of his hand. "If we're going to go out to eat, I need to go to my place and change." She stood from the bed.

He stood up next to her and put his arms around her waist. "You go and change while I grab a shower."

She gently kissed his lips, and then whispered, "About last night ...."

He tilted away from her, raising a skeptical eyebrow. "What about last night?"

A big smile lit up her face. "I had a really great time."

"There are many more nights like that to come for us, Allison."

She warily cocked her head to the side. "Not if you keep calling me Allison."

"Especially if I keep calling you Allison."

She stepped out of his arms. "We'll see about that."

Al left the bedroom and retrieved her flip-flops from the living room floor. She gave him one last smile before darting out his door.

Grady let out a long breath while silently thanking divine intervention for bringing them together. When he turned for the bathroom door, he shook his head in disbelief over his good fortune.

"Hell of a woman. And now, she's mine."

Chapter 13

As Grady studied a map of the Audubon Zoo, the bright spring sun was beaming down on a circular pond, with a dark green elephant sitting on a rock in the center, spewing water playfully from its trunk. Beside him, Al was taking in the children splashing around the edges of the pond while watchful mothers looked on. The sounds of animals calling from other parts of the zoo floated in the air, along with the intermittent squeals of happy children. Grady was still trying to decipher the map when a gentle breeze from the nearby Mississippi River made the flimsy paper billow in his hands.

"We can head to the Asian Domain for the elephants … which is this way." He motioned to his right. "Or we can go left and see the primates." He nodded to Al. "Your call."

She waved to her right. "Elephants. You always have to start with the elephants at Audubon Zoo. It's a tradition."

Grady folded up the map and took her hand. "Elephants it is."

They strolled down a wide sidewalk surrounded by tall oak trees and lush green gardens with signs pointing to the Asian Domain.

"Who brought you to the zoo when you were little?" Grady probed, squeezing her hand.

"My dad. It was the one place we both loved. We were the animal freaks in our family. My mother and Cassie were allergic to everything under the sun, so my Dad and I would run away to the zoo and take in the animals."

"Sounds like you two were pretty close."

She shrugged. "When I was little, yeah, we were close, but about a year before he took off, he pulled away from me. By then, he was fighting all the time with my mother."

"Fighting? What did they fight about?"

"Money. He never made enough of it, and she never liked to stop spending it."

"I thought your mother had money."

"When they first got married, she had a lot of it. After a while, I guess they just went through it all. My mother never worked a day in her life, until my father left. She had a business degree from Tulane, but when the time came to look for a job, all she could do was secretarial work. She worked for an accounting firm in the Central Business District."

"You ever hear from your father?"

Al shook her head. "Nope. The last day I ever spoke to him was the day he left. I hugged him good-bye and then went to school. When I came home, he was gone. I think my mother knew where he went, but she never told Cassie or me."

Grady tried to think of something encouraging, but his mind went blank. What could he say about a man who walked away from his children?

Ahead, a circular ring was filled with huge rocks and dirt. Rising behind the ring was a square, red-bricked building with an arched open entrance in front and a small cupola on top. Running around the perimeter of the ring were smaller red-bricked housing facilities for the elephants.

Grady stuck his nose in the air. "You can smell the elephants ahead."

"I love that smell. Makes you know you're in a zoo."

"I'm surprised you didn't become a vet, instead of a nurse."

"That would have taken way too long in school," she maintained. "I needed to hurry up and make money to help Cassie pay the bills."

"What did Cassie do for a living?"

She let go of his hand. "She was a dancer, like you." She steadied her eyes on the elephant enclosure before them. "She got into it when the money started running out. In the beginning, a few of my father's old friends gave her jobs waiting tables in their clubs. One thing led to another, and she eventually ended up on the stage."

He reached up and turned her face to him. "Why didn't you tell me that?"

"Does it matter?"

"It matters to me, Allison. It explains why you have a soft spot for everyone in our business."

She gave him a reassuring smile. "Yeah, I always try to rent to dancers because of Cassie. She would have wanted that."

He stood back from her. "What was she like?"

"Cassie?" She rolled her eyes and softly laughed. "A big kid. She was outgoing, beautiful, goofy, and had a million friends. Boys were constantly following her, and she was the life of any party. She was the happiest person I'd ever known."

Two small elephants came out of the main gate and entered the ring in front of them. The lumbering animals picked up dirt from the ground and tossed it over their broad backs.

"It sounds like you loved her a great deal," Grady voiced, observing the elephants.

"I adored her. She was my big sister."

One of the elephants let out a long, loud cry.

"How did she die?"

Several children began running toward the ring, anxious to see the elephants. Al smiled as the children scurried around them. For several seconds she said nothing, but simply took in the exuberant faces. When her gray eyes returned to Grady, they were swimming with sadness.

Devastated by her sorrow, he put his arm around her shoulders. "Forgive me. I shouldn't have asked you that question."

"No, it's all right." She raised her head and shook off her melancholy. "I just don't like talking about how Cassie died. I know it happened a long time ago, but sometimes there are moments it feels like yesterday."

Grady draped his other arm around her. "What do you say we go and see the monkeys?"

Al nodded. "I like monkeys."

Grady took her hand and led her away from the elephants. "Come on, we've got lots to see."

* * *

They had stopped at the Cypress Knee Café inside the Louisiana Swamp Exhibit for soft drinks, and were sitting on the pier overlooking the green, algae-filled swamp below. Across the swath of water, a narrow shoreline was covered with a handful of alligators and a few brave turtles, catching the afternoon sunshine.

"Did you like to go to the zoo when you were a kid?" Al queried, sitting across a wooden picnic bench from him.

"My father didn't believe in wasting time on things like going to zoos or on vacations. When we had free time, my brother and I were expected to fill it with profitable pursuits, like part-time jobs or doing chores to earn our allowance. After we graduated from high school, Dalton and I were expected to pay our way through college. That's why I took up dancing, because the grants and loans weren't cutting it." He explored the small crowds scattered about the pier.

"Sounds like your father was pretty strict."

Grady put his paper cup of sweet tea down on the picnic table. "Not strict, disciplined. He grew up poor and worked hard to get ahead. Dad was an executive with a big advertising company in New York City. He started as an accountant and worked his way up to CFO. We lived in an affluent part of Connecticut, belonged to the nearby country club, and were always seen at the local charity fundraisers my mother was involved with." He shrugged his broad shoulders as the sunlight glistened in his short, blond hair. "I'm not knocking how we were raised. My dad made sure me and Dalton appreciated what it took to have the kind of life we did. He fought to make us tough, perhaps a little too tough."

"What makes you say that?"

Al noticed how more than a few of the women seated around them kept turning their hungry eyes to Grady. His good looks and ripped body beneath his snug T-shirt had attracted more than a few second-glances as they had meandered around the park.

"After I found out my parents were killed in that car accident, I kept hearing my father's voice in my head saying, 'Be strong, stay tough, and no matter what, don't show your emotions.' Took me a while to realize that my father was wrong. If you don't acknowledge your emotions, you just end up alone."

"You father sounds a lot like my mother. She always taught us to never to get too close to anyone, because they would only hurt you in the end."

He rested his thick arms on the picnic table. "Is that why you kept pushing me away?"

"Partly." She shrugged, making her silky blonde hair fall about her shoulders. "I also needed to know that I wasn't going to end up as just another … Cathy."

Grady grasped her outstretched hand. "You are so much more to me. I hope you realize that now." He shook his head. "Why didn't you talk to me about this before, instead of torturing me?"

Al coyly smirked. "Sometimes a man needs to go through a good bit of hell before a woman can let him know heaven."

His heart soared. "I like that. Might have to—"

"Excuse me?" a dark-haired woman with beady green eyes intruded. She pointed at Grady. "Aren't you a stripper at that club? What's it called … The Flesh Factory? I saw you there the other night."

Grady sat back and crunched his lips together, appearing irritated. *Great. This is all I need.*

"Yeah, I, ah, dance there," he told the woman.

The woman's small eyes immediately twinkled with interest. "You were really good. I saw you dancing with this woman on the stage and the two of you were … well, really hot."

Grady stood from the table, angrily snatching up his paper cup of sweet tea. "Glad you liked the show."

Al took the hint and rose from her seat, holding her soft drink in her hand.

"I even told my girlfriends about you," the woman gushed. "I'm gonna bring them back to see you. You're incredible on stage."

Grady forced a polite smile on his lips. "Thanks." He reached for Al's hand. "We've got to be going." Pulling Al away from their picnic table, he headed to the garbage cans at the end of the pier.

"Does that happen a lot?"

"At least once in every town," he confessed, throwing his paper cup into a trashcan.

Al pitched her soda into the black barrel of trash and observed his pensive brow. "You don't like being recognized, do you?"

"No. It's not like I'm an actor or politician. I take my clothes off for a living. It's not something to be proud of."

She came up to him and squeezed his hand. "I like what you do."

Unable to look at her while his anger festered, he kept his eyes on the swamp. "Well, you're the only one. When my old man found out what I was doing to pay the bills at Yale, he called me a worthless son of a bitch and never spoke to me again. He never came to my college graduation or attended my wedding."

She tugged on his hand, pulling him toward her. "He was wrong about you, Grady. You're not a worthless son of a bitch. You're a very special … son of a bitch."

Pivoting his eyes to her, he chuckled. "How come I only feel special with you?"

"Because you make me feel the same way," she declared.

Grady reveled in the way her hair shined in the bright sunlight, and how her features glowed with affection. He yearned to capture that moment. To lock away the memory forever, so he could look back and know for that brief instant he had been happy.

Al sheepishly grinned and then pulled at his hand, urging him down the path.

"Where are we going now?"

Al said nothing, but kept grinning at him as she guided him off the path. She hastened across the grass to the side of the path, and moved toward a row of trees and shrubs that were planted in front of a small structure. When they came around the ridge of greenery, a storage shed built out of cinderblocks manifested before them.

Grady spied the isolated building. "What are we doing here?"

Al nudged him behind the shed, and he laughed out loud at her bravado. When she pushed him up against the wall of the shed, pulling at his T-shirt, Grady quit laughing and started getting turned on. He liked her this way; forceful and demanding.

"The way that woman looked at you back there, it reminded me of that night I went to your club," Al said, her hands on his chest. "I saw all of those women wanting you, but they couldn't have you."

He tossed his arms around her. "I could only see you that night."

Al nestled against his body. "When you danced with me, I fantasized about you taking me, right there on the stage so everyone could see. I wanted to show all of those other women that you were mine."

He breathed in her lavender-scented hair. "That would have been a hell of a show."

"Still could be." Her hand went to the crotch of his jeans, fondling him. "You ever want to do it in public?"

Grady gaped at the minimal covering of brush in front of the shed. "Here?"

"I've always wanted to have sex at the zoo." She nuzzled his neck. "Are you afraid we'll get caught?"

Grady could feel the blood rushing through his veins when she said those words. He crushed her to him. "Hell no."

She nipped his chin. "Prove it."

Taking up her challenge, he spun her around and pressed her body into the wall of the shed. Quickly lowering the zipper on her jeans, he tugged the snug material down her hips, and then let the jeans drop to her ankles. Pushing her panties out of the way, he grinned as his hands squeezed the cheeks on her smooth, round ass. Al groaned when he spread her cheeks apart, and slipped his fingers into her folds. He got hard when he felt how wet she was.

"You like being bad, don't you?"

She backed her butt into his him, rubbing against his erection. “Does that surprise you?”

Grady shoved two fingers deep into her, making Al grunt with surprise. “No, I had a feeling you were this way, but you don’t like to show it.”

“I—I never felt comfortable enough with anyone to … be bad.”

His lips skirted along the right side of her neck. “What about with Geoff?”

“Geoff?” Her cynical snicker intrigued him. “Geoff and I have never been … well, he was never adventurous, not like you.”

Grady liked hearing that. He was thrilled that he could give her something that Geoff couldn’t. Quickly unzipping his jeans and removing his cock, he teased her with his tip. “Tell me, is this a fantasy of yours? To have sex in public.”

“We can talk about that later. Just hurry. Before someone comes,” she begged, trying to back into him.

“No, you’ll tell me now.” He moved his hips away from her butt. Taking her hands, he shoved them into the wall of the shed, pinning them above her head. “What fantasies do you have?”

Al’s divine creamy ass beckoned to him, but he summoned his self-control, determined to get her to speak.

“I want to fuck … in dangerous places. You know, where there is a chance of getting caught.

“Places like the zoo?” he whispered.

“Anywhere in public. I just want to know how it would feel … with you.”

Thankful that she was finally opening up to him, he let up on her hands and reached for his back pocket. Retrieving his wallet, he was grateful that he had restocked it with condoms before heading up to Al’s place that morning. Taking a foil packet from his wallet, he quickly returned it to his back pocket.

After slipping on the condom, his arm went around her waist, pulling her to him. When he eased his fingers into her folds, spreading her open, he could feel her relax against him.

He entered her with one swift motion, penetrating all the way inside of her. Al moaned as he started moving in and out.

Deliberately, he took his time, relishing the feel of her. He wanted to enjoy her fantasy and was delighted that she had finally shared something so intimate with him.

The first time she came, Grady held her close, and when her body drooped in his arms, he started pounding into her. He gave into his impulse, wanting to go hard and deep. Al was grunting against the force of his penetrations; he could feel her body tensing as her second orgasm crested much faster than the first. Her nails dug into his arm, her head rocked back, and just when he felt she was going to scream, Al tucked her head, shuddered, and didn't make a sound.

Her silence made his final thrusts all the more exquisite. When he finally came, he bit down on her shoulder, desperate to stifle his groan.

They did not take long to enjoy the aftermath of their lovemaking, opting instead to dress quickly and move away from their hiding place. Just as they stepped out from behind the line of dense foliage, a small gaggle of children ran by the path in front of them, screaming at the top of their lungs.

"Where were they a few minutes ago?" Grady cracked. "We could have used all that screaming then."

Al's airy giggle warmed his heart. She trotted ahead to the path, and he watched her ponytail of long blonde hair dance in the light breeze. On the path, he caught up to her and took her hand.

Strolling along, he wondered how he had been so lucky to have finally found a woman who made him feel as if the world was a place of endless possibilities. In a few days, he had gone from his dead-end, day in and day out existence, to appreciating that life was about those special moments and not the monotony.

* * *

The sun was sinking in the western sky when they returned home. As they climbed the steps to her third-floor apartment, Grady wished their time together did not have to come to an end.

"Maybe I could come by after I finish up at the club?" he suggested, as she put the key into the lock of her apartment door.

Al turned to him. “That might be pretty late, and I have a case in the morning.”

He took a step closer to her. “Then why don’t you go and take a long nap, so when I come by you’ll be fully rested. We don’t have to do anything tonight. I just want to be with you.”

Al rested her hand on his chest. “I guess you could come by for a little while.” Her hand caressed the thick muscles in his chest and then she smiled. “But I can’t promise that nothing will happen, especially if you take your shirt off.” She curled into him. “Or your pants.”

Grady threw his arms around her and kissed her lips. Al quickly opened her mouth, hungrily accepting him. He wanted to carry her into her apartment and take her to bed, but then he remembered the club.

If he was going to take a permanent position at The Flesh Factory, he would have to keep Matt Harrison happy, and make all of his shows. He didn’t want to risk losing his paycheck, especially now that things were looking up in his personal life.

He reluctantly let her go. “I’ve got to get to work.”

She stepped back from him. “Go on. I’ll be here when you get back.”

He kissed her lips once more. “I don’t know how I’m going to get through two shows, knowing you’re waiting for me.”

She returned to her door and pushed it open. “Oh, I’m sure all those screaming women will help keep your mind occupied.”

He waited as she walked through the entrance to her home, and then added, “All those women don’t mean anything. It’s just a job.”

She took her keys from the lock. “I know.”

“I don’t want you to think that I would ever—”

“Grady, it’s all right. I don’t mind.” She waved to the stairs behind him. “Go to work.”

He turned to the stairs, but before he reached the first step, Al called to him.

“Just make sure they don’t get close enough to grab your ass, all right?”

Chuckling, he faced her. "They won't, I promise."

Al shook her head and quickly closed the door.

Encouraged by her jealousy, Grady happily trotted down the stairs. She was beginning to care for him; he could sense it. However, he knew that the comment she had made would be the first of many about keeping the women off him at the club. With time, her comments would take on a more demanding tone, and eventually turn into ultimatums. He had seen the strain his choice of employment could put on a relationship. Now, more than ever, Grady had to start making plans for getting out of the skin game. If he wanted a future with Al, he had to begin looking for another job.

But what am I good for? Who would hire me?

The idea of returning to the corporate world did not appeal to him, but it would be more palatable to Al than dancing. A strange shiver of deja vu overtook his body as he recalled the exact same scenario with Emma. He had walked away from dancing to make her happy, but had not been happy with where he ended up. He wanted to believe that things would be different with Al. Grady felt like the sand in his hourglass of hoped for dreams was running out, and that Al was his last chance at finding that place between happily ever after and happy for now.

Chapter 14

The Flesh Factory was packed and the tables in the pit were overflowing with women. The music was vibrating through the walls, and the high-pitched screams were grating on everyone's nerves. It was one of those nights where the dancers were getting groped a little too much by the patrons, the bartenders were getting snippy with all the orders of white wine spritzers, and the management was aggravated with the staff's complaints. It was what was termed in the business as a Full Moon Night, when all the bitches came out to play.

"Jesus, they're brutal out there tonight," Lewis uttered, as he came in the dressing room door, pulling bills from his G-string. "I swear, one old lady out there was going to give me a blow job right on stage."

Sitting with a towel around his waist, Grady wiped his hand over his sweaty brow. "I know. I damn near got a hand job from one woman."

"Probably the same woman." Lewis began counting up the bills in his hands. "At least the tips make up for it. I got almost two hundred out there tonight."

Grady nodded in agreement. "Yeah, tips were good tonight."

Lewis went to the dresser and grabbed a towel draped on top of it. He began wiping the sweat and oil from his body. "Did Matt give you a lot of shit for missing the other night?"

Grady picked at the towel around his hips. "No, quite the opposite. He offered me a permanent job, dancing here. No more traveling."

"Yeah, I knew he would have to fill Colin's spot in the line up."

"Colin?" Grady furrowed his brow at him. "Colin quit?"

"No, got fired." Lewis tossed his towel on the dressing table. "Matt got wind of an altercation between him and Beverly."

Interested in hearing more, Grady leaned forward in his chair. "What do you mean by an altercation?"

"Colin had been sleeping with Beverly. She wanted to call it off, he didn't. Then things got out of hand. He hit her; a few times from what I hear."

"Are you sure Matt didn't beat her up and is looking for a scapegoat?"

"Nah, Matt wouldn't touch anybody. He's not the type. I think he knew about Colin and Beverly, but didn't care. If you ask me, that marriage has been over for a while now."

Grady fell back in his chair, dumbfounded by the news. "Are you sure about this?"

Lewis stepped out of his G-string and reached for a thick white robe hanging behind the dressing room door. "I saw Colin packing up yesterday. He told me Matt canned his ass because of Beverly. Ed, the guy who shares his dressing room, is the one who told me about Beverly getting beaten up. Apparently, Colin is a pretty angry man where women are concerned."

"Shit," Grady whispered, and ran his hand over his face.

Grady envisioned what could have happened to Matt if he had not found Doug when he did. He was not sure how he was going to break the news to his friend about what had really happened to Beverly, but he had to set the guy straight. Doug was giving his heart to a woman that did not want it, and would eventually hurt him. Grady had been on the receiving end of such betrayal in the past, and did not wish that kind of heartache on anyone.

"Is there a problem?" Lewis asked, tying off his robe.

"No," Grady told him. "I guess I'm just kind of shocked about Colin, that's all."

"The guy was an asshole. He started a lot of fights around here with customers and other dancers. The place is better off without him." Lewis smiled. "But hey, it's great news for you. No more traveling. I think that landlord of yours will like having you as a permanent tenant."

"Yeah, she might."

"How is it working out with her?"

Grady slyly grinned. "Better than I'd hoped."

"When I saw you two dancing together, I knew it was only a matter of time before what was going on vertically went horizontal."

"You've got a way with words, Lewis."

"I'd better. I've got the MA in English from Duke to prove it."

"No shit." Grady shook his head. "I've got a BA in finance from Yale."

"What strange bedfellows this economy has made, eh?"

"Indeed," Grady confirmed.

A loud rap on the door made both men turn. Lewis went to the door and when he opened it, Nick Davies from the bar was frowning at them.

"Paulson, there's a woman asking for you. Says she's your landlord. I thought it might be important, so I said—"

Grady jumped from his chair. "Where is she?"

"At the bar," Nick replied.

Grady was scrambling toward the door when Lewis stopped him. "You can't go out there in that." He gestured to the towel around Grady's waist. "You'll be torn to pieces by that crowd."

Grady glimpsed his towel. "I'll change."

"No," Lewis asserted. "I'll go and bring her back here. You stay put."

"What about Matt's no girls backstage rule?"

Lewis waved off his concern with a curt grin. "She's not a girl; she's your landlord."

"Thanks, Lewis."

"Hey, anything for another Ivy Leaguer." Lewis walked through the entrance, pushed Nick out of the way, and then shut the door behind him.

Grady reached for his jeans and briefs hanging over his chair by the dresser. Another knock at the door, took Grady by surprise. He hastily zipped up his jeans and ran his hand over his sweaty hair, trying to make himself look presentable for Al. But after pulling the door open, he was stunned to see Matt Harrison standing before him.

Wearing a tailored brown suit and yellow tie, with his silver-tinged black hair neatly combed back and flashing his gold Rolex, he appeared to be every inch the wealthy executive, not the owner of a strip club.

"Hey, Grady, got a minute? I wanted to talk to you about our little arrangement. See if you made up your mind about dancing permanently here at The Flesh Factory."

Matt slinked into the room, and Grady nervously checked the hallway. Deciding to leave the door open, Grady hoped Lewis would know to get Al out of there before Matt saw her.

Grady turned his attention to Matt. "Sure, we can talk."

Unfortunately, when Grady stepped into his dressing room, Matt shut the door.

"You thought about what I said?"

Grady anxiously kept his eyes on the closed door. "Yeah, I thought about it."

"Look, I'm not gonna play games with you. I like you; you're not stuck up or want to be catered to like some of these guys around here. Plus, you look good on the stage and the women like you, so I think you would do well here. What do you say? Do you want to become a headliner here?"

"Actually, Matt, circumstances have changed for me and I've decided I want to stay in New Orleans. I would like to accept your offer."

Matt raised one black eyebrow. "By circumstances, I assume you mean a girl?"

Feeling self-conscious about his semi-naked appearance in front of Matt, Grady went to the chair by the dresser and picked up his T-shirt. "I just mean circumstances."

"It's that broad from the other night, isn't it? You two looked awfully good together. I wondered if you knew her."

Grady pulled on his T-shirt. "You can call my agent, Burt Conroe, with the details."

"Sure, I'll call Burt and we'll hack out a contract." Matt smiled, appearing happy that he had gotten what he wanted. "I'll even give you Colin's old dressing room, too. You can move in there anytime you like."

"I'm happy here." Grady paused, remembering what Lewis had told him earlier. "I heard you fired Colin," he added. "Is it true?"

Matt's happy smile disappeared. "Yeah, he got to be too hard to handle. That boy had one too many bad habits, if you know what I mean."

Grady was just about to inquire which of those bad habits Matt was referring to when the dressing room door flew open. Lewis and Al stepped inside and stared at Matt and Grady. Grady blew out an uneasy breath, waiting for Matt to let into him for breaking his rules.

"Allie Cat? Is that you?" Matt went to Al, throwing his arms around her.

"Hey, Uncle Matt." Al gave the man a warm hug.

"Uncle Matt?" Grady exclaimed.

Matt turned from Al. "Yeah, this is my Allie Cat. I started with her old man in a club a few doors down from here. I knew her sister Cassie, too. She used to dance for me. Everybody up and down Bourbon knows Al. She's been hanging out in all the clubs since she was in diapers." He glanced back at Al. "I haven't seen you since … well, it's been a long time."

"You didn't tell me you knew my boss," Grady vented.

Matt motioned between Al and Grady. "You two know each other?"

"Oh yeah, this is a hell of a lot better than Shakespeare," Lewis commented, backing out of the room and shutting the door.

"Grady is my tenant," Al told Matt. She then smiled knowingly at Grady. "He's also a very good friend."

Matt interpreted the smile on her face. "Just a friend?"

Al stepped further into the dressing room. "Please, Uncle Matt."

Matt raised his hands, assuaging her disapproval, and then a thought hit him. "You were the girl on the stage with Grady the other night. I thought you looked familiar."

Al nervously tucked a strand of blonde hair behind her left ear. "I, ah, just came to see his show."

"You reminded me of Cassie up there. You moved just like she did on the stage."

"I'm no dancer," Al argued.

"It ain't about being a dancer in this business. You know that." He turned to Grady. "I guess I can see why your circumstances have changed. You just make sure you do right by her. She's like a daughter to me."

Grady cleared his throat. "Yes, sir."

Matt went to the door and then turned back to Al. "Don't wear him out too much tonight, Allie Cat. He's got two more shows tomorrow night."

She smirked at Matt. "Glad to see you haven't changed, Uncle Matt."

Matt opened the door. "You know me, baby. Once a skin man, always a skin man."

Matt stepped out into the hall and closed the door, chuckling as he went.

As soon as Grady was sure Matt was gone, he went to Al's side and slipped his arms around her waist. "When were you going to tell me about Uncle Matt?"

"I knew he owned the club, but I didn't think he would remember me. Matt was one of my dad's old friends. He helped Cassie and me after Mom died. I haven't seen him since his wedding to Beverly."

"You were at his wedding?"

She nodded. "Beverly invited me."

Grady's face became serious as he stared into her eyes. "Then you must know what kind of games she has been playing with Doug."

She stepped out of his arms. "I know Doug is one of many men in and out of Beverly's life. I've tried to warn him about her, but he never listens."

"Did you know Beverly ended up in the hospital two days ago, and told Doug that Matt beat her up?"

"Matt? No way." Al vehemently shook her head. "He may be many things, but he has never raised a hand to any woman. It was probably one of Beverly's other boyfriends."

"It was. Another dancer here at the club named Colin. Matt fired him for it."

"Sounds like Beverly's MO. She's always had a thing for dancers."

"Doug needs to know how Beverly really is," Grady insisted.

"He already knows, Grady. He knows all about Beverly's other men, but he still won't let her go."

Grady ran his hand over his short blond hair. "I had no idea."

"'Love makes for strange lovers,' my mother used to always say. I don't know why Doug puts up with Beverly, but he does. Maybe Matt stays married to her to spare his kids the pain of divorce … or to keep everyone from finding out about his other life. God knows, Matt was never really into women."

Grady stared at her in disbelief. "You knew about that, too?"

"My father used to call Uncle Matt queer when I was a kid. I didn't know what it meant, but when I got older, I figured it out."

Grady shook his head while muttering, "This really is a small town."

Inching closer, she ran her fingers along the ropelike muscles in his forearm, tracing the large veins with her fingertips.

"You're oily."

"I didn't wipe off the oil from my show yet. I was hurrying to dress so I could get to you." That lustful tingle began in his groin as he watched her slender fingers stroke his arm. "What are you doing here? I thought we were meeting back at your place."

"I couldn't sleep, so I decided to catch your show." Her alluring grin was fueling his desire. "Sorry to say, I missed it," she admitted with a sexy sigh.

Unable to resist her any longer, Grady slid his arms around her. "That's a shame. I would have liked dancing for you."

Her hands gripped his damp T-shirt. "Maybe you can give me a private dance?"

He kissed her neck. "I have to warn you, I'm not cheap."

"What will a private dance cost me?"

His lips brushed against her chin. "I'll dance for you, if you show me your cupola."

Her airy laugh instantly brightened the dismal dressing room. "I'll think about it." Her eyes drifted to the silver-sequined costume hanging from a hook on the wall behind him. "How do you come up with your routines? I mean, the choreography and costumes." She nodded to the silver costume. "How did you think up that one, for example?"

He followed her eyes to the costume. "That?" He let her go, walked over to the wall, and lifted the silver costume from the hook. "I had this made when I returned to dancing. I'm not sure where I came up with the idea. I guess I was thinking of some flashy outfit to hit the road with. It seems pretty silly now, but I was trying to be original. The dance moves take shape after I have the outfit. What I really try to do with the costume and dancing is create a character the audience can get lost in. Something that fulfills the fantasy."

She glided up to him, smiling seductively. "Grady, you're the fantasy, not the character. What all those women want out there is the body they see on stage. How you dress isn't important. It's how you move. That's what turns them on. It's what turned me on."

He replaced the costume on the hook. "Really?"

"Yeah. The way you sway your hips." She curled her hand around his right hip, lowering it to his butt. "The way you shake this." She patted his behind. "Very enticing."

"Enticing?" He chuckled and took her hand. Spinning her around, he pressed into her back. "I could say the same thing about you. Every time you walk away from me," he thrust his hips into her, "I get turned on by your ass."

Holding his arms against her chest, she swayed her hips from side to side, purposefully rubbing against his cock. "Is my ass turning you on now?"

He buried his head in her hair as a rush of white hot heat shot up from his groin. "Damn, that feels good." He lowered his hand to her crotch and slipped it between her legs, pressing into her. "I know something that would feel a whole lot better."

"Ever done it in a dressing room?" she whispered. "With a fan?"

"No," he conceded, beginning to sway his hips in time with hers. "Dressing rooms aren't places where you get a lot of privacy. People are always walking in and out."

"Let's give it a try." She pushed his hand deeper into her. "Because I'm not sure I can wait much longer for you."

"No need to wait." He lowered the zipper of her jeans, and slid his hand into her panties. "I can satisfy you right here, right now." Grady bit down on her earlobe as his fingers found her folds. Easing into her wet flesh, Al steadied herself against him and opened her legs wider.

"I love it when you're wet for me."

His forefinger found her clit and he rubbed hard against it, making her gasp with pleasure. God, he loved the sound of a woman getting turned on. Setting her clit between his thumb and forefinger he pinched it and Al shuddered.

"Yeah, you like that, don't you, baby?" he cooed in her ear, pinching her again.

She was rocking in his arms as he methodically rubbed her clit between his fingers, feeling the tension rising in her muscles. He held her close and luxuriated in the silky texture of her wetness as his cock got hard. He wanted to bend her over, fuck her from behind, but he held back. This was for her and only her. When she finally let go he thought he would hear her scream, but instead she trembled against him and then sagged in his arms.

He gave her a few minutes to catch her breath while rubbing his hand along her back. When she zipped up her pants and spun around in his arms, she showed him a perturbed frown.

"That wasn't quite what I had in mind." She cupped his erection. "Sure you don't want more?"

He pecked her lips and moved her hand aside. "No, I want to leave you hungry for me."

Al's frown disappeared as her eyes swept over his chest. "I don't think I'll ever stop being hungry for you."

"Now that is what a guy really likes to hear." He touched his forehead to hers. "Why don't we go back to your place? Perhaps you could let me loose in that fancy kitchen of yours, so I can whip us up a midnight snack. I might even be able to put a dent in that insatiable hunger of yours. What do you say?"

"Grady, I have an 8 A.M. case," Al complained.

He walked awkwardly to the dressing room door, his hard on rubbing against his jeans. "I promise to get you to bed at a reasonable hour."

"'A reasonable hour?' I don't like the sound of that."

"You can trust me, baby." He opened the door. "I'm a man of my word."

"Trust you?" She moved toward the door. "We'll see, Grady."

"Ernest Hemingway once said, 'The best way to find out if you can trust somebody is to trust them.' So trust me, Allison." He nodded to the hallway. "Go pull your car in front of the club while I finish packing up and," he glanced down at his crotch, "calm down."

She stood at the door, scrutinizing him with her cautious eyes. "Trusting is difficult for me, Grady."

"Me too, but I would like to start trusting someone … and I would very much like that someone to be you."

"I'd like that, too." She kissed his cheek, and then quickly spun away.

Leaning out the door, Grady watched her slender hips saunter down the hallway. A kick of uncertainty hit his gut as he thought of trusting Al with his heart.

Can you really trust her? his bothersome inner voice nagged.

He had been so long on his own that the idea of trusting another seemed like a foreign concept to him. Despite his reservations, Grady was convinced of one thing; if he did not take a chance with her, he would regret it for the rest of his life. No, it was time for a fresh start and a new outlook. He just prayed that Al was the woman he had been hoping for … the one who could heal his tattered soul.

Chapter 15

After hurriedly depositing his bags inside his apartment door, Grady followed Al's seductive hips up the stairs to her third floor home. As she placed the key in the lock, he kissed the nape of her neck.

Al's body shuddered when he began to fondle her breasts.

"Can't you wait until we get inside?" she protested, struggling with the lock.

Grady bit down on her neck and whispered, "Hurry."

When the dead bolt gave way, Grady kicked the door open and pushed her inside.

Al chucked her keys to the floor while Grady shut the door. She surrendered to his arms and eagerly kissed him. Her kisses were like fire against his lips. Never had he known such a sensation with a woman; it was as if his every nerve was buzzing with electricity. Christ, he wanted her so much. He ached to be inside of her.

His lips were inching down her neck when she mumbled, "What about our midnight snack?"

"It can wait," he returned and slammed his mouth into hers.

Al tugged at his T-shirt, quickly lifting it over his head. She threw the shirt to the nearby deep red sofa while Grady slipped off his tennis shoes. She took Grady's hand, leading him across the darkened room toward the moonlight creeping in through the picture window. When they came to the built-in bench below the window, she pushed him down on the taupe cushions and stood before him. Her eyes were intently focused on his as she slipped her T-shirt over her head and then slowly unzipped her jeans. Rocking her hips back and forth, she slid the fabric down her slender thighs. Enthralled, Grady watched as she stepped from her jeans and reached behind her back, removing her bra. She smiled sheepishly at the floor when her breasts fell free. The gesture almost sent Grady's blood pressure through the roof. It was so sexy, and at the same time, so innocently sweet. He wanted to take her in his arms and never let her go.

After she dropped the bra to the floor, she took his hands and brought them to the waistband of her tan cotton underwear. Grady eased the panties down her legs and she held on to his shoulders as he helped her step out of them. Naked before him in the moonlight, she was the most beautiful creature Grady had ever seen.

His fingers traced the contours of her thighs, and then he placed his hands around her slender hips. Leaning forward, he kissed her stomach and breasts. Al climbed onto his lap and straddled his hips. With Grady kissing her as his fingers pinched at her pink nipples, she began rocking her hips against his crotch, enticing him. Reaching between her legs, he teased her wet flesh and Al hugged his neck when he flicked her clit.

She fumbled with the zipper on his pants, but Grady lifted her from his hips and laid her back on the bench. He raised her left leg in the air, kissed her ankle, and slowly moved his lips along her inner calf, nipping at her inner thigh until he reached the valley between her legs. When his mouth settled over her clit, Al gasped with pleasure. Her hands tugged at his hair as his tongue swirled around her most sensitive spot. She arched on the bench and bent her head back when his gentle motion grew more demanding. He could feel the tension in her body rising. She was reaching for the wall behind her as her gasps became cries of desperation. Right before she was about to come, Grady pulled away and her body caved with abject disappointment.

"Don't stop," she begged.

Grady kissed her thigh, and then spread her folds apart. His tongue circled around her swollen clit and then he gently grazed his teeth against her flesh. Her body lurched upward as if hit by a bolt of lightning, and then she screamed. As the orgasm cascaded through her, Grady slipped his fingers inside of her, feeling her pulsate.

"I love making you come," he whispered.

Al's body was limp with satisfaction as he rolled her over. He pulled her hips up, forcing her to her knees. He quickly unzipped his jeans and lowered them over his hips. As he ran his hands over her creamy white ass, his erection throbbed with need. Spreading her legs apart, he opened her folds. With one powerful push, he entered her.

Al grunted as he backed out and dove even harder into her.

"Yes," Al whispered as she rolled her head back. "Again."

He smacked hard into her once more and she groaned. She spread her legs wider apart and raised her hips even higher.

"Go deeper," she pleaded.

With his hands, Grady squeezed her butt cheeks together and pushed with brutal force to enter into her deepest reaches.

"Oh, God," Al cried out.

Grady grunted as he made every penetration as hard and deep as he could. The snug fit of her around him was driving him crazy. With every thrust, he felt his orgasm rushing forward. Soon he was pounding into her, the sound of their hips slapping together filled the air. Then, she cried out with ecstasy. He could not control it any longer and he tugged her hips closer to his with a frantic desire to end his torture. The white heat from his groin took over his mind, blotting out everything except the sensation of being in her. He moaned and clung to her just as his climax barreled through him.

For several seconds he was too numb to move and simply kept his arms locked around her waist.

"That was better than before," Al whispered beneath him.

Grady backed away from her and sat back on the bench with a thud.

"It's official, you're killing me," he breathlessly joked.

Al snuggled against him. Grady put his arm around her shoulders and pulled her close.

"You didn't use anything, did you?"

Stunned, Grady realized she was right. He had forgotten to put on a condom, having been so caught up in the act.

"Damn it," he cursed and rocked his head back. "I completely forgot."

"I didn't mind. I actually liked it better that way."

"Yeah, me too. But it was foolish of me. I know you don't want kids, and—"

"I never said I didn't want children, just a husband," she cut in.

"What if something did happen tonight?" He kissed the tip of her nose, "Or perhaps another night … would you want my baby?"

She rested her head against his chest. "With all my heart."

The rush of relief that surged through him took him by surprise. There it was; the moment he had been waiting for from her. That glimmer of emotion that told him she cared for him, just as much as he cared for her.

Grady pushed her naked body back on the bench. "In that case, to hell with condoms."

"We need to continue to be careful, Grady. We barely know each other and a child is a lot of responsibility. Then there is the added problem of our age difference. How would we—?"

"Allison," he interrupted. "Stop talking." He kissed her lips and folded his arms around her. "We are what we are, and I wouldn't change any of it for the world." He slid his jeans off, kicked them away, and then climbed on top of her.

"What happened to your promise to get me to bed at a reasonable hour?" she asked, reaching around to his tight, round ass.

"I haven't forgotten, and we'll get to bed … eventually." He spread her legs apart. "When I've had enough of you."

She reached down and stroked his growing erection. "Enough? We'll see about that."

His lips hovered over hers. "Yeah, we may be here a while."

* * *

Standing over Al's island cooktop, dressed only in his jeans, Grady tended to the grilled cheese sandwich in the pan before him.

"I like your kitchen." He waved his spatula at the oak cabinets and beige granite countertops that were set against the dark hardwood floors. "I especially like the posters."

On the eggshell-painted walls were various posters of renowned New Orleans restaurants, with a few signed by the chefs who cooked there.

"Did all these guys stay with you?" Grady questioned, admiring a brightly colored poster of a New Orleans courtyard.

Al browsed the posters from her stool next to the cooktop. "Not all of them, no." Pulling at the lapel on her green silk robe, she motioned to a poster on the far wall next to her built-in refrigerator. "Max Kramer, who worked as a sous-chef at Andouille, got some of the posters for me at a fundraiser. A few of the others my mother collected. She always admired chefs, even wanted to be one. She's the one who got to know some of the bigger chefs in town. She started the collection, I just added to it."

He flipped over the sandwich in the frying pan. "Why didn't your mother become a chef?"

"Because she couldn't cook worth a damn!" Al's laughter filled the kitchen. Grady's gut tingled when he heard her girlish giggle. "Lord knows, my mother tried. She was always preparing these weird dishes for Cassie and me to try, but they were pretty bad."

"Did she ever take classes?"

"No, but she made Cassie take them, hoping it would help Cassie find a husband." Al's eyes stared off into the distance. "My mother always wanted grandchildren. She used to do anything and everything to get Cassie interested in marriage, but she never did."

"You've never been interested, either," Grady reminded her.

"Unlike Cassie, I never found the time to get serious with anyone. In my twenties, I was too busy going to school and working. After Cassie died, I was going to graduate school, working, and running this place. There was no time for dating. After I got my masters, and started working as an anesthetist, I dated a few guys and kind of hoped maybe I would settle down with one of them, but …."

"Geoff came along," Grady stated, finishing her words.

"I met him soon after I started working for the group I belong to. We had worked together for two years before the affair began. Even then, I thought it was just a fling, but as time went on I discovered it wasn't."

He turned off the heat from the cooktop and carried the pan to a white china plate on the counter. "When are you going to tell him it's over?"

Al lowered her eyes to the beige granite countertop. "I'm not sure. I have that early case with him in the morning."

Grady placed the sandwich on the plate. "Tell him then,"

"I can't tell him then, Grady." Al reached for the plate. "Besides, maybe we should wait a bit to see if this thing between us works out. We've only just started and things can change."

"What things?" he demanded, depositing the pan in the sink with a loud bang. "This is a relationship, Allison, not a passing fancy or a fling. Or do you plan on staying with him and just keeping me on the side? You know how I feel about being a meaningless fuck … and that is not what we have."

"I just want to wait to say anything to Geoff. Can you blame me? You could still disappear in four months."

"I am serious about us. I won't disappear," he shouted. "Matt offered to make me a headliner at his club. I said yes, so I could be with you."

She picked at the sandwich, tearing off a corner as the melted cheese inside stretched like string. "What if you get bored, Grady? Wanderers often think they want to settle down, but after a time they get bored and move on. I've seen it before in this house, with a lot of men just like you. My father was a wanderer; marriage and kids nearly destroyed him. When he couldn't take it anymore, he left." She popped the piece of sandwich into her mouth.

"I would never walk out on my wife or kids," Grady assured her.

She dropped the sandwich on the plate. “My father said the same thing to my mother once.”

“Allison, I’m not your father.”

She wiped her hands together. “You know, when you call me Allison, sometimes you sound just like him.”

Grady marched to her side. “Don’t do this. Don’t push me away because you’re afraid we won’t work out. The way to make sure it does work out between us is to believe it will.”

“We barely know each other,” she asserted, standing from her stool.

“You know Geoff better, is that it?” he bellowed. “How can you possibly want to stay with a man that is never going to treat you with the respect you deserve?”

“Respect?” she yelled. “With Geoff it was never about respect. I knew what I was doing when we started. I had to give him what he wanted. I had no choice but to—”

Grady gripped her arm. “What do you mean you had no choice? Of course you had a choice, Allison.”

She threw off his hand and turned away. “You don’t understand.”

He came up behind her, set his hands on her shoulders, and turned her to face him. “Explain it to me.” Grady stared into her eyes, replaying her words in his head. “Is there more to this? Does he have something on you?”

“Something?” She gave a heartless, cynical laugh. “I should never have said anything to you. This isn’t your problem.”

“Allison, what in the hell is going on between you two?”

She went to the sink and rested her hands on the counter’s edge. For several seconds, she kept her back to Grady. When she finally faced him, she was pale and her gray eyes were deeply troubled.

“Ten years ago, the house needed a hell of a lot of repairs and I didn’t have the cash to make those repairs,” Al slowly began. “I went to a bank to take out a loan against the equity I had in the house, but I didn’t qualify. When I mentioned it to Geoff, he made a few phone calls to some bankers he knew, but said I could not get the loan without a cosigner with good credit. He volunteered to help me, but on one condition." She tilted her head to the side with a half-smile.

Grady wiped his hand over his face as the reality of her confession hit him. "Jesus, I can't believe he did that to you."

Al dropped her eyes, while she hooked a blonde lock of hair behind her right ear. "He had been hitting on me since the moment I started working with him. He knew I would never consent to being his mistress, but he wanted me. I just didn't realize how much." She raised her eyes to Grady. "I was going to turn down his proposal. Then one day, an agent who always sent his clients to me called and said he was going to start boarding his people someplace else, because he was getting complaints about the conditions in my house. He also said he wasn't the only one getting complaints. I didn't have a choice … I needed to get ahold of some ready cash to fix up my house and keep renting my rooms. Otherwise, I was going to lose everything. When I went to Geoff and agreed to his terms, he promised he would take care of me, and make it so I could always keep my home." She ran her hands up and down her slender arms. "I know what that makes me, Grady, but there are some things in life you would rather die than give up. My home is all I have left. I can't lose it."

"So you stayed with him all these years for the house?"

"I know it sounds silly, but after a while it turned out to be more than just about the sex, and we actually began to care for each other. He even told me he loved me and was going to leave his wife for me, but I never wanted him as a husband. I knew eventually he would run around on me, too. The gossip around his office was that I wasn't his first mistress, and I'm pretty sure there have been others while we've been together. In the end, I got to keep my house, and he has given me everything I have asked for and more. A new car, clothes, a gourmet kitchen, all the things a man gives his mistress."

Grady pulled her into his arms and held her close, feeling like a monumental ass. "I'm sorry. For a man who has always been judged for doing what he does for a living, I didn't even think twice about judging you. I was wrong. Forgive me."

She sighed against him. “There’s nothing to forgive.” She eased back from him. “You were judging me, just like I was judging you.”

“Do you still have the loan?”

She nodded. “It’s a thirty year mortgage, but I’ve managed to pay down the loan by about half in ten years.”

“How much do you owe?”

“Fifty thousand.”

He let her go and took a moment to think. When he looked up at her again, he said, “I can get you the money.”

“I don’t want your money, Grady.”

“Why not? Then you could be free of him.”

“Don’t you see? I would just be trading Geoff for you. I would owe you then, Grady. You would be doing just what he did to me.”

Grady held her face in his hands. “I want to help you, Allison.”

She removed his hands. “It’s my problem. I’ll handle it.”

“It’s our problem,” Grady corrected. “If we are going to make this work, they’re not just your problems anymore; they’re our problems.”

“Grady, there is no we or us.” Her eyes darted about the kitchen as she tried to contain her frustration. “We’ve only known each other for a few days. You can’t just jump into my life and think you’re going to solve all of my problems and then live happily ever after with me. It takes time to get to know each other.”

“I don’t need time. I know how I feel, and I want more with you. I don’t want to see how it goes or wait to see how things work out. It’s all or none with me.”

“I can’t give you any more that what we have right now. I’m still not sure, Grady, can you understand that? I just need some time to—”

The ringing of the phone from the living room next door interrupted her.

“Who in the hell would be calling at this hour?” Grady shouted.

Al said nothing, but walked through the arched entrance to the kitchen and into the living room. Grady quickly followed her.

She pulled her cell phone from her black handbag and checked the caller ID. Giving Grady one apprehensive side-glance, she turned away and answered the call.

"Yeah," she quietly said into the phone.

Grady instantly realized who was calling her in the middle of the night. The idea of Geoff having so much control over her infuriated him. With every passing second, he felt his grip on his anger slipping away. Unable to stand it anymore, he wrenched the phone from her hand and lifted it to his ear.

"She'll have to call you back," he growled into the speaker, and then hung up the call.

Al's eyes ripped into him. "How dare you—?"

"How dare I?" He was floored by her response. "After what we just did, how can you stand there and talk to that smug son of a bitch?"

"I have to! I've got to keep kissing his ass to keep my house!"

Grady went to the sofa and picked up his T-shirt. "You say you know what taking up with Geoff made you, but do you know what it makes you if you stay with him knowing how I feel?" He went to the door. "I may sell my body on that stage every night, Allison, but I have fought like hell to try and hold on to my dignity through the years. I wonder if you can say the same thing." He yanked the door open and bounded into the hall. "When you're ready for a real relationship, you know where I am." He slammed the door closed.

How can she consider staying with that ... that asshole!

Incensed, Grady trotted down the stairs to his apartment. Once inside, he banged his front door closed and went to the kitchen. Frantically searching the cabinets, he finally found the last traces of the bottle of Jim Beam, left over from his night with Doug. He reached for the bottle and eagerly downed the remaining dregs of dark liquid.

Wiping his hand over his mouth, he could still feel that gnawing in the pit of his soul. Glancing down at the bottle, Grady thought back to his night with Doug and all the things he had told him about his relationship with Beverly. Grady had a sudden desire to vent his frustrations, and he knew of no better place than in a bar, pouring his heart out to a bartender who also happened to be a friend.

Chapter 16

The crowd inside Pat O'Brien's main bar had thinned out tremendously since Grady had first arrived. Familiar tunes from the seventies, eighties, and nineties could be heard as patrons, still nursing their house specialty drinks, sat by the bar. Amazed by the popularity of the colorful beverages, Grady considered what was wrong with good, old-fashioned stand-bys like bourbon and vodka.

"I think your bar must sell more of those big red things—"

"Hurricanes," Doug interjected, standing behind the bar.

"Yeah … they drink them more than anything else in here," Grady admonished from his bar stool. "I personally think those damn things get you drunk faster than the Jim Beam we downed the other night."

Doug picked up the empty glass in front of Grady. "You want another JD on the rocks?"

Grady nodded. "I'm not drunk yet. So keep them coming until I pass out."

Doug shook his head and dumped the glass in a sink behind the bar. "Whatever you two had a fight about, it's no reason to sit in here and get drunk, Grady. You should have stayed and talked it out with her."

Grady snorted with contempt while Doug filled a fresh glass with ice. "Why? She won't call it off with the other guy, and she doesn't believe me when I say I want to make it work between us.

She thinks I'll bolt at the first itch to hit the road again. How in the hell do I convince her that I'm done with that life?"

Doug reached behind him for a bottle of Jack Daniel's. "You'll never convince a woman, you know that. What's the old saying? 'Man has will, but woman has her way.'"

"It's Oliver Wendell Holmes, actually," Grady corrected.

"Whatever." Doug shrugged. "Weren't you married? Didn't you pay attention then? Women are only convinced by actions, not words. You can tell her you will never leave, but until you stay and are at her side for the long haul, she'll never believe you." He poured the dark brown liquid in the glass until it reached the rim. "Al's a real tough nut to crack where men are concerned … hell, where people are concerned. She keeps her emotions hidden from everyone. You two have been an item for what, two days? You're just going to have to give her time."

"You've been with Beverly for two years, and she still has not left Matt for you. How much more time are you going to give her?"

Doug placed the glass of Jack Daniel's on the bar in front of Grady. "As long as it takes. I love her. You'll put up with a lot of crap when you love someone. I'll stand by her, be there for her, and hope the day comes when she realizes what a piece of shit Matt Harrison is."

Grady lifted his drink. He peered into the dark liquid, summoning the courage to tell Doug what he needed to hear before he wasted any more of his heart on a woman who could never love him. "Matt Harrison didn't beat her up, Doug."

Doug reached for a bar towel and pretended to wipe up a stain. "I figured that, but I never pushed her about the truth."

Grady gaped at him, dumbfounded. "You know about the other guys?"

Doug threw the towel down on the bar. "I know. I've always known. When we're not together, there is some other guy she's with. It's usually another stripper. She's got a thing for strippers. When those guys are finished with her, she comes back to me. She always comes back to me. That's how I know she loves me."

"She just loves Matt's money more," Grady commented, raising his glass to his lips.

Doug leaned against the bar, nodding. "I think she loves the life. Being married to a man who can move mountains is important to her. When you come from nothing, you don't want to give up the only something you've got." He placed his hand on his thick chest. "Me? I'm just a bartender going nowhere fast. But if I were a man like Matt Harrison, she would be with me, of that I have no doubt."

Eyeing Doug's white, long-sleeved shirt and red bow tie, Grady wondered why the man had not strived for more.

"You could do better, Doug. Go to school and get a degree. It's a start, and who knows, you might meet someone else. A pretty undergraduate that likes your dark, swarthy looks."

"Dark, swarthy looks? Hey, I might not be blond-haired and blue-eyed, but when I danced, the ladies went for my looks more than you California-beach guys."

Grady took a long sip from his drink, relieved that for a moment he had not thought about Al. The burning pain in his gut returned whenever he did think of her, and he would toss back more Jack Daniel's to try and make that pain go away.

"Anyway, I was a terrible student," Doug went on. "Damn near failed out of high school. The only thing I was good at was running track. I started dancing right after graduation, to pay for my car, when my parents cut me off. I'm not smart enough for college, like you or Al. You guys planned ahead and always have something to fall back on. My backup plan is right here." He patted the bar.

When Doug's profile caught the light from one of the spotlights hanging above the bar, Grady saw the lines of worry etched in his friend's brow. Doug may have always strived to appear relaxed about his future, but Grady could see that the years of uncertainty were beginning to wear the man down. Such faces haunted the minds of painters and poets, because any chance to capture the haggard look in a man's eyes might show the world how treacherous and unyielding the weight of life could be.

"You could always go back to dancing," Grady proposed, tearing himself away from his contemplation.

"I thought about it, but I'd need to get a new agent who could schmooze the club owners that Matt Harrison isn't friends with." Doug nodded to Grady. "You ever thought about doing that?"

"Doing what?" Grady quizzically returned.

"Being an agent. You're smart, know financial stuff, and probably could work out better deals than the guys out there now. None of them have ever danced. Might be nice to actually have an agent who knows what it's like to be a stripper."

"Never thought about it." Grady briefly contemplated the glass in his hands. "I've read enough contracts to know what needs to be in them and what doesn't."

"I think you would be better at that then being a stock broker. That isn't you, but this could be."

Grady took another long sip from his glass. "I wonder what Al would say about that." He shook his head. "Probably would hate the idea."

"Did she tell you why she wouldn't leave the plastic surgeon?" Doug probed, leaning into the bar.

"Money."

Doug appeared surprised. "Really? I never figured Al to be the gold-digger type. If anything, she's more of the kind to make it than sleep with it."

Grady put his drink down, baffled at how the alcohol was not easing his troubles. "She's not with him for his money. Apparently, she owes him. He helped her get a loan to keep her house, and then he used it to keep her."

Doug winced. "That's pretty cold. Who would want a woman that way?"

"A proud peacock," Grady mumbled.

Doug shook his head, grinning. "I think you and I are in the same boat, my friend. We've given our hearts to women who are already tied to other men. Mine is married, and yours might as well be."

Grady picked up his drink again and knocked back a big gulp. "Yeah, but how do we cure ourselves of this mess?"

Doug searched the crowd gathered in the main bar. "I could see if Cathy is around."

Grady sank down lower on his stool. "Please tell me she's not here."

"No, you're safe." Doug snickered at his reaction. "She left with Randy right before you showed up. She also asked me if I knew about you and your condition … should I even go there?"

Grady smacked his glass down on the bar. "That was Al's idea of humiliating me. Cathy showed up at the house, and I let Al tell her I was leaving to go to Atlanta to treat my disorder."

Doug raised his dark eyebrows. "What disorder?"

"Tinea cruris."

Doug's dark eyes went wide. "Wait … jock itch?"

"Yeah. Can you believe it?"

Doug laughed so loud that many of the patrons in the bar turned his way to see what the commotion was about.

Grady smiled at his amusement. "I couldn't believe Cathy thought it was some deadly disease. I was damn near ready to kill Al for coming up with such a thing, but it got her to leave me alone. Otherwise, Cathy was probably going to stay camped out on my doorstep."

"Wish I could have been a fly on the wall for that one," Doug chuckled. "I knew she was a bit dense, but … Jesus."

Grady picked up his glass and analyzed the dark liquid.

"It won't help, you know?" Doug berated. "I've been there, and all the alcohol in the world won't erase her from your mind."

"What would you suggest … a gun?" Grady joked, as he put the drink back down on the bar.

Doug picked up his half-empty glass and took it away. "No. Go back to the house and talk to her."

"In the morning," Grady countered. "She needs to sleep. She's got an early case."

Doug poured out Grady's drink in the sink behind the bar. "Ten bucks says she's awake, worrying about you."

"I thought you said she was a tough nut to crack where men are concerned." Grady stood from his stool.

"Tough, but obviously not impenetrable." Doug scanned the nearly empty bar. "Why don't you wait a few minutes, let me clock out, and you can give me a lift home?"

"I walked here," Grady clarified. "It's too hard to find a place to park in the French Quarter. It's easier to walk everywhere."

"Then I'll walk home with you," Doug offered.

"I thought you had to work until four?"

Doug viewed the clock on the far wall by the jukebox. "It's really slow, and they don't need two of us to close the bar. I'll let the other bartender know I'm leaving."

"All right, I'll wait for you." Grady sat back down on his stool.

As Doug took off for the other end of the bar to speak with an older man dressed in an identical long-sleeved white shirt and red bow tie, Grady let his eyes wander to the smattering of customers. By the wall next to the jukebox, he spotted a couple sitting at a table, deep in conversation. He watched how the woman caressed the man's hand, smiled into his eyes, and appeared to be everything that a woman in love should be: happy, content, and complete.

Grady thought of Al and the way she had first looked at him when they met at the French Market. Over time, her eyes had changed from cool and distant to warm and inviting. He wondered if what he had initially seen in Al's gray eyes had not been so much dislike for him, but distrust for what he represented; a man she desired. He knew she had been attracted to him at their initial meeting, but it was not until he had held her in his arms and made love to her that he realized just how utterly explosive that attraction had been. Never had a woman consumed him quite like Al. Even Emma, with her cold, dictatorial personality, had never compared to the burning desire he had for Al.

Grady wiped his hands over his face and wanted to laugh out loud at his dilemma. Here was the woman he had always wanted, but she was just out of reach.

"Ready?" Doug inquired, as he came up to his stool in front of the bar.

Grady stood up, pushing his concerns aside. "You sure you can just take off like this?"

"Yeah. Management is always looking to save a buck here and there."

When they emerged from Pat O'Brien's, Grady felt the rush of alcohol he had consumed finally kick in. He swayed slightly and then breathed in the crisp night air, righting himself.

"All that JD just hit you?" Doug queried, keeping his eyes on him.

"I'm fine," Grady fussed.

Doug motioned down St. Peter Street toward Royal. "Just in case, we'll walk slow."

"Good idea," Grady concurred.

When they came to Royal Street, they turned left, heading toward Esplanade.

Grady surveyed the empty street. "I'm lost."

The dark shadows beneath the balconies of the tall Creole townhouses reminded him of the creepy funhouse rides he used to go on as a child. They stepped into blackness, only to emerge on the other side into a moonlit darkness.

"You probably take Bourbon Street back to the house, right?"

Grady nodded. "Only way I know."

"Royal is quieter than Bourbon at night, and there are far fewer noisy drunks. I prefer going this way."

"I think I prefer having more people around," Grady affirmed, feeling a little vulnerable amid the empty sidewalks.

"I like the quieter side of the French Quarter," Doug professed. "Although, I usually have my gun with me. Just in case."

"Now that I know you won't shoot Matt, I'll give it to you when we get back."

"Thanks for the vote of confidence."

They walked on as their footfalls echoed around the tightly packed buildings on either side of the street.

"If you hadn't gotten involved with Beverly, would you have stayed in New Orleans?" Grady interrogated. "Or would you have moved on?"

"I don't think I'll ever leave New Orleans," Doug confessed while they ambled past St. Ann Street. "Never been anywhere like it. The people down here have such love for their city. They adore every dirty street, every broken water pipe, every cracked sidewalk, and every pothole. Didn't know such love ever existed, but it's alive and well, and living in New Orleans."

"That's quite a testament."

"It's quite a city." Doug shrugged as he put his hands in his black trouser pockets. "It has its problems, too, don't get me wrong, but somehow the problems seem to blend with the benefits. Besides, this place is more like home to me than where I came from."

"And where is that?"

Just ahead, something caught Doug's attention and his gait slowed. "Springfield, Missouri," he mumbled.

From out of the darkness, beneath one of the balconies, a man appeared. He was wearing dark clothes, white tennis shoes, and as Grady felt those hairs stand up on the back of his neck, he saw a flash of something in the man's hand.

"Doug?" Grady said under his breath, watching the man approach.

Doug removed his hands from his pockets and moved closer to Grady. "I see him. Just be cool."

"Wallets!" the man snarled, holding up a .9 mm pistol to Doug's face.

Grady's stomach shrank and the alcohol in his system sped through him, making him feel lightheaded. He stood frozen, staring at the gun and praying he survived to see Al once more.

"Hey, man," Doug slowly spoke up. "Just take it easy with that thing."

Grady saw the gun in the attacker's hand and his eyes rose up the long sleeve of the dark hoodie jacket to the face of their assailant. He couldn't have been more than sixteen, Grady surmised. With round brown eyes, dark, coffee-colored skin and a boyish fullness to his face, Grady could tell by the boy's trembling grip on the gun that this was not a seasoned criminal.

"Wallets, now. Give 'em here." The young man held out his other hand as he kept the gun poised on Doug.

"All right." Doug kept his voice soft and even. "It's in my back pocket." He nodded to Grady. "Give him your wallet."

"Real slow, man," the kid barked.

Doug slowly reached around to his back pocket and was pulling out his wallet when a flash of light from a door to their left distracted him. The diversion made the young man look away for a split second, but that was all Doug needed. He lunged at the mugger.

Grady stumbled backward when the young boy and Doug fell to the ground.

"What in the hell is goin' on out there?" a man's voice called.

The stranger came out of the brightly lit doorway and saw Grady standing there while the young boy and Doug wrestled on the ground.

Grady spun his eyes away from the man in the doorway and was about to go to Doug's aid when a shot rang out. The gun clanked to the ground and Grady watched in shock as their assailant jumped to his feet and ran away.

When Grady returned his eyes to Doug, his friend was lying on the sidewalk and holding his belly. A patch of blood was spreading on the front of his white shirt.

"Doug!" Grady shouted, and rushed to his side.

He immediately saw the gunshot wound in his abdomen. The man from the doorway came up to Doug.

Grady saw the fear in the baldheaded man's brown eyes. "I'll call 911," the stranger shouted, and headed back inside the open doorway.

"Shit, this hurts," Doug whimpered as the blood from his shirt began to seep to the sidewalk.

Grady put his arm under Doug's shoulder and held him up from the cold cement. "Hold on, Doug. Help is coming."

Doug's bloody hand grabbed ahold of Grady's blue T-shirt collar. "I don't want to die … not like this, not here."

Grady helplessly watched while the color ebbed from Doug's face. His dark complexion was turning ash white, and the light in his eyes was quickly dimming.

"You hold on, Doug," Grady ordered.

"Can you tell Beverly …?" His eyes closed and then popped open again, as if he were fighting to stay alert. "Tell her that I was thinking of her." He winced and blinked his eyes. "This hurts, Grady. It really hurts."

Sirens erupted in the background. "You hear that, Doug? They're coming. Don't you stop fighting, they're coming."

Doug's blood began to pool around Grady's blue jeans as he sat on the sidewalk, holding his friend up from the ground.

"I can hear them," Doug weakly voiced. He turned his eyes to Grady. His body relaxed in Grady's arms and he seemed to calm a little. "Just like the cavalry." Then, Doug went limp.

"Doug?" Grady shouted, holding Doug's motionless figure.

Please, God, no!

Grady heard the sirens fast approaching. Within a minute, he could see the red lights coming down Royal Street. He tried to stay calm as a thousand regrets flooded his mind. The entire evening flew across his memory, and he yearned to find some logic as to why this had happened. He should have given Doug back his gun, he should have insisted they stick to the busy sidewalks of Bourbon Street, and if he would not have gone to Pat O'Brien's to drink, Doug would not have walked home with him. Guilt, remorse, and terror seized Grady's heart while the blood poured from Doug's wound and his breathing became shallow. Grady feared that if he did not get help soon, he would never get the chance to tell Doug just how sorry he was for their being in the wrong place at the wrong time.

Chapter 17

The waiting area of the University Hospital Emergency Room was overflowing with people who were coughing, groaning, chatting, texting, and watching the early morning news on the television bolted into the wall next to the bright orange admitting desk.

Grady was sitting in an orange chair with a bowl-shaped seat that was welded to a row of seven other chairs. Still wearing his bloodstained T-shirt and blue jeans, he anxiously awaited word on Doug's status. When he had first entered the emergency room, the world outside of the glass doors had been cloaked in night, but trickles of sunlight were now sneaking their way across the drab, gray floor.

He had replayed the entire incident in his head, desperate for some hint as to the identity of the mugger, and when things had gone terribly wrong.

A pair of brown loafers came into focus in front of Grady's chair. "Mr. Paulson?"

A short, fat man with bushy black eyebrows and sallow skin was standing over him.

"Are you Grady Paulson?" he asked, checking a notepad in his hand.

Grady stood from his chair and studied the man's snug brown pants, protruding gut, and ketchup-stained yellow tie. "Yes, I'm Grady Paulson."

The man's thick lips turned upward in a smile, making his small, hazel eyes disappear behind the round bags underneath.

"I'm Detective Villere, NOPD. I need to ask you some questions about the shooting. You got a minute?"

"Sure. Nobody has come out here and talked to me since Doug first arrived. That was hours ago and I'm still waiting for news."

The detective waved the notepad in his hand to the red double doors marked ER/Trauma Room. "From what I've been told, your friend was in real bad shape when he was brought in, and they had to take him up to surgery right away."

"Surgery?" Grady's heart sank. "When did that happen?"

"Sorry, Mr. Paulson, that's all I know."

Grady searched the packed waiting area, figuring the sooner he got the detective out of his hair, the faster he could get back to Doug. "Where do you want to talk?"

The detective crooked his finger at him. "Follow me."

Grady followed the heavyset man to a corner of the room with an unmarked orange door. The detective pushed the door open and hit a switch on the wall to his left.

"Conference room," he proclaimed, walking through the doorway.

Grady noted the round table off to the side surrounded by heavy wooden chairs with brown upholstered seats. Despite the peaceful prints of ocean views on the walls, the buzzing fluorescent lights above made the room appear dingy and depressing.

Detective Villere closed the door and went to the table. He waited for Grady to take a chair before he put his notepad down and had a seat across from him.

Before he spoke, Detective Villere consulted his notepad. "I got some information from the officer who arrived at the scene and found you with the victim. There was also a Mr. Schneider at the scene. He called 911, is that right?"

"The guy who walked out the door? I never got his name. He saw what happened, and after Doug was shot went and called for help."

"His name is Harold Schneider and he owns the building your friend was shot outside of," Detective Villere explained. "There has been a rash of hold ups in the Quarter lately, and your description of the shooter matches several we've gotten from other victims."

"Are you sure?" Grady shook his head in disbelief. "The guy that held us up was just a kid, couldn't have been more than sixteen. The way he was holding on to the gun made me think he had never done that before."

Detective Villere made a note on his pad with a pen that was slightly chewed at one end. "How was he holding the gun?"

"He was shaking when he held it. He looked completely terrified."

"The officer who interviewed you at the scene says you got a good look at him. You gave a pretty detailed description. Do you think you could identify him in a line up?"

"I think so. I mean, it was dark and he had a hood over his head, but I still got a good look at his face and his eyes."

"We'll probably need you to come in to look over a line up later on." He consulted his pad once more. "Now, I was told when Mr. Schneider opened his front door, your friend …." He glanced down at his pad.

"Doug Larson," Grady inserted.

"Mr. Larson jumped the suspect. Why did he do that? Were you two drinking prior to the hold up?"

"I was, but Doug was sober. We were coming from Pat O'Brien's, where he works. As for why he did it … I have no idea." Grady combed his hand through his hair. "He told me to be cool and not try anything. I thought if we handed over our wallets, the kid would run off. I never expected Doug to jump him."

"The shooting happened during the struggle, correct?"

Grady nodded. "Yes, that's right."

"We collected the gun at the scene. It was reported stolen by a liquor store owner in the Quarter last week, during a robbery."

"Could it be the same kid?"

Detective Villere shrugged. "Could be. Or it could be someone in his gang who gave him the gun, or in his family."

"His family?'

"Oh, yeah." Detective Villere rolled his eyes. "We get a lot of crime in this city, which should come as no surprise to you. New Orleans is a pretty dangerous town. Criminals here are born out of gangs, drugs, poverty, or a combination of all three. I've seen a mother stand next to her bullet-riddled sixteen-year-old son in an ER, take the cell phone from his dead body, and pass it on to her twelve-year-old son. Drugs can be a family affair down here, and sometimes that is the only income a family has. These kids are raised to believe they won't live to see twenty-five. They become so numbed to killing, that after a while they're like zombies, and kill anyone who crosses their path."

"I had no idea," Grady muttered.

"In case it was more than a simple robbery attempt, I need to know if Mr. Larson had any enemies that may have wanted him hurt or killed?"

Grady sat very still for a moment, debating the necessity of telling the detective everything about Doug's past with Matt Harrison. He knew if he said anything, Matt would know where it came from, but he also believed that if Matt would have wanted Doug out of the way, he would have done it by now.

"No, I don't believe Doug had any enemies," Grady finally disclosed.

"What about you? Is there anyone who would have wanted you out of the way?"

"Me?"

"Where do you work, Mr. Paulson?"

Grady sat back in his chair. "What has that got to do with the robbery?"

"You told the officer at the scene that you were employed as a stripper at The Flesh Factory. Could this have been a hired hit man by a jealous husband or lover?"

"No," Grady barked. "I just dance there, nothing else."

"I want to make sure I cover every angle here. I know your club and the guy that runs it. Matt Harrison is friendly with a lot of the higher ups in the local mob. If he wants you gone, you're gone."

Detective Villere sat back in his chair. "Now, do you want to tell me what you know about Harrison's wife and Doug Larson?"

Grady shook his head. "Well, if you already know about the two of them, why ask me?"

"Did Mr. Larson tell you of any problems with Beverly Harrison or her husband lately?"

"Only that Beverly was in the hospital recently for falling down the stairs. He blamed Matt and claimed she was covering up for him."

The detective dropped his eyes, checking his notebook. "Or she was covering up for one Colin Caffranelli, a dancer at your club, who turned up floating in a canal in City Park yesterday. He had been shot once in the back of the head."

Grady lowered his eyes to the table, trying to hide his shock from the detective.

"Did you know Mr. Cafranelli?"

Grady raised his eyes to the detective. "I knew him. I was told he was fired."

The detective's small, hazel eyes coolly explored Grady's face. "I'm not going to sit here and play games, Mr. Paulson. From what I have learned, you're an upstanding guy who travels around the country making a living dancing in these clubs. You never get in trouble and have never been arrested. But this city is different from the others you've been in. Here, everyone is interconnected. When a man who is sleeping with a prominent nightclub owner's wife gets killed, and then the next day another one gets shot in an apparent hold up, I've got to wonder if something else is going on."

"I've told you all I know," Grady calmly attested.

The detective sighed and then gleaned his notebook again. "You're staying in the same house as Mr. Larson, correct?"

"On Esplanade Avenue, yes."

"Al Wagner's place, I know it well."

Grady frowned. "You do?"

Detective Villere shrugged. "I've been there a few times. Not all of Ms. Wagner's clients are as upstanding as yourself."

Grady smirked. "And not all cops are corrupt, right, Detective?"
"Touché, Mr. Paulson."

Grady folded his arms over his chest, uncomfortable with the way the interview was beginning to feel more like an interrogation.

"Do you have any contact information for Mr. Larson? Family, perhaps?" the detective persisted.

Grady shook his head. "I got the impression he wasn't very close with them. All I knew was that he was from Springfield, Missouri, and as for family there … I have no idea."

The detective nodded. "We've been in touch with Ms. Wagner already. She told us the same thing."

Grady thought of Al and what she was going through. He wished she was there with him. He wanted to hold her close and feel the warmth of her next to him.

Detective Villere stood from his chair and reached into the back pocket of his pants. After pulling out a worn billfold, he removed a white business card and handed the card to Grady.

"You can call me if you think of anything else. If anyone from Mr. Larson's family happens to contact you, please have them give me a call."

Grady stood from the table, taking the business card. "Sure will, Detective."

"We have all your contact numbers in case we need to talk again."

"Do you really suspect Matt Harrison had something to do with this?" Grady pressed.

The detective pensively let go a long breath, making his stout waistline bulge out slightly. "Honestly, no, but I had to ask. From what you described of the shooter, this sounds like a straight up robbery gone bad. Mafia types like Matt Harrison don't hire young kids to pull the trigger for them. If it had been a hit, Mr. Paulson …." The detective slowly grinned, making his small eyes disappear behind his pasty skin. "You wouldn't be standing here, talking to me. Hit men don't leave witnesses behind to testify against them." He picked up his notepad from the table. "I'll be in touch."

The round detective waddled to the conference room door. After he had stepped from the room, Grady's body sagged with relief. He slumped back down in his chair, trying to digest all that he had been told.

He put his elbows on the table and held his face in his hands. *How in the hell did everything turn to shit so quickly?*

He sat back and pulled his cell phone from his pocket, wanting to call Al, only to realize he did not know her cell phone number. In their short time together, he had forgotten to ask her for it. As he thought about their whirlwind romance, he came to grips with the fact there was a lot he did not know about her. Little things that lovers shared, they had not had the time to discuss, making Grady feel all the more ashamed of his behavior the night before. He should have been more patient with her, and understood, not belittled her fears.

Standing from his chair, he was anxious to return to the waiting room, in case someone came looking for him with news on Doug. Just as he was about to open the conference room door, someone stepped inside.

"Detective Villere told me you were in here," Al softly said.

She was wearing her jeans from the night before with a simple white T-shirt. Her long hair was pulled back in a ponytail and her eyes were red and slightly swollen.

Without hesitation, Grady threw his arms around her and pulled her to him. "I wanted to call you, but I didn't have your number."

She nodded and pulled back from him, eyeing his bloodstained clothes. "The police called me just as I was about to head to work this morning. They told me what happened and that they were looking for any information on Doug's family. I got here as soon as I could."

"The detective told me he's up in the operating room. That's all I know. When I got here, they were asking me about his medical history, if he was allergic to anything, his blood type … hell, I didn't even know his middle name." Grady backed away from her and went to the table.

"What happened?" she gently pressed, coming up to him.

Grady lowered his tired body into a chair. His head ached, his eyes felt like sandpaper, and he desperately needed a cup of coffee. He wiped his hand over his face and when he gazed up at Al, he suddenly felt as if the world had just stopped spinning.

"After our fight, I went to see Doug at Pat O'Brien's to get drunk," he mumbled. "We were walking back to the house and this kid—a real young kid—came out of the shadows and pointed a gun at us. Before I knew what was going on, Doug was on the ground wrestling with him, the gun went off, and there was blood everywhere." He tugged at his blood-soaked T-shirt.

"We need to get you home." She gestured to his T-shirt. "Get you out of those clothes, and let you get some sleep."

"Sleep?" Grady snorted. "I'll never be able to sleep again. I keep seeing him lying on that sidewalk, the blood just gushing from his body. The whole time I kept thinking, 'What do I do? If only Allison was here, she would know what to do.'"

She stepped beside his chair. "Grady, there was nothing more you could have done for him. You stayed with him and that is all that matters. He is getting the best care possible." Her hand caressed his cheek. "When the police called me and told me about the hold up, I thought initially it was you in the emergency room. Then, when they told me it was Doug, I was … relieved you were okay. But Doug …." She paused and shook her head. "He never deserved this. He's a great guy who wouldn't hurt a soul."

Grady took her hand and held it tight. "I'm so sorry about last night. I should never have gone off on you like that. You were right; we need some time to get to know each other. If I would have listened to you and stayed, then perhaps Doug would not be where he is right now."

"Grady, don't you blame yourself for this. It was a stupid accident. If anyone is to blame, it's me. I drove you away last night because I was afraid. I've never been anything more than a diversion to Geoff. Until I met you, I thought that was all I was good for."

He stood from the chair and cupped his hands about her lovely face. "You are a woman with so much to offer any man. I'm the one who isn't good enough for you."

She softly laughed, and the sound lifted Grady's debilitated spirit. "Listen to us. We're two people so chewed up by life that when someone wonderful comes along, we only wonder what we did wrong, instead of being happy that we finally did something right."

The door to the conference room swung open and a lanky man dressed in green scrubs, black clogs, and a long white coat walked in. He had dark, curly hair, soft brown eyes, and looked like he had not slept in a week.

"Are you two here for Mr. Larson?"

Grady took Al's hand and led her from the table. "Yes, I'm Grady Paulson and this is his landlord, Allison Wagner."

"I'm Dr. Phil Rotolo, senior general surgery resident here at University Hospital. I just finished operating on your friend." He closed the door behind him and came into the room.

"How is he?" Grady quickly inquired.

Dr. Rotolo kept his brown eyes on Grady, looking very worried. "The bullet lacerated his liver and nicked his abdominal aorta. He lost a lot of blood. Because of that, we have to wait and see if his organs were damaged by being without perfusion for so long."

Grady turned to Al. "What does that mean?"

"Sometimes if vital organs do not get enough blood flow, they shut down. It starts with the kidneys and liver, and can eventually progress to all the organs."

"Obviously you're not just a landlord," Dr. Rotolo surmised.

"I'm a nurse anesthetist with the Jackson Group."

Dr. Rotolo sighed. "Then you know what we're up against."

She nodded.

Grady looked from Dr. Rotolo to Al while a sinking feeling took over his insides. "What are we up against?"

Al's sigh confirmed Grady's worst fear. "We may not know for another twenty-four hours or so, if he will pull through this, Grady."

"He could still die?" Grady all but shouted.

"If his organs did not get enough blood, then they're already dying," Dr. Rotolo explained. "His body will begin shutting down. If that happens, there is nothing else we can do."

"Goddamn it," Grady roared, and turned away.

"He's in ICU, sedated, and on a lot of pain medication," Dr. Rotolo spoke up behind him. "Even if you two did visit him, he wouldn't know you were there. The best thing to do is to go home and wait. By tomorrow morning, we'll have a better idea of where we stand."

Grady faced the doctor. "Thank you."

Dr. Rotolo flashed a weak smile. "I wish I could give you better news about your friend, but it is just too early to tell, one way or the other." He turned around and headed to the conference room door.

Al put her arm around Grady's waist. "Let's go home, Grady. There's nothing more we can do here."

Grady let Al usher him from the conference room and out into the ER waiting area. As they crossed the waiting room and headed toward the entrance, Grady became mesmerized by the play of light through the thick glass doors. Stepping through the ER entrance, the sunlight enveloped Grady's body. In that instant, he realized how fragile life was. In a flash, all a person's dreams and hopes could be snuffed out by a single stupid mistake, leaving one to debate if there was any meaning to this existence. Perhaps life was nothing more than a vain attempt to steal a few desired moments of happiness from the unkind clutches of a cold and heartless universe.

Chapter 18

When they returned to the house on Esplanade, Al took a stunned and silent Grady to his apartment and removed his bloody clothing. After tossing his jeans, briefs, and T-shirt in the trash, she led him into the bathroom.

She turned on the hot water in the shower. "This will help you to relax."

"I can't relax," he confided. "How can I relax after everything that has happened?"

She guided him to the shower. When Grady stepped beneath the rush of hot water, he closed his eyes and thought of Doug. He did not want to enjoy the cascade of massaging water on his face, and felt guilty for being able to stand in his shower and do something as mundane as bathe, while Doug was lying in an ICU bed, fighting for his life.

A pair of hands began kneading the muscles in his back and neck. "You can't blame yourself," Al whispered in his ear.

Grady whirled around and saw her naked body squeezed next to him in the tiny shower stall. He slid his arms around her and put his forehead against hers.

"How do you know what I'm thinking?"

"Because a good man would feel guilty about what happened, and not relieved that it didn't happen to him."

"Am I a good man? I don't know anymore."

"You're a good man, Grady Paulson. I wouldn't be here if I didn't believe that."

She kissed his lips and instantly Grady was consumed by his desire for her. He wanted to forget about Doug, and to stop the endless slideshow of blood, pain, and fear in his head. Needing a moment of peace with her, he opened his mouth, wanting more of her. He pushed her back against the tiled-wall of the shower stall. Giving in to the madness surging in his veins, his hands roamed the curves of her body. He lifted her right leg and wrapped it around his waist. Driving his fingers deep into her warm folds, she shivered.

"I need you, right now," he murmured against her cheek.

Al held on to his shoulders as his fingers became more insistent, delving deeper inside of her.

"Then take me, Grady."

He lifted her other leg and hooked it around his hip, eager to enter her, but the cramped shower stall made it hard for him to maneuver their bodies around. Frustrated, he held her to him and shoved the glass shower door open. Dripping wet, he carried her to the vanity and lowered her on to the counter. Glancing down at her nimble body dripping with water made him grow hard. Driven by his desire, he pushed her back on the vanity, pulled her bottom to the edge, and lifted her legs. Unable to wait, he entered her with one forceful thrust. When Al uttered a brief whimper, he froze.

"Shit, I hurt you. You weren't ready for me. I shouldn't have done—"

She placed her finger against his lips. "You didn't hurt me." Al's legs went around his waist and she encouraged him to go deeper. "You can never hurt me, Grady."

He gently kissed her lips and began moving inside of her. He wanted to go slow, to bring her to orgasm again and again, but he was unable to control his passion. Instead, he pushed into her as fast and as deep as he could go. He wanted to be selfish and satisfy his own lust, to help quell his fury. Within seconds, the burning in his stomach was replaced by the demand of his cock. He grunted as he moved feverishly in and out of her. With one last urgent thrust, he came inside of her, groaning against the intensity of his orgasm.

Catching his breath, he heard the running water of the shower behind them.

"I—I'm sorry," he whispered.

"Shhh, don't apologize. I understand."

He embraced her wet body, and then he felt the chill in the bathroom. Pulling away from her, he turned off the shower and reached for a towel on the rack by the shower door. Coming back to her, he covered her with the towel and began rubbing it against her skin. Grady kept his eyes from her face, ashamed of how he had just acted.

Lifting her from the vanity counter, he carried her to the bedroom and pulled back the blue comforter on his sleigh bed. He deposited her beneath the sheets and then climbed in next to her. After pulling the covers around them, he wrestled the towel from her body and dropped it to the floor.

"Next time it will be better, I promise," he vowed, spooning behind her.

"I know, Grady. You just needed to forget."

"You're too good for me."

Al traced her fingers up and down his arm draped over her chest. "I could say the same thing about you." She wiggled around to face him. "Try to get some sleep."

"I'm not going to be able to sleep."

"Please try. You will be able to deal with everything a little better, if you get some rest."

Grady let out a long breath. "What are his chances?"

"Depends on a lot of things."

"Tell me the bottom line, Allison."

"The bottom line?" Al sat up next to him. "Not good. If he does recover, there's a pretty good chance he'll have some kind of permanent damage or disability."

"Disability?"

"Brain damage. The brain is an organ just like the heart or liver. If it goes without blood for too long, it dies, or pieces of it die. They won't know what, or if, there is any damage until they see if he comes around."

Grady ran his hands over his face. "I can't believe this is happening."

Al gently stroked his hair. "Get some rest, Grady."

"Just stay with me for a little while. That's all I need."

Her hand continued to move rhythmically back and forth through his hair. "I'll stay as long as you want me to."

"Stay forever, then."

He waited, his heart pounding, for her response.

"Shh. Sleep, Grady."

Letting it go, he lost himself in the motion of her hand. Suddenly, Grady felt exhausted. All the worry, fear, guilt, and regret stilled within him. All he could feel was Al's gentle caress. His breathing slowed and his eyes closed, and within seconds blackness overcame his thoughts, allowing him to drift away.

* * *

When Grady's eye's opened, the late afternoon sun was beaming in through his bedroom window. He reached beside him and discovered a mound of twisted covers, but no Al. When he stood from the bed, his muscles ached and his head was foggy. Events of the previous night quickly came back to him, turning his stomach into a complex nest of knots.

He glanced about the bedroom and remembered Al rubbing his head as he drifted off to sleep. Reaching for a clean pair of jeans hanging in his closet, he went to his bathroom, eager to get upstairs to her and see if there was any news on Doug.

Standing before her apartment entrance, he gently knocked on the tall door and waited. When Al opened the door, she was dressed in a pair of fitted gray warm up pants and a pink tank top. In her hand was a tall glass, filled to the rim with orange juice.

He pointed to her glass. "Breakfast?"

"Actually, it's orange juice and vodka. Want one?"

"Yeah, that sounds really good."

Grady shut her door and followed her through the living room to the kitchen.

"Have you heard any word on Doug?"

"Not yet," she responded. "But it's too early to know anything. We probably won't hear of any change until late tonight or tomorrow."

After they made their way through the arched entrance to the bright kitchen, Al went to the built-in refrigerator.

"Did you get any sleep?" she asked, pulling a carton of orange juice from the refrigerator.

"Some. I didn't even hear you leave."

She went to one of the window cabinets by the sink and retrieved a tall glass. "I waited until you fell asleep and then snuck out."

"Why did you leave? Did I snore?"

"No." She poured the juice into the glass. "I had to make arrangements for someone to cover my cases for the next few days."

"What did Geoff say about that?"

She returned the orange juice to the top shelf of the refrigerator and opened a cabinet door below the sink. "I haven't told him yet. I spoke with the medical director of the group I work for and said I needed to take a few days off." She reached inside the cabinet and pulled out a bottle of Grey Goose Vodka.

Al came up to Grady and handed him the glass of orange juice.

"Can you afford to do that?" he inquired, taking the glass.

She unscrewed the cap on the bottle of vodka. "I'm allowed time off, and if Geoff has a problem with that, he won't say anything to my boss. He doesn't want them to know about us." She began adding the vodka to his glass of orange juice. "Say when."

But Grady never told her to stop. When the orange juice was nearing the rim of the glass, she pulled the vodka away and recapped it.

"Do you plan on becoming an alcoholic?"

"At times like these, I wish I could."

"Booze will only make you do stupid things you'll just regret later on. You have to face what's in front of you, no matter how much it hurts. If you don't, you'll just allow life to get the better of you and become as bitter as the booze you drink."

Grady watched her replace the vodka in the cabinet. "Who was the alcoholic in your life?"

She turned back to him. "What do you mean?"

He rolled the drink in his hands. "Only people who have lived with alcoholics would know that. Mine was my old man. Drank like a fish and was as bitter as hell about his life. Probably why he pushed my brother and me, so hard. Who pushed you?"

Al collected her drink from the countertop by the refrigerator. "My sister, Cassie. She was always a party girl, but after our mother died, the drinking got a lot worse."

"Matt said she danced in one of his clubs. Is that when it began?"

Al shook her head. "It was real bad by then. She used to get drunk to dance. Then she would drink to be able to flirt with the customers. I knew what was going on, but I couldn't stop it. She always said the booze helped her to dance better."

Grady peered into his drink. "My mother always tried to talk to my father about his drinking, but he would just shut her down with some comment about her being a nag or a pest. The night my parents died, they were coming back from a party. The police said quite a few people at the party tried to take my old man's car keys away, but he insisted he could drive." Grady took a long gulp from his drink. "Last night, I kept thinking of them, and how I felt when my brother told me about their deaths. It was like all those emotions came back after the shooting. I thought I had put it behind me."

"Grief has a funny way of sneaking up on you when you least expect it. I know there are days when I can't stop thinking about Cassie. The pain I felt when she died comes back as sharp as the day it happened."

"I guess time heals all wounds, but life keeps them from closing completely."

Al inspected the dark circles under his eyes and the deep lines across his pale brow. Taking his hand, she put her glass down on the beige granite countertop. "I want to show you something."

Grady put his glass down next to hers. "What?"

"My cupola."

They made their way across a small connecting laundry room, with a few shelves and a stacked washer and dryer in a corner. Passing through another door, Grady noticed the smaller room contained a plain wooden desk with a laptop and printer on it. Next to the desk was a gray metal file cabinet, and there was a bulletin board—cluttered with business cards—on the white-painted wall next to the door.

"My office," she told him. "I handle all the rental business in here." She motioned to a short wooden door, almost the size of an attic door, cut into the wall in the corner of the room. "That's how you get to the cupola." She went across the room and yanked on the old brass handle on the door.

Moaning with resistance, the door slowly opened. Al stepped into the darkness on the other side and Grady followed her. On the opposite side of the door, a pair of very narrow winding steps led steeply upward. As he climbed the steps, Grady's hand skimmed over the deep, red-bricked walls next to him. The air was damp and musty smelling. The small space made him feel claustrophobic, and he was just about to ask how much longer when sunlight could be seen from the top of the stairway. Reaching the last of the steps, his head emerged from a square hole in the floor of the cupola above.

He stood from the opening in the floor and took in the red-stained floors, conical ceiling lined with red-stained beadboard, and high white railing composed of thick latticework. When he spied the panoramic view of the French Quarter, his breath caught in his throat.

"Wow, no wonder you never let anyone up here. What a great view."

In the distance, the tops of the assorted Creole townhouses and cottages seemed to stretch upward and touch the clear blue sky. He could see to the far reaches of Canal Street at the other end of the French Quarter. To his left, the top of a ship moving down the river could be detected over the rooftops. Even the tall oaks cluttering Esplanade Avenue could not reach as high as the cupola.

The city seemed so vibrant and clean from up there. There was no hint of cracked sidewalks or filthy streets, and the only smell he could detect was the hint of sultry spring lingering in the air. Even the din of the Quarter was muffled, with only the occasional croon of a lonely brass horn or pounding drumbeat creeping upward from the clubs below. He marveled at the late afternoon sky and yearned to reach up and caress a passing puffy, white cloud.

"I used to come up here all the time when I was a kid," Al confessed, leaning against one of the white-painted wood posts topped with scrolled brackets. "Me and Cassie would make plans up here. We dreamed of getting out of New Orleans and having a life outside of the city."

"You wanted to leave New Orleans?"

"Yeah, when I was a kid I couldn't wait to get away. After Cassie died, I realized the city was a part of me. I couldn't stand to be away from the heavy, humid smell of the place, the music from the French Quarter, or the eclectic quirks of the people. I knew no matter where I went, I would end up coming home. So, I stayed."

Grady leaned on the rail next to her. "This is breathtaking. I can see why you don't let your tenants up here. I'd want to keep this for myself, too."

"That's not why I don't bring people up here."

Grady played with the long ponytail of blonde hair against her back. "Then why do you keep this place off limits?"

She kept her eyes ahead, staring off into the distant French Quarter. "This was Cassie's favorite place on earth. Whenever she got in trouble, which was almost every day, she used to come up here and hide from my mother. Near the end of her life, she spent a lot of time in this cupola. She was drunk more than sober, those last few months. I always attributed her latest binge to some break up with yet another loser she had attached herself to. It wasn't until the autopsy that I found out she was three months pregnant."

Grady reached his arms around her. "What happened?"

"She must have come up here after a show. I had been asleep in my room, but the gunshot woke me. When I got to her, she was already dead. Self-inflicted gunshot wound to the head, that's what the autopsy said, but that wasn't what killed her. I never understood why a broken heart never qualified for a cause of death in medicine. I think that kills more people than guns, or booze, or drugs. In the end, it's their heartbreak that does them in; the method they use to finish the job is just a technicality."

He closed his eyes and cursed his inability to sense her distress. From the beginning, he had known her sister's death still grieved her. He had never imagined that after seventeen years the reason still ate away at her soul.

"I should have known." He squeezed his arms tightly around her. "I should have guessed there was more to it than you let on."

"It's been over and done for a long time, Grady. I should put it behind me."

"'There are better things ahead than any we leave behind.'"

"Who said that?" she asked, gazing out to the French Quarter.

"C.S. Lewis."

She ran her hands up and down his thick arms, teasing his skin. "Where did you learn all of these quotes of yours?"

"I used to read a lot as a kid. I remember things that make sense to me."

"You're not a stripper, Grady. You're too smart to be dancing on the stage for a room full of drunk housewives."

"You know, they're not all housewives," he cheekily returned.

She shook her head. "You know what I mean. You need to get back into business. I think you need to feel useful to be happy."

"Perhaps, but it's going to take a lot of knocking on doors and handing out a ton of resumes to find a job in this economy."

"Is there something else you can do?"

He remembered Doug's suggestion at the bar. "Doug told me I should become a talent agent and book strippers on the circuit. God knows, I've been in damn near every club there is to dance in for men."

She circled around to face him. "I think that's a great idea. I can help you get clients. I'll call a couple of my father's old friends who still have clubs on Bourbon. We can have your clients stay here at the house. I can help you get started."

He was stunned by her reaction. "You would help me?"

"Absolutely," she affirmed, looking happier than she had been in the past twenty-four hours.

"Perhaps I could give it a try, but I would have to fit it in around dancing at the club. I've still got bills to pay until that takes off. I have to keep a roof over my head."

She rested her head against this chest. "Maybe we could work out a payment plan on your rent, so you could stop dancing and spend all your time working on getting clients."

"What did you have in mind?"

The ringing of her cell phone from the back pocket of her jeans made Al instantly pull away. She anxiously grabbed for the phone and answered the call.

"Hey." She spun away from Grady. "Now is not a good time," she softly said into the speaker. "I need some time off. I've got—" She shook her head and frowned. "No, I don't need you to come over."

Grady grew enraged when he realized who was on the other end of the line. He debated taking the phone from her and telling Geoff to shove his job up his ass, but Grady was reminded of the last time he had done that. He was too emotionally exhausted to go down that road again and decided not to interfere.

"I'll call you later." She hung up her phone.

"Geoff?" Grady glowered at her.

"Don't look at me that way. He was worried and wanted to know why I called in for the next few days."

"You didn't tell him?"

"No. How can I explain about Doug? Geoff wouldn't understand."

Grady angrily folded his arms over his chest. "Why not?"

"Geoff thinks I get too involved with the people who live under my roof. He's been begging me to get rid of my renters for years."

Grady turned away. "Then you would be even more dependent on him to be able to keep your home."

"I know that, and that's why I keep telling him no. I'm trying to lessen his grip around my neck, not add to it."

Grady barreled up to her, his eyes filled with rage. "How can you stay with a man you feel that way about? Obviously, you don't care about him."

"I shouldn't have said that. It came out the wrong way."

"No, it didn't, Allison. Can you stand there and tell me you actually have feelings for Geoff?"

"You don't spend ten years with someone and not have feelings, Grady." She shoved the cell phone in her back pocket. "How long after you knew it was over with your wife did you stay?"

Grady was taken aback by her question. "I told you, I caught her—"

Al moved toward the opening in the floor. "In my experience, affairs come after two people have given up, not before. Otherwise, there would have been no affair in the first place." She started down the steps back into the house.

"You've never been married, Allison," he called, following her into the stairwell. "Having an affair with a married man for ten years does not give you the right to pass judgment on those of us who have been married."

Halfway down the dark stairwell, she turned to him. "Maybe it is because I've been involved with a married man that I have a better perspective on marriage than you, Grady. Don't think just because you were married that your emotional commitment is any different from mine. I know a lot of married people who are a hell of a lot more miserable than people having affairs."

As Grady struggled down the narrow staircase to keep up with her, she popped out of the doorway below and into the house. When he emerged in the office, he caught sight of the back of her jeans heading into the laundry room adjacent to the kitchen. Fast on her heels, he reached the kitchen and grasped her arm, stopping her.

"Why don't you ever talk about leaving him?" he bellowed.

She shirked off his arm. "I told you, I can't walk away until I can either get him off my note or pay it off myself."

"I said I would give you the money."

She threw her hands up. "You just don't listen, do you, Grady?"

Marching through the archway from the kitchen to the living room, Al headed to her apartment door.

"Where are you going?" he shouted.

She opened the door. "I'm not going anywhere. You are." She pointed outside to the hall.

"Are you going to throw me out every time we have an argument?"

"Sounds good to me."

Grady's cell phone in his back pocket began ringing. When he pulled the phone from his pocket and saw the local number, his heart came to a standstill.

"Hello?"

"Mr. Paulson, this is Dr. Rotolo at University hospital. I needed to call you about Mr. Larson."

Grady locked eyes with Al. "How is he?"

"I'm sorry, Mr. Paulson, but the blood loss was just too much for Mr. Larson's body. We did everything we could … but your friend passed away about an hour ago."

Grady closed his eyes, trying to hide the truth from Al for a moment longer. "I understand."

"The police were never able to find any next of kin. The only phone number they could dig up was disconnected," Dr Rotolo explained. "We have his effects here, and since there is no family to take responsibility for him, I wasn't sure if you wanted—"

"I'll come down to the hospital right away," Grady told him, his voice cracking under the weight of his emotions.

"There's no rush, Mr. Paulson. You can go to admitting and take care of everything when you're ready." Dr. Rotolo paused. "Again, I'm very sorry."

"Thank you," Grady whispered, and then hung up the phone.

When he found the courage to raise his eyes to Al, he saw a single tear streaming down her cheek. He watched the teardrop trickle along her pale skin and remembered how Doug had once called her "a tough nut to crack." Grady wondered if his friend would have reconsidered his statement, seeing the fragile woman before him.

Al wiped her tear away. "I'll go with you to the hospital."

Grady's arms went around her. He suddenly needed to feel her warmth. He felt cold, colder than he had ever been.

"You stay here," he breathed into her hair.

Al eased away from his tight embrace. "You need me with you."

In her eyes, he saw the change. She had gone from vulnerable to stalwart in a matter of moments. Her strength deepened his affection for her.

Patting her shoulder, he put on a brave half-smile. "I'll go and get his things. I need to do it. Besides, the doctor said they were never able to get ahold of any family. There is no one to take responsibility for him."

"I've never left any of my tenants for the city to bury before, and I won't start now. I can make the funeral arrangements while you're at the hospital."

He pulled away from her. "You've done this before?"

"A few times. A lot of people in your business don't have any family to speak of, and I figured someone should see to their funerals."

Grady rubbed his thumb along her tear-stained cheek. "You're a kind soul, Allison."

"No, I just believe that even if someone has lived a not so wonderful life, they deserve a dignified end." She stepped back from him. "They'll want a funeral home preference when you go to the hospital to sign for his body. Tell them Lake Lawn in Metairie."

He shook his head. "I'm sorry about before. I just want to—"

"Later, after we have dealt with Doug, we can argue, yell, talk, whatever you want." She waved at the open door. "I'll be here when you get back from the hospital.

He kissed her lips. "I'll cook us dinner when I get back, and then we can get good and drunk. How does that sound?"

Her smile was mixed with warmth and sadness. "Sounds like something Doug would have appreciated."

"Yeah, he would at that," Grady agreed.

Her gray eyes were on him and her small brow furrowed. "What about the club? Aren't you supposed to dance tonight?"

"I'll stop by the club on my way and talk to Matt. We need to have a chat."

Al tipped her head to the side. "About what?"

He shook his head, trying to appear casual and not wanting to tell her about all that the detective had inferred. Grady wanted to protect Al for as long as he could.

"I just think he should hear about Doug from me," Grady lied.

Al stepped toward the door. "Then, I guess I'll see you when you get back."

He put on an upbeat smile for her. "You can count on it."

Grady left her apartment and headed to the stairs, feeling the heaviness in his heart cutting off his air. The walls were closing in, but he fought to remain calm, at least until he was away from her. He did not want to let Al see what Doug's death had meant to him. He had never watched someone die. Holding Doug on that sidewalk, as they waited for help, was the closest he had ever come to death. Images of Doug's bloody body had never been far from the forefront of his thoughts. Making his way across the landing, he could feel the bitter taste of fear rising in his throat. Choking back the rush of emotions, he concentrated on the task at hand. He needed to get to the club and find Matt.

Much of what Detective Villere had said was still rolling around in his head. Confronting Matt Harrison could be dangerous, but he needed to know, once and for all, that Doug's death was just a senseless crime, and not a calculated act of revenge.

Chapter 19

The closest parking spot Grady could find to the club was over a block away. When he reached the entrance to The Flesh Factory, the sun was low in the afternoon sky and just about to dip below the rooftops.

Inside, they were gearing up for a busy night ahead. Tables were being set up around the stage by the waitstaff, while technicians were adjusting the spotlights. Grady spotted Nick and another bartender putting away glasses and stocking supplies behind the bar.

"You're early," Nick commented, when Grady came up to the long bar.

"Is Matt here yet?"

"Check backstage. He's probably back there," Nick told him.

Grady went to the door on the left of the stage and walked inside. Backstage, he found Matt sitting at his wooden desk located against the red-bricked wall. He was talking on his cell phone when he saw Grady coming toward him. He immediately stood from his desk and waved Grady closer. With a sullen expression, Matt tugged at the collar on his rumpled white shirt. His blue suit jacket was hanging from the chair behind him, and his gray tie was slightly askew, making the fastidious businessman appear somewhat disheveled.

"You go ahead and make whatever arrangements you want. I'll call you back, baby." Matt hung up the phone. "I already heard about Doug Larson."

"We need to talk," Grady asserted, glancing about the open backstage area.

"Yeah, I figured as much." He motioned to the door that led to the dressing rooms. "We can talk in your dressing room. Lewis isn't here yet." He grabbed his suit jacket and slipped it around his shoulders.

The two men retreated down the dark hallway behind the stage door and headed toward Grady's dressing room.

"How did you know about Doug?" Grady demanded, while Matt shut the dressing room door.

"Detective Villere of the NOPD homicide division paid me a visit. Seems he had a little chat with you at the hospital about Doug. He said he even flat out accused me of having Doug eliminated because of Beverly." Matt went to the dresser and rested his hip against it. "He said you never cracked during his questioning. He gave me the impression you frustrated the hell out of him. I want to thank you for backing me up."

"Did he tell you about Colin?"

"Yeah." Matt nodded. "He asked me what I had to do with the guy's death, which was nothing. I may have fired the little shit for hitting Beverly, but I didn't kill him for it. If I knocked off all the guys in this club that slept with my wife, I wouldn't have a business left."

"What did happen to Colin?" Grady interrogated.

"I heard he had a problem with more than his temper. The boy was dealing drugs on the side. After I fired him, he was going to skip town still owing some impatient men a lot of money. You can imagine how that went down."

"I can understand why you fired Colin, Matt, but why blackball Doug?"

Matt let go a long, thoughtful breath. "Beverly cared for him. Hell, she didn't just care; she was in love with him, for Christ's sakes." He tossed up his skinny hand. "I learned a long time ago to ignore my wife's indiscretions. She would always come back to me when it was done, but Doug was different."

"You didn't have anything to do with his death?"

"Nah, I wouldn't hurt the guy." He shook his head. "If Beverly found out, she'd probably kill me; or worse, divorce me. I just turned a blind eye to it and figured one day he would move on. Unfortunately, this is New Orleans, and what happened to Doug happens to a lot of people in this town. It was just a stupid accident."

Grady moved toward the dressing room door. "I'm on my way to the hospital to claim his body. After that, I'm going back to spend some time with Al, so I won't be dancing tonight."

Matt held up his hands, giving in. "I already made arrangements for someone else to dance in your place. After I found out about what happened to you and Larson, I knew you would need a few nights off to get your head together."

"I appreciate that."

"How are things with you and Allie Cat?"

Grady sighed. "We're trying to make it work."

"She's worth it, Grady. When Clarence, her old man, came to me and asked me to watch over his two little girls, I felt responsible for everything that happened in their lives. After Cassie …." His voice faded. "I never forgave myself for not stepping in sooner and getting her out of the clubs. I knew it was eating her up inside, but I never knew she was … suicidal."

Grady opened the dressing room door. "Al told me about what happened. Did you know who the father was?"

Matt knitted his brow. "The father?"

"The father of Cassie's baby. When she died she was three months pregnant. Al didn't tell you?"

The color drained from Matt's face and he fell back against the dressing table behind him. "Jesus, I didn't know."

"I thought she told you."

Matt stood from the desk, taking a moment to collect his thoughts. "Cassie was seeing an employee of mine, Kirby Marchand, a few months before she died. Kirby was a bouncer at one of my clubs. He was also married with a baby on the way. I knew he was no good for Cassie, but when I tried to talk to her about him, she blew me off … like Cassie blew everybody off. You couldn't tell her anything. She was stubborn like that."

Grady rubbed his hand over his face, feeling tired and raw. "You ever tell Al about Kirby Marchand?"

Matt shook his head. "We didn't speak after Cassie's death. Al had just finished nursing school and was preoccupied by her career. When I saw you with her the other day, it was the first time we had really spoken to each other since Cassie's funeral. There's no point in saying anything now. It's in the past." Matt walked up to Grady and reached into his blue jacket pocket. "Before I forget, I have something for you." He held out a white envelope to Grady.

"What's this?" Grady took the envelope.

"Your new long-term contract. I didn't send it on to Burt yet. I figured I would let you look it over first."

"Thanks, I'll read through it and get back to you." Grady shoved the envelope into the back pocket of his jeans.

"If you ask me, you're wasting ten percent of your salary on an agent, Grady. You're a smart, Yale educated guy. You should be able to handle your own negotiations."

"I've been thinking about just that, Matt. Al wants me to get into being a talent agent for some of the dancers in the Quarter. Who knows?"

Matt raised his dark eyebrows. "You want clients? I've got guys and gals in a couple of my clubs, looking for a good agent. Problem is, most of the agents out there don't take on dancers just starting out. If you'd be willing to represent some new talent, I could send some people your way."

"I'll think about it, Matt."

"You'd be a much better agent than a dancer. Don't get me wrong, you're a great dancer, but you've got a good head on your shoulders. Seems a shame to waste it. You can't do this forever. You've got to plan ahead."

"Thanks for the advice." Grady gave him a curt nod of his head. "I'd better get going. I've got to go to the hospital and get Doug's things."

"That's already been taken care of, Grady."

"What are you talking about?"

"Beverly saw to everything." Matt placed his hands in his blue suit trouser pockets. "When you walked in, I was on the phone with my wife. I told her about Doug. At first, she cried like hell, and then insisted on going to University Hospital to make arrangements for him."

"Beverly is making the arrangements?"

"She wants to do it. I can't refuse her. Hey, I know it sounds strange as hell, but it would make my wife happy, and I always want to make her happy. I may not have liked the guy, but I won't begrudge him a decent burial. Anyway, Beverly said he had no family … none that wanted him, anyway."

Grady stared at Matt with a newfound appreciation. "I've got to say, Matt, that is very magnanimous of you."

"Hey, I may own strip clubs, sell watered down liquor, hang out with some shady friends, and have a not so great marriage, but I'm not a heartless bastard. I run clean joints with professional dancers and make sure all my people—customers and dancers—are satisfied at the end of the day. That way I can sleep at night and not end up with a bullet in the back of my head." Matt paused and his face sobered. "There's a fine line between dealing in the right side of sin and the wrong side of it. With one, you skirt around the edges of what society thinks is acceptable; with the other, you get lost in that world where human life becomes just another commodity. That's the true art of sin, my friend, knowing how far you are willing to go before you know you are about to go over the edge."

Grady thought of Al. Before he came to New Orleans, he would not have been willing to go very far for any woman; now, it was all he could do to keep from tumbling over the edge.

"I'll be getting back to Al," Grady said, moving toward the door.

"Take care of her, Grady. Make sure you keep her happy."

"I'll try my damnedest, Matt." Grady opened the door. "What else can I do?"

* * *

Returning to the house on Esplanade Avenue, Grady bounded up the stairs to Al's third-floor apartment and enthusiastically rapped on her door.

When Al opened the door, she did not appear very pleased to see him, and stood in the doorway, blocking his path. Her usually vibrant eyes were subdued and her thin, pink lips were not smiling, but pulled back in a worrisome grimace.

Alarmed by her appearance, he rushed toward her. "What's wrong?"

"Who is it, darling?" a man's voice called from inside the apartment.

Grady's blood turned to ice when he heard that voice. "Is Geoff here?"

"Grady, please," she softly said. "He just showed up. Come back later when—"

Grady pushed the door open, cutting off her words. He stepped into the apartment and saw Geoff stretched out on her comfy red sofa with a glass of white wine in his hand.

Geoff banged his drink down on the thick coffee table when Grady barreled up to him.

"What's he doing here?"

"Geoff, stop it," Al snapped. "I told you what happened last night. Grady and I have been through a lot together, and he came to see how I was."

"Come on, Allison, I know what he's after," Geoff roared. "He's just another one of your dirtbag tenants looking to score with a rich woman, so he can be set for life."

Grady gestured to Allison. "Hey, asshole, at least I'm not some pretentious prick keeping a woman under my thumb by holding a mortgage over her head."

Astonished, Geoff moved out from behind the coffee table. "You told him? What are you doing telling some thug about our financial affairs?"

"He's not a thug, Geoff," Al hollered. "He went to Yale and has a degree in finance."

"Who gives a shit?" Geoff bolted to her side. "He's lying to you, just like they all do. Every time one of his kind come into this house, you believe everything they say, let them skip the rent, and then when they drop dead in your rooms, you bury the stupid bastards. When are you going to learn you can't keep associating with this element?"

"Geoff, enough!" Al exclaimed. She strode up to Grady. "You need to leave."

"I'm not leaving him alone with you," Grady loudly balked.

"He's no better than the other one," Geoff declared, coming up beside her. "He was in love with you and tried to turn you against me, too."

"Doug wasn't in love with me," Al argued, as she stood between Grady and Geoff. "He was my friend, and he didn't believe that you were good enough for me, either."

Geoff's nostrils flared and his brown eyes widened. "Good enough for you? Jesus, Allison, when are you going to wake up and see this one is just as worthless as the dead guy?"

Grady pushed past Al and headed right for Geoff. His fist hit the doctor squarely on the left side of his jaw, sending him backward. Grady's right pinkie exploded with pain, but he kept on, balling up his right fist to continue his assault on Geoff.

"Grady, no!" Al screamed behind him.

Geoff caught himself on the arm of the red sofa and stood up again to face Grady. He raised his arm and swung at Grady, but years of dancing had made Grady fast on his feet. He dodged Geoff's blow and popped back up, punching Geoff once more. When his hand connected with Geoff's face, he felt the man's nose cave under his fist.

Blood poured from Geoff's nostrils as he staggered about, but Grady was not about to let him get off that easily. He cocked back his arm and swung with all his might into Geoff's face, hitting him across the cheekbone.

Geoff fell to the floor and Grady grabbed at his right hand.

"Enough!" Al screeched.

Grady turned and saw the fury in her face and realized he had gone too far.

She ran to Geoff's side, while he moaned and rolled around on the floor, grabbing his face.

"Get out of here!" Al shouted at him. "And don't ever come back!"

Grady stared at her in amazement. *Are you kidding me?*

How could she be upset with him? He had done what any red-blooded male would have done in the same situation. Infuriated that she would take the side of the idiotic Geoff, Grady marched to the door holding his throbbing right hand.

"You son of a bitch," Geoff cried out in a high-pitched voice. "I'm going to call the police."

"You do that, asshole," Grady challenged and made his way to the open front door.

Grady ran down the stairs to his apartment and slammed the door closed. Holding his right hand, he paced like a caged animal in front of the french windows that overlooked the second-floor balcony.

He could not believe she had done that. It was as if everything they had shared together meant nothing. The same bitter taste he had known after Emma's betrayal returned and burned the back of his throat. He had trusted another woman, changed his future plans for her, and she had stomped all over his heart. Grady wanted to laugh at his stupidity, but his anger overwhelmed him, making him kick the coffee table in front of him.

You're a fucking idiot, Grady Paulson, that confounding voice chastised.

Pain from his injured pinkie made Grady bend over. He went to the kitchen, opened the freezer door, and retrieved a plastic bag of crushed ice he had kept since first injuring his finger. Gently wrapping the bag of ice around his finger, he returned to the sofa.

When he sat down, something tugged at his back pocket, distracting him. Grady removed the white envelope Matt had given him from his pocket. Looking over the envelope, he shook his head. Maybe staying in New Orleans was a mistake, and another city was just what he needed.

After staring at the envelope for several minutes, he became curious about what the contract contained. He put the bag of ice aside and ripped open the envelope. Spreading the folded white pages out on his coffee table, he was thankful for the diversion as he perused the pages one by one.

A knock on the door pulled him away from the contract. Thinking it was Al, he scrambled from the sofa and leapt for the doorknob. But when he opened the door, it was not Al waiting for him.

Suzie was wearing another of her flimsy nightgowns covered by a sheer robe, which left nothing to the imagination. Tears, trailing black lines down her freshly powered cheeks, marred her mascara, while her sultry red lips were quivering.

"I heard about Doug." A blonde tendril fell from her upswept hairdo as she held up a bottle of Jim Beam. "I thought perhaps you might like some company." She nodded to the bottle. "He mentioned somethin' about you two getting wasted on Beam a few nights ago. I thought we could send him on his way with a bang."

Grady eyed the bottle and was overcome with images of Doug. "Thanks, Suzie, but I don't think I'm in the mood for company."

"I heard you were with him. Is that true?"

"We were heading back from Pat O'Brien's when this kid came out of nowhere. He flashed a gun and before I knew what was happening, Doug and this kid were on the ground wrestling over the gun." Grady's mind replayed the incident as he stared into Suzie's empty brown eyes. "It was … I don't know where to begin."

She stepped inside the door and took his hand. "Baby, you need to get good and drunk, and tell Suzie all about it."

He put his arm about her waist, keeping her from coming any further into his apartment. "I really need to be alone."

She worriedly searched his face. "You're sure?"

"How did you hear about it so fast?"

"Honey, it's all over the news. When a bartender gets shot in the Quarter, it's news down here. It's a violent city, and when good people get hurt, the media jumps all over it."

Grady shook his head. "I would never have thought something like that would make the local news."

"Told you this was a weird place. They celebrate their victories as loudly as they rant about their mistakes." She backed out of the doorway and then handed him the bottle of Jim Beam. "You take this. If you're gonna be alone, at least you can get drunk and enjoy it."

He held the bottle, contemplating the benefits of drinking until he could forget about Al.

"Thank you, Suzie."

"Any idea when the service for Doug will be? I know he didn't have any family. He told me once his folks threw him out after high school, and he hadn't spoken to them since."

Grady suddenly felt guilty that he knew so little about Doug's life. He should have tried harder to know more.

"Beverly Harrison is taking care of the arrangements," he told her. "I guess there'll be some kind of announcement in the paper about the funeral."

Suzie smiled, making her eyes appear unusually warm. "So she came through for him in the end. Doug loved the hell out of that woman."

"You knew, too?"

She waved to the bottle in his hand. "You weren't the first in this buildin' to spend a night getting' drunk with him and listenin' to him talk about Beverly."

"But I was the last," Grady professed.

Suzie's eyes immediately filled with tears. "Yeah, it's kind of sad, ain't it? I mean you start out in life so full of hope and with so many shiny dreams. Then, you grow up and people begin to rip apart your dreams until they ain't shiny no more. Your hope dries up, and one day you're stuck tendin' bar because you fell in love with the wrong kind of woman. Just when you think it can't get no worse it does, and poof … it's all over." Suzie ran her hands up and down her slender arms. “Makes you wanna get your shit together, you know? Give up dancin’, get a life, a husband, a family.” She arched a well-plucked brow at Grady. “You ever think about gettin’ out?”

He bobbed his head. “I’ve been seriously considering it.”

“Yeah? Well, good for you. You get out and get a good life. You deserve it.”

He ran his right hand over his chin. “I don’t know about that?”

Suzie pointed to his right hand. “What happened to your finger?”

“I just hit it on something.”

“Better get some ice on that.” She thumbed the hall behind her. “I’m gonna go. You take care, Grady.”

“You, too, Suzie.” He held up the bottle in his left hand. “And thanks for this.”

“You drink one to Doug for me.”

“I’ll do that.”

He waited while she walked down the hall to her apartment door. After she reached for the doorknob, she gave him one last flirty wave and disappeared inside.

Grady took the bottle of Jim Beam back to the sofa and twisted off the cap. Taking a long sip, he sat back. Closing his eyes, he relished the burn when the alcohol hit his stomach. He quickly took another sip, and then another, trying to put as much bourbon as he could in his system, thinking that the more he drank the better he would feel. As he sat on the sofa with his finger throbbing and his heart in shreds, he remembered something Doug had said the night before.

I’ve been there, and all the alcohol in the world won’t erase her from your mind.

Grady held up the bottle. “This is for you, my friend, wherever you are.” Grady put the bottle to his lips and drank back several long gulps.

When he finally came up for air, his throat was on fire and his belly ached, but he felt better. He rested his head on the back of the sofa and focused on forgetting about Al. The only problem was the more he tried to forget her, the more he realized that sometime during the past few days he had fallen in love with her.

Shaken by the reality of his situation, he wondered where he had gone wrong. Grady found it odd how love and death could change the course of a life in a matter of seconds.

One moment you're alive, and the next you're dead. One day you are content with the way things are, and then the next you are obsessed with the life of another.

Love and death seemed inexplicably tied to the human condition, because we were all meant to suffer through one, and eventually be taken by another. Except, Grady reasoned, death was meant to put an end to one's misery, whereas love was usually what brought that misery on in the first place.

Chapter 20

A loud banging woke Grady from fitful dreams about drowning in pools of blood. His eyes flew open and slivers of the early morning sunshine were dancing through the french windows of his living room. He wiped his face and then spied the nearly empty bottle of Jim Beam on the sofa next to him. At that moment, his pinkie began throbbing.

"Shit."

Then, banging erupted again from his apartment door, compounding the pounding in his head.

Stumbling from the sofa, he went to the door and angrily turned the key in the deadbolt before pulling it open, desperate to make the banging to stop.

"Are you Grady Paulson?" a police officer inquired, standing next to another uniformed officer from the NOPD.

Grady wiped his eyes, thinking this was still part of his dream. "Yeah, I'm Paulson."

"Grady, what's going on?" Suzie inquired, coming down the hall. "I heard all the banging and …." Suzie gawked at the two policemen. "How'd you guys get in the building?"

"Ma'am, please," the second officer said, holding up his hand to Suzie.

She was dressed in a more concealing white terrycloth robe than the sheer number she had sported the night before. Grady surmised the police had awakened her out of bed because her hair was slightly askew, and she was not wearing an ounce of makeup.

She appeared much older than he had originally thought, and also much more vulnerable.

The first officer held up a piece of paper to Grady. "Mr. Paulson, you're under arrest for the assault and battery of a Dr. Geoffrey Handler." The other officer grabbed Grady's arm and spun him around. "You have the right to remain silent, anything you say can and will be—"

"Are you kidding me? That son of a bitch!" Grady shouted as handcuffs were slapped over his wrists. "Where are you taking me?"

"Central lock up to be processed," the first officer told him, taking Grady's keys out of his door.

"Should I get Al?" Suzie fretted from her apartment door.

"No, don't," Grady insisted. "I'm sure she already knows."

"Do you want me to call someone?" she pressed.

After shutting his door, the police officers led him to the stairs.

"Call Matt Harrison at The Flesh Factory," Grady shouted to her. "He'll know what to do."

The officers walked on each side of him while they made their way down the stairs and out the front doors. He was loaded into the back of the police car, and after making himself comfortable, something made him raise his eyes to the third-floor balcony. There, leaning against the wrought iron railing and drinking from a mug, he saw Geoff taking in the show. Grady was furious when he realized who had let the cops into the house. As the police car pulled away from the curb, Grady kept his eyes on the balcony. It seemed Geoff had carried out his threat to press charges, after all. The only problem for Grady was how he was going to finagle his way out of this mess.

* * *

After being fingerprinted, photographed, and thrown into an eight-by-eight holding cell, all Grady could do was nurse his hangover, hold his throbbing pinkie, and think. The gray cement floor and gray cinderblock walls surrounding him stunk of urine, cigarette smoke, and body order. There were no windows, and the only familiar noise interspersed amid the sound of slamming jail cell doors, coughing, cursing, and conversation, was the buzzing of the fluorescent lights overhead. To keep his mind off the pounding in his skull and the queasy feeling in his stomach, Grady mulled over his problems.

He sat on the cold steel bench in the corner of the empty cell and debated whether or not Al was a party to his arrest. He found it hard to believe that after all they had shared she could be so deceptive. Then, Grady recalled how Emma had lied to him about her affair. Instead of making sense of it all, he was more confused than ever. Perhaps Grady had been wrong about Al. In the end, maybe all Geoff's money and connections did matter to her. Despite all of that, something within him refused to accept the fact that she could be so cold-hearted. He remembered the smell of lavender in her hair, felt the way she had responded to his touch, and knew he was not ready to give up on her … at least, not yet.

As time passed, Grady considered how long it would be before he could get out and be able to talk to her. He convinced himself that if he could only have a few minutes alone with her, he could convince her that Geoff was the wrong man to hold her trust. Rubbing his hand over his stubble-covered face, he thought about how she had looked at him the night before. The anger in her eyes and the way she had told him to leave and never come back.

"Maybe I am a fucking idiot," he whispered, sitting back on the uncomfortable bench.

"Paulson, Grady Paulson," an Orleans Parish Prison officer called from outside the gray bars to Grady's holding cell.

Grady stood from the bench. "I'm Paulson."

"You're free to go," the officer announced.

Grady approached the cell door. "What?"

"The charges were dropped right after you were brought in." The officer opened the cell door. "You can go right down this hall and collect your things from the main desk." He pointed down the gray corridor that led to a single metal door.

Grady nodded and quickly headed down the hall, passing a number of similar holding cells containing up to ten men. Suddenly, he felt fortunate that he had not had to share his cell with anyone else. At the main desk, he was handed a large manila envelope with his keys, shoes, and watch, and was asked to sign his release form.

Stepping outside into the sunshine, a wave of relief washed over him. Grady admired the flawless blue sky, sucked in the fresh air, and wanted to dance right in middle of the street. His celebration was short lived, however, when a yellow cab stopped in front of him and a grizzly driver stuck his head out the window.

"You need a ride?"

"Yes, I do." Grady opened the back of the cab and climbed in. "Esplanade and Burgundy," he told the driver.

Less than ten minutes later, Grady was standing outside of Al's mansion on Esplanade, looking up at the third-floor balcony and thinking of Geoff sipping his coffee as he was hauled off in a police cruiser.

Pulling out his keys, he opened the black gate and headed to the front doors. He stepped inside and peered up the stairs, debating the stupidity of going to Al's apartment door and beating on it until she answered.

"To hell with it," he muttered, and trotted up the stairs.

He reached the second-floor landing and was about to head up to Al's place when he glimpsed someone parked outside his apartment door.

When he came around the landing, Al stood from the floor, wiping her hands on her blue jeans.

"I wanted to make sure you were all right."

"Was that before or after I was carted off to jail for hitting Geoff?"

"I didn't know he had pressed charges until Suzie came and told me the cops had taken you away."

Grady stepped past her and opened his apartment door. "How could you not know? He was standing on your balcony this morning as I was led away in handcuffs, Allison. What did he do, sneak out of bed in the middle of the night and slip down to the police station while you were asleep?"

He walked inside his apartment and Al followed him in the door.

"He left last night after your fight, but he promised he would not do anything to hurt you. He came by this morning, but I thought it was to check on me, not let the cops in. After Suzie told me what happened, I confronted him and told him to drop the charges against you or it was over between us."

Grady tossed his keys on the coffee table. "Somehow, I don't think Geoff dropped the charges because you asked him to. He doesn't operate that way." Grady went to the french windows at the end of his living room and gazed out at Esplanade Avenue. "What did you promise him in return for letting me off?"

"Nothing," she proclaimed.

He turned to her, smirking. "Do I look stupid, Allison? He sent me to prison with a specific purpose in mind, and only dropped the charges when he got what he wanted. He wasn't out to get me; he was out to get you."

She held her head high, keeping every hint of emotion from her eyes. "Geoff agreed to drop the charges because I asked him to."

His aggravation growing, Grady ran his left hand over his short blond hair. "You expect me to believe that?"

She glared at him. "Yes! You would have been convicted and maybe sent to prison, and I—"

"I could have handled it. I didn't need you sacrificing your life for me."

"I didn't sacrifice my life, Grady. I simply realized I was making a mistake by getting involved with you. Now you have your freedom, so you can head back out on the road where you belong."

He threw his hands in the air. "Where I belong? I thought I belonged with you?"

"You read way too much into a few rolls in the sack." She turned for the door. "I don't want you, Grady."

He ran up behind her and held her arm. "Don't do this. You cannot give yourself to a man who can never love you, or appreciate you, like me."

"Love? You don't love me, Grady." She removed his hand from her arm. "You're just looking for someone to save you. I'm tired of saving people. I've spent so many years trying to make sure people like you didn't make the same mistake Cassie did. It's taken me this long to discover I can't save anyone. We can influence, prod, cajole, and hope that we have changed a life, but in the end, change is something someone decides on, not something that is decided for them."

"I don't believe that. Yesterday you were ready to pay for Doug's funeral, and today you're giving up?"

She took a step away from him. "I'm not giving up, I'm just changing course. After your fight with Geoff, I realized he was right about my associating with dancers. So, I'm going to get out of the rental business and take back my home."

"How can you afford to do that? I thought you needed the income from the renters to keep your home."

"Geoff assured me that he can compensate me for losing the rental income, and promised I will never have to sell my home."

"So that's it? He let me go, but in exchange you have to give in to his demands." He tilted closer to her. "I know you, Allison. You're not this cold, uncaring person you're trying so desperately hard to be."

She went to the door. "You don't know me, Grady … you never did, and don't ever call me Allison again." She stepped through the front door and banged it shut.

Grady tried to think of a hundred reasons to run after her, but his feet never moved from his spot on the floor. He knew in his heart that she had sacrificed her happiness for him, but she would never admit it. Geoff had found a way to tighten his hold on her. Until Grady could break Geoff's financial grip, he felt there was little he could do to win her back.

Fed up with his situation, Grady gave into his body's loud protests for rest. His pounding head had lessened to a slight throb, his finger still ached, and his body was numb with exhaustion. The events of the past two days, and his added hangover from the night before, made him seek refuge from his weariness on the brown sofa.

Sinking into the soft cushions, his mind continued to fill with scenarios and possible solutions to his troubles. Another thought rose above the chatter in his head; maybe it was time to walk away from Al and move on. The shred of doubt that sliced through his being smacked him like a sock to the jaw.

You always knew you could never hold on to a woman like that.

He detested that voice of reason but began to wonder if it had been right all along. He had never believed himself a quitter, however time and circumstance had weakened his resolve. Before the break up of his marriage, and working years on the road as a stripper, he would have done everything to win Al back. Now, he wondered if she was not better off. He hated Geoff, that was certain, but a plastic surgeon could give her more security than a mediocre male stripper. He may not have liked how Geoff had kept her, but at least she was being kept, and would never want for anything. That, more than his feelings for her, was beginning to undermine his desire to remain in New Orleans.

"It would be best if I left town," he whispered as his heart began to ache. "Might make it easier for both of us."

Chapter 21

Four days later, Grady was retrieving the only decent suit jacket he owned from his closet. Shaking out the wrinkles, he heard a light tap on his door.

When Suzie saw him standing in the doorway, her brown eyes immediately zeroed in on his crooked tie.

"Let me fix that." Suzie straightened the knot on his black tie.

Grady slipped the dark gray jacket over his shoulders. "Can you believe it's the only tie I own?"

Noticing the way her black cotton dress clung to her ample bosom, Grady lowered his eyes to Suzie's pointy black stiletto high heels. He wanted to suggest a more modest pair of shoes, but decided the day was going to be difficult enough without belittling the woman's choice of footwear.

"You ready?"

"As ready as I'll ever be," Suzie sighed.

They were making their way to the front doors when Suzie halted on the dark oak staircase and wistfully took in the paintings on the walls.

"I'm gonna miss living here."

Grady headed past her on the steps. "You find another place to live yet?"

She followed him to the first floor. "There's a place further up Esplanade; it's not as nice, but it's reasonable. I called them yesterday when I got my letter, and they said I can move in next month. At least I'll be able to get out of here before Al's deadline."

"You would think she might have given everyone a little more than four weeks' notice," Grady griped, reaching for the doors.

"Her letter said she was flexible if people could not find another place in time."

Grady opened one of the oak and glass doors for her. "I doubt she'll be very flexible about letting people stay on."

"Are you still leavin' next week?"

He nodded, while holding the door for her. "Yep. My agent found Matt a replacement for me at the club. Five more days and I'm out of here."

Suzie paused in the doorway. "Are you sure you don't wanna stay?"

"Positive. I'll be better off somewhere else."

Suzie walked outside. "Keep tellin' yourself that, Grady. Maybe one day, you'll sound like you believe it."

* * *

Lake Lawn Metairie Funeral Home was located next to the vast complex of Metairie Cemetery. Originally built as Metairie Race Course in 1838, the site became a cemetery in 1872, and still housed the largest collection of elaborate marble tombs and funerary statuary in the city of New Orleans.

As Grady drove his car through the black gates that led to the funeral home, he spotted a modern mausoleum built of white stone and art deco stained glass on his right. He was taking in the grand structure when Suzie began dabbing a tissue at her eyes.

"Are you all right?"

"I hate funerals," she asserted from the passenger seat. "I never go to these things because they make me so emotional, but I wanted to be here for Doug. He was real good to me."

Grady parked the car in front of a plain, one-story, orange-bricked building with a tall, white steeple on the roof.

He worriedly counted the small number of cars in the parking lot. "I sure hope we're just early; otherwise, this is going to be a real cozy affair."

Suzie searched the parking lot with her watery eyes. "Who else is gonna come besides the few of us at the house and the guys he worked with at Pat O'Brien's? I don't think he had any other friends."

Grady turned off the engine. "You want to go inside or sit out here for a while?"

Suzie's lower lip quivered ever so slightly. "Just give me a minute."

"Take your time," he assured her, checking his stainless watch. "The service doesn't start for another twenty minutes."

A red Porsche 911 Carrera pulled into the lot and parked a few feet over from Grady's Honda.

Suzie's eyes immediately perked up as she spied the car. "Nice," she mumbled.

Grady's apprehension grew and he waited to see who emerged from the car. Within seconds, Geoff climbed from the driver's side, adjusted his dark sunglasses, and then fastened the buttons on his black suit jacket.

Grady's anger quickly retreated when Geoff casually stepped around to the passenger side of the car. Grady sucked in an anxious breath. After Geoff opened the passenger door, Al stood from the car, wearing a demure black dress with white fluting about the hem and neckline.

"Oh, look," Suzie chirped, pointing to the couple. "There's Doc Handler." She paused as Geoff placed his arm about Al's waist. "Well, well, would you look at that? Never thought she would go for a married man."

"He's the reason you're having to move out of the house," Grady explained. "It seems the good doctor doesn't want Al renting to our kind anymore."

"Ha! That's a good one. Half his business is strippers and dancers. Every girl I know workin' on Bourbon goes to Doc Handler. Don't know where he thinks he's gonna get business from if word gets around about that."

Grady waited to see if Al would spot his car in the parking lot, but Geoff quickly ushered her toward the orange-bricked building.

"Maybe we'd better go in now, Grady."

Grady never took his eyes off Geoff and Al as they entered the front glass doors of the funeral home.

"Sure, Suzie, let's go."

He escorted Suzie to the front of the funeral home, fighting to keep his anger in check.

"You okay?" Suzie worriedly pressed.

"Yep," Grady grumbled, opening the door for her. "I'm fine."

"You're sure?" she pestered, walking through the entrance.

"Fine," he muttered.

She put her hand on his chest, stopping him. "You're not fine, Grady. Every time you say you're fine, you look like you're about to rip somebody's head off." Suzie straightened his black tie. "You know, I may not be the smartest girl around, but I can tell when a man is head over heels for someone. If you want her, Grady, you're gonna need to let her know how much."

Grady stretched his neck against the confining tie. "She made her choice, Suzie."

Suzie inspected her handiwork. "But did you?"

"I'm moving on."

She snickered and patted his chest. "Yeah, I'll believe it when I see it."

Taking his hand, Suzie led him into a small reception area just beyond the entrance. The pale yellow walls had several niches filled with holy statues of Jesus and The Virgin Mary. A stunning fresh floral bouquet of red roses and white carnations was on a small table. Next to the table, standing signs announced the names of the services being held down each of the two wide corridors leading to the right and left.

Grady saw the Larson name on the sign to his left and waved Suzie ahead. The corridor was decorated with tasteful, tall stained glass windows set into the walls and lighted from behind by a flickering array of candles. At the end of the corridor, double wooden doors were left open, and a row of wooden pews could be seen inside a viewing room. Next to the doors, a wooden table with an open sign-in book and a small arrangement of yellow and green carnations stood waiting.

They reached the table and Suzie picked up the pen. "If somethin' happens to me, make sure they cremate my ass. Don't have one of these things for me." She nodded to the nearly blank page in the book. "This is sad. There are only three names here."

Grady stood beside her and read over the page. Al was the last to sign in, with two other names before hers that Grady did not recognize. Grady stood by as Suzie signed her name, adding an abnormally large amount of swirls and dotted hearts.

"Your last name is Rabinelli?"

"My first husband's name was Rabinelli," Suzie clarified.

He took the pen from her hand. "First husband?"

"Yeah." She peeked inside the room beyond the open doors. "Husband number two was named Smith, so I figured my first husband's name sounded more … mysterious for my stage name."

"Stage name? What about your maiden name?"

"Steinberg ain't exactly the best name for a stripper, unless you're dancin' at a bar mitzvah."

Grady began jotting his name down on the book. "I can see your point."

"Where I came from, everybody grew up and either married a good Jewish boy or a good Italian boy. I married a not so good Italian boy who started me strippin'. My second husband was a not so good Jewish boy. He owned a string of nightclubs in Jersey and got knocked off by the mob for embezzlin' funds. I figured maybe with number three, I'll find that good boy my momma wanted for me."

Grady dropped the pen on the sign in book. "I hope you do, Suzie."

Suzie's face fell as she stared into the room and sighted the open casket. Grady followed her eyes to Doug's body in the coffin. He put his arm around her shoulders and felt her trembling.

"We can stay out here, if you want."

She removed another tissue from her black handbag and shook her head. "No, I'll be all right. It's just a shock to see him in that thing. I was hopin' Beverly might have cremated him. I didn't think we were gonna have to actually see him, you know?"

Grady squeezed her right shoulder. "Just remember, it's not Doug in there. He's gone to a better place."

She turned to him, her brown eyes round and tear-filled. "You believe that? I mean, that we go to a better place and all. I always wondered if maybe bein' a stripper meant God thought us less important than all the good people."

"God doesn't judge us, Suzie, only other people do."

Suzie dabbed her eyes once more and directed her attention to the coffin. "I hope you're right, Grady. I hope God understands that what we do ain't who we are."

Beyond the doors, Grady beheld a small churchlike room with dark red carpet, an arched wood ceiling, and light blue, stained glass windows along the left wall.

Suzie gripped his hand like a terrified child.

He gave her a supportive smile. "Come on. Let's send Doug on his way."

"But on his way where?" Suzie questioned, staring nervously at the coffin ahead.

Grady's eyes settled on Al's long blonde hair in a front pew. "On his way west," he proposed, remembering what Al had told him of her sister. "He's heading west."

* * *

The Lake Lawn Mausoleum burial plot Beverly had reserved for Doug was located in one of the expansive corridors inside the towering white building Grady had passed at the entrance to the Lake Lawn Metairie Complex. The thick atmosphere in the corridor smelled of mold and decay, blended with the heady aroma of lighted candles that shimmered inside glass sconces outside dozens of other burial sites.

While the preacher droned on about ashes, eternity, and dust, Grady's eyes drifted to the surrounding plaques on the other crypts, announcing the birth and death dates of the occupants. He thought it rather innocuous that a lifetime of accomplishments, mishaps, misdeeds, and probably a bit of sin, could come down to two dates that neither defined who you were, or how you had lived.

As Suzie stood in front of him and made yet another heartfelt sob into her tissue, Grady patted her shoulder for encouragement. He found his eyes once again veering over to Al and Geoff, standing off to his far right. Grady gritted his teeth when he saw the way Geoff's hand stayed glued to Al's waist. Occasionally, he would pat her behind, making Grady's blood boil. Geoff's dark sunglasses partially hid the bruises on his face, but Grady was happy to see some discoloration edging out from underneath the dark lenses.

"You want to tell me what she is doing here with him?" Matt Harrison whispered behind Grady.

Matt had opted to keep to the rear of the small group gathered outside of the burial niche, while Beverly took her place front and center next to Doug's casket.

Grady took a slight step backwards to stand next to Matt. "She was involved with him before we began, and she has chosen to stay with him."

"But he's married to one of the big money Browns."

Grady dipped his left shoulder toward Matt. "Married, but hasn't been faithful for a long time. He has kept Al on a tight leash for years."

Matt's dark eyebrows went up. "Meaning?"

"He cosigned a loan for her to keep her house and is holding it over her head."

Matt placed his hand over Grady's shoulder and urged him away from the funeral party. Just as the two men were quietly walking away, Beverly gave out a monumental cry.

Matt rolled his eyes. "She's emotional about all of this, but I'm not complaining. Doug's death made her start confiding in me again. I guess she had no one else. We're talking now, something we haven't done in a long time." About twenty feet away from the handful of mourners, Matt came to an abrupt halt. "Now, what's this bullshit about Handler and my Allie Cat?"

Grady felt a twinge of guilt for walking away from Doug's service, but he figured his friend wouldn't have wanted it any other way.

"Geoff has had his hooks in her for a long time," Grady disclosed. "He's been holding money over her head to keep her with him. Son of a bitch even had me arrested for assault and battery. Then he promised to drop the charges against me, if Al gave him what he wanted."

Matt frowned, making his dark eyes appear slightly menacing. "Which was?"

"To make her stop keeping tenants in her home. He's agreed to make up for her losses, but she has to give up boarding strippers, and me."

"To think I let that man work on my wife's tits." Matt paused and grinned at Grady. "Did you assault him?"

"I broke his nose," Grady confessed with a smug smirk.

"Hence the dark sunglasses. I noticed he hasn't taken them off since he arrived." Matt took a moment while keeping his attention on the funeral party. "Is her hooking up with the doctor why you turned down my offer to headline at my club?"

"I can't stay in New Orleans. I can't watch her throw her life away like this. She doesn't love him, but—"

"She will stay with him to protect you," Matt inserted.

"I offered to get the money to pay off Geoff. I told her I would risk going to prison, but she would hear none of it." Grady shook his head. "You know how stubborn she is. Don't get me wrong, I would stay and fight, if I thought I had a chance with her, but I know I don't. She won't talk to me or return any of my phone calls."

Matt peered over at Al. "Maybe I can help."

"How?" Grady demanded, intrigued.

"I know somebody that might not be too happy about Handler's financial arrangement with Allison." Matt shrugged his slender shoulders, placing his hands in his black trouser pockets. "They may even want to put a stop to it."

Grady's blue eyes explored Matt's face. "Who do you know?"

Beverly's intermittent bursts of sobbing made Matt look toward the mourners gathered at the burial site.

"Let me make a phone call or two. I'll let you know what I find out later at the club." Matt gave Grady a pensive side-glance. "You're dancing tonight, right?'

Grady nodded his head. "I'll be there."

"Good." Matt returned his gaze to the funeral party. "Let me get back to Beverly before I get a lecture in the car on the way home about how I abandoned her at her lover's funeral."

Grady took a step toward the ongoing funeral. "That sounds a bit … disturbing, Matt."

Matt lightly slapped his hand on Grady's shoulder. "Hey, welcome to my marriage."

Chapter 22

The Flesh Factory was packed. The women filling the pit were unusually rowdy for a Thursday night. Lingering clouds of smoke hovered in the air as catcalls and whistles perforated the eardrums of many of the bartenders and dancers catering to the demanding crowd. The waitstaff of men, dressed in bow ties and briefs, had to fight to keep their clothes on amid the zealous, and very inebriated, customers.

After doing a celebratory bump and grind with a bashful, blonde bride-to-be, Grady quickly fled the stage, ignoring heated demands for encores. Toweling off while he toted his tuxedo costume across his right arm, he passed Lewis in the hallway leading to the stage.

"They're ruthless tonight," he warned the winged man.

Lewis rolled his eyes. "I heard." He motioned to their dressing room door. "There's a Detective Villere waiting for you. Nick showed him back to our dressing room."

Grady's robust grin fell from his face. "When did he get here?"

"About five minutes after you went on."

Grady quickened his step down the hallway, anxious to see what the detective wanted. He had heard nothing from the man in days, and hoped he had news on Doug's assailant.

When Grady stepped in the room, he found the round detective eyeing his silver-sequined G-string laid out on the dresser next to his bright silver costume for his second show.

"That don't scratch your balls?" the detective posed, pointing to the G-string.

"Yes, but we must suffer for our art," Grady extolled as he secured a white towel around his waist.

The detective's hazel eyes scrutinized Grady's washboard abs and defined, muscular arms. "You guys stay in really good shape."

"Sort of have to be in this business."

Detective Villere snorted. "Some business. My niece told me about these places, but I've never been in one. Strip clubs with women, I've been in plenty of times, but never with men."

Grady shut his dressing room door. "What can I do for you, Detective?"

Detective Villere's eyes followed Grady across the room as he went to put his black tuxedo costume down on a chair by the dresser. "Are you still willing to ID the kid who shot your friend in a line-up?"

Grady froze, still holding his tuxedo jacket. "You found him?"

"We think we've found him, but I need your positive identification to make sure. We tracked the gun through some snitches we have in a few of the local drug gangs. They said the gun was passed off to a kid looking to join up." Detective Villere came closer to Grady. "Part of the initiation was to shoot some gay guys in the Quarter. I guess he thought the two of you were a couple."

"Why gay men?"

"Who knows?" The detective shrugged. "I've heard of drug gang initiations where they had to rape a woman, shoot a cop, or kill some random target. I've been doing this for twenty years, and there are times when things I see on the street still shock me."

Grady tossed his black jacket on the chair. "If I identify the shooter, then what?"

Detective Villere sighed and turned his eyes to the floor. "Then there is a trial, or in this case a court hearing, because our suspect is a juvenile. He's fifteen."

"Fifteen?" Grady bellowed.

"I've had twelve-year-olds up on murder one. Their age don't matter much when you're dealing with drug-related crimes."

"Will I have to come back to the city to testify for that hearing?"

Detective Villere appeared surprised. "You're leaving?"

Grady turned to the black tuxedo costume. "I'll be moving on to Atlanta next week for a three-month gig."

"You move around a lot?"

Grady reached for a hanger dangling from a hook in the wall. "Part of the job."

"Just stay in touch. If you ID this kid, we'll need you to come back for a hearing. Because he's a juvenile, if he's found guilty, he'll be sent to a juvenile detention facility until he's twenty-one."

Grady snorted with disbelief as he hung up his jacket. "Doug dies and all he gets is six years. Seems like pretty worthless justice, if you ask me."

Detective Villere moved toward the door. "Justice was never meant to satisfy the innocent, just punish the guilty." He opened the door and glanced back at Grady. "Can you come by the Eighth District Police Station, around two tomorrow afternoon, to look at a few mug shots?"

"Yeah." Grady nodded. "I'll be there."

Just as Detective Villere was about to walk out the door, Matt appeared in the hallway outside.

"Hey, Chris. You here for the booze or the broads?" Matt joked, taking the detective's outstretched hand.

"Neither, Matt." He jutted his thumb at Grady. "Just having a word with my witness. How's Beverly doing?"

"You know Bev, crying her eyes out and shopping to feel better." Matt chuckled. "Adele and the kids all right?"

"Great," the detective replied. "Thanks for asking." Detective Villere paused. "We'll talk soon," he added, shook Matt's hand and headed down the hall.

Matt came into the dressing room and closed the door.

"I'm confused." Grady obstinately put his hands on his hips. "What was all that between you and the detective? I thought you said he was out to get you."

Matt nodded. "He is, but we're civil with each other outside of that. His wife and I dated in high school, so I can't be a total asshole to him. Adele and I are still good friends."

Grady was bowled over. "I can't believe this. You actually dated his wife?"

"Years ago, before I got into working the clubs. That's the way of things in New Orleans. Everybody knows everybody."

Grady shook his head, trying to absorb the absurdity of the situation. "No wonder Suzie thought this was a weird town. Are any criminals actually convicted of anything here?"

"All the time. But it's usually because they were sloppy, stupid, or didn't contribute enough to the DA's re-election campaign."

Grady cocked one eyebrow at Matt. "Which I'm sure you do."

"Every time any politician in this town asks for money for their election, I contribute. I would be a fool not to. Over the years, I've learned to pay the right people, so I can operate my businesses without any problems. It may not be the way things are done in other cities, but it is the way things have been done since New Orleans began."

Grady began to press the Velcro seams on the sides of his tuxedo pants together. "Maybe it's good I'm getting out of here. Imagine my morals if I stayed."

"I need to talk to you about your leaving," Matt declared, coming up to Grady. "Remember when I told you I know some dancers that might be interested in being represented by you?"

"Yes, but that was when I was going to stay."

"I know, but I spread the word around. I've got quite a few dancers looking for a new agent. I thought I might see if you're still interested."

"You know why I'm leaving, Matt."

"I predict that things are getting ready to change for you. You might want to stick around for a while."

Grady dropped his tuxedo pant leg, letting the material fall to the chair. "What did you do?"

"I made a phone call."

"To whom?"

"My landlord, Beth Brown. I told her what was going on between Handler and Al, and she wasn't too happy about it."

"What's her interest in their relationship?"

"Beth is Handler's wife. Her family bought up a bunch of properties in the French Quarter, years ago, when they owned the big dairy. One of the buildings they own …." He pointed to the floor.

"Son of a bitch," Grady whispered. "Handler gave me the impression his wife knew about his affairs."

"Knew about Allison, yes, but she didn't know about the car, the loan he cosigned for her, or the truth about why he was beaten up. The good doctor just said he was jumped by the jealous boyfriend of a patient in the parking lot of his medical building. Considering Handler's wife is the money behind the marriage, she wasn't too pleased that her family money was being spent to keep Geoff's mistress in a manner way beyond what they had agreed on."

"Agreed on?"

"It seems Mrs. Handler gave Geoff some ground rules for keeping his mistresses, discretion being one of the biggest. Geoff was supposed to keep his relationship with Allison out of public view. When I saw them together at the funeral and told Beth about how attentive Geoff was, she became very angry. It did not take much to get her to start telling me all about her real relationship with her husband."

Grady briefly pondered the information, but then he picked up his tuxedo pants and began to reattach the breakaway seems. "All of that might change Geoff's relationship with Allison, but it won't change anything for me."

"What are you talking about? It means he'll probably stop seeing her to appease his wife; otherwise, it will cost him."

"I'm glad Allison will be out from under his thumb," Grady commented, never taking his eyes off his costume. "I'll still be heading out of town next week."

"What about the guys I know looking for an agent? Aren't you interested in seeing if you can make a career change?"

Grady dropped the fabric. He stood up and leveled his eyes on Matt. "I'm a male stripper, Matt. I don't know the first thing about being an agent. I would probably just screw it up, like everything else in my life."

Matt took a step closer to him. "You're a lot like Allison, did you know that? I used to watch her and Cassie, whenever Clarence brought them to one of his gigs. I used to sit them down at the bar and make them Shirley Temples, only Cassie would pretend her drink was something exotic, like a rum punch. She would wave to every customer in the joint and chat up anyone who would listen." He shook his head, smiling. "Not Allison, though. She would sit on her barstool and watch her sister, never saying a word. I asked her once why she never talked to anyone in the bar, and you know what she told me? 'Because who would want to talk to me? Cassie's the interesting one.' Ever since then I've always called her Allie Cat, because she would sit and watch everyone with her big gray eyes."

Grady scowled, seeming unconvinced. "Nice story, Matt, but Allison and I are nothing alike."

"Yes, you are," Matt countered. "You both think you're not deserving of happiness. Allison attached herself to a married man and was willing to give you up, because she thought she didn't deserve to you." Matt waved a bony hand down Grady's physique. "Now you're going to run away from the one woman who made you feel like you were worth something. When you were with her, you saw yourself as a hell of a lot more than a male stripper. And you know what? You are worth something, Grady. You just had to have someone else wake you up from this coma you've been walking around in. Now that your eyes are open, you can't go back. You have to try to be that man, the one you always dreamed of being."

Grady shook his head. “She doesn’t want me. She made that very clear.”

“She doesn’t want to want you. I discovered something else about Allie Cat all those years ago. She’s stubborn as hell. Sometimes stubborn people need to be made to realize what they have before it packs up and leaves town.”

“Nice try, Matt. But I’m going. We’re over.”

“Personally, I think you’re making a big mistake, Grady.” Matt turned for the door. “But what do I know? I’m just a skin man, not a matchmaker.” Matt opened the door and walked into the hallway.

Grady ran his hand over his chin, thinking of Al. He had moments of weakness where he longed to see her again, but wasn’t sure if he should. Their last encounter had left him bruised and broken. Another might destroy him for good.

Get out while you still can, reason counseled. *You’ve got nothing left for you in New Orleans.*

In the pit of his gut, he feared that his irksome inner voice was right. The only question that remained was why was his heart still not convinced?

Chapter 23

Located on Royal Street, in the heart of the French Quarter, the New Orleans Police Department Eighth District Station was more like an antebellum home than a place for law officers. The Greek Revival building had white Corinthian columns surrounding a yellow plaster exterior, and a white post-railing on the roof, detailed with ornamental urns.

Grady browsed the building and then the assortment of police cars and motorcycles parked out front. He thought it almost a shame that something as grand and elegant as that old building would be home to those who spent their careers wrestling with the ugliness of the city. It was as if the buildings of New Orleans, with their unique beauty, hid the real secrets of those who inhabited them. Stashing away a multitude of sins behind romantic balconies, charming doorways, and enchanting decorative facades, only added to the mystique of the Big Easy.

"Right on time," a man's craggy voice called to Grady.

Glancing to his right, Grady spied Detective Villere sporting a casual brown blazer and khaki pants. A brown belt held in his wide girth and also showed off his shiny gold badge.

"I saw you from my office window," the detective revealed, pointing to a window to his right. "Come inside."

Once they entered the thick glass doors, a whir of activity greeted Grady. Police officers—some dressed in their uniformed blues and some in street clothes—scurried around a large main floor. There were glass partitions along the edges of the room, allowing visual access to all of the offices. On the main floor were an assortment of metal desks laid out in rows, where uniformed officers fielded phone calls.

"I'm over here," Detective Villere said, motioning to his right.

Grady followed him to the small office.

"Kind of makes it hard to have any privacy." Grady waved at the glass office walls.

"They designed it that way. I guess the city wanted to make sure we were doing our jobs." The detective went to a standard issue metal desk—no different from the ones on the central floor. He picked up a brown manila folder, opened it, and placed it before a black and gray metal chair in front of the desk. "Look these over and see if you recognize anyone," he directed.

Grady moved closer to the desk and had a seat. He began carefully examining six mug shots, stapled to the inside of the folder. At first, none of the faces looked familiar, and Grady was about to turn to the detective when something about one of the pictures caught his eye.

The face was of a very young man with coffee-colored skin and a round, almost cherubic-looking face, but it was the eyes that resonated with Grady. It was the same terrified look he had seen in the eyes of the assailant that night. He stared at the picture and slowly other details about his very young assailant came back to him.

After a few more seconds, he pointed to the mug shot. "That's him."

Detective Villere checked the mug shot. "You're sure?"

"I remembered the look in his eyes. It's the same as the kid in that mug shot. It's the same guy."

The detective picked up the folder. "That's the kid we have in custody." He shut the folder. "Now that we have a positive ID, we can get him to talk."

"Talk about what?"

"If he knows he was identified, he'll probably be willing to tell us who gave him the gun, hoping that will lessen his jail time."

Grady sat back in his chair. "Does all of this ever get to you?" He waved his hand over the desk. "I can't imagine doing this for a living."

"Funny, I can't imagine doing what you do for a living. With me, I'm getting satisfaction by getting bad guys off the streets and keeping people safe. What do you get from your job?"

Grady ignored the question. "How would putting Matt Harrison away give you satisfaction?"

The detective shrugged. "Personally, I like the hell out of Matt. Professionally, he makes my skin crawl. However, it's who he hangs out with that really interests me."

"Can you really separate your personal feelings from your professional ones?"

The detective rested his hip against his desk and folded his arms over his ample belly. "When you dance with those women on the stage, do you keep your professional feelings for them separate from your personal feelings?"

Grady was about to answer when he thought of his dance with Al. It was the one time when his personal feelings and professional feelings had melded into one.

"I used to think I could, but lately …."

"Then, my friend, it's time for you to get out of that game. When your professional life clashes with your personal life, you're going to have to give up one or the other. If you don't, you'll be miserable with both."

Grady stood from his chair. "That's worth thinking about."

The detective moved away from his desk toward the open office door. "You're a bright man, Grady Paulson. I did some checking up on you. BA in finance from Yale, upper management at Lehman Brothers; you were going somewhere. I think you could get back on track, if you found your melch."

"My what?"

"Melch: the thing that makes it all worthwhile." Detective Villere smiled and placed his hand over his chest. "For me, it's my wife and kids. They are what I go home to every night that makes all I go through here bearable." He paused. "So, who do you go home to?"

"Haven't had a home to go to in a while," Grady divulged.

Detective Villere held out his hand. "I hope you find one soon, Grady."

Grady shook his hand. "We're done?"

"All done," Detective Villere confirmed. "Let me know where you end up, in case we need to speak with you again."

"I will." Grady moved toward the door.

"And Grady?" the detective called to him.

Grady turned to see the detective looking out a window to Royal Street.

"Good luck with the girl," he added.

"What girl?"

Detective Villere just smiled and shook his head.

Grady walked out the door of the Eighth District Police Station and observed the bustling French Quarter around him. The warm air held a myriad of enticing aromas wafting up from Brennan's Restaurant on the next block. He was about to step from the curb when he spotted a red BMW 325i parked next to the police station entrance. Curious, he took a step closer, but quickly discovered the car was empty. Shaking his head and disappointed by the flurry of hope in his gut, he was about to turn away from the car when he heard a woman's musical voice behind him.

"I was told I could find you here."

Grady slowly spun around.

Al was standing by the curb, her blonde hair flowing about her shoulders, wearing a pair of green scrubs and holding up a brown paper bag in her hand.

His heart momentarily thrilled at seeing her. Then Grady remembered how she had pushed him away, and his resolve hardened against her. "What are you doing here?"

"I thought we should talk. I think there are some things we should settle between us."

Grady surveyed the smattering of people strolling along the sidewalks on either side of the street. "Who told you where I was?"

"Uncle Matt. I called the club looking for you and he picked up the phone. We chatted for a while … mostly about you."

"I'll bet that was an interesting conversation," he mumbled.

"The reason I'm here is because I need to give you something."

Grady took a step closer to the curb. "What do you need to give me?"

She held up the paper bag in her hand. "I got you these from the French Market."

Grady pointed to the bag. "What is it?"

"Strawberries."

He eased in front of her. "Why are you bringing me strawberries, Allison?"

"To tell you how I'm sorry I am about all the things I said … and that you were right about Geoff. He was a proud peacock." She rolled her eyes. "He fired me today."

Grady fought to keep his smug grin in check. "Did he?"

"He said his wife wanted him to work with only male anesthetists."

Grady took the bag of strawberries from her. "What brought that on?"

"I'm not sure. I went into work this morning and he called me into his office. He just gave me his keys to my place and said it was over."

Grady put the bag behind his back, eyeing her reaction. "How do you feel about that?"

"Relieved," Al sighed. "He also told me he would make sure the note on my house was signed over to me. No strings attached."

"I'm glad for you," Grady admitted, keeping the emotion from his voice. "I know how much you love your home."

"Now you and the others don't have to move out. With Geoff no longer holding my purse strings, I can stay in the rental business."

Grady cast his eyes to the street. "Well then, you can find a new tenant for my place. I've decided to head back out on the road. I'll be leaving next week."

"You weren't going to tell me?"

His eyes veered back to her. "I was going to slip a note under your door." He held up his right pinkie. "But I figured it would be safer to just leave my keys and my excuses with Suzie."

They stood for a few uncomfortable minutes as the sound of the French Quarter surrounded them. There were a million things Grady wanted to say, but he said nothing as his grip on his bag of strawberries tightened.

Finally breaking their agonizing silence, Al waved at the police station. "Did they find the guy who shot Doug?"

Grady pulled the bag of strawberries from behind him and brushed out the creases he had made in the bag. "Yeah, it was a fifteen-year-old kid. They'll probably need me to come back to testify at a hearing."

Al took a step closer to him. "Maybe when you come back the watermelons will be out."

"Maybe so." He held up the bag. "Thank you for these." Grady made a move to leave when she stopped him.

"I was hoping we could at least be friends."

That familiar burn in his gut for her sparked to life, but he refused to give in to it. "I can't be friends with you. I can't go backwards. There's been too much between us."

She inched closer. "I know that, but I was hoping you would give me another chance." Al came right up to him. "I was wrong, Grady. Wrong to turn to Geoff, wrong to not trust my feelings for you, and wrong to let you slip away."

The pain of her rejection was still fresh in his heart, but intermingled with it was a glimmer of hope that maybe all was not lost. "What feelings for me?"

She smiled and his defenses crumbled. "The ones I have been denying since the moment you hit on me in the French Market."

He studied her gray eyes, weighing her sincerity. "I didn't hit on you."

"Of course you hit on me, Grady. It was obvious. That line about—"

"Fine, I hit on you. Let's get back to the part where you were going to tell me how you feel about me."

She ran her hand up his T-shirt. "So you admit you liked me from the beginning, too?"

"At this particular moment, I'll admit to anything." He dipped his head to her. "Just tell me how you feel. I need to hear it."

"How I feel?" Al caressed his cheek. "For the first time in my life, I feel alive, completely alive with you, Grady Paulson. If you go, I'm afraid I'll disappear into my empty life and never know that sensation ever again. If you stay … well, I think we might just have a chance at happiness together. What do you say?"

"Are you sure you want a future with me? I want you, Allison, but I want all of you … I don't want to win you by default."

"You're first in my heart Grady, then, now, and always." She stood back from him, wearing that wonderful grin that always got to him. "Besides, I always hated peacocks. They're way too noisy, and they like to peck at your shoes."

His reservations retreating, he shook his head at his inability to resist her. "Where did you learn that about peacocks?"

Al stepped back to the curb. "The zoo, naturally." She went to the driver's side door of her red car. "Get in," she instructed.

Grady moved toward the passenger side door. "Where are we going?"

"To talk about our future together."

"What if I don't want to talk?" he pressed, raising his eyebrows suggestively.

She eyed the police station next to the car. "We could take the opportunity to explore another one of my fantasies. You ever had sex in a police station?"

Laughing, Grady opened his car door. "Get in and take me home before you get us both arrested."

"You don't want to try?"

He saw her standing next to the car, the light breeze dancing in her hair, and suddenly he knew he would never leave her. He couldn't. Like the crusty Detective Villere had suggested, he needed to find the thing that made his life worthwhile. In that instant, Grady knew he had found his melch. Without Al, he was lost.

"Why don't we save that one for the honeymoon?" He climbed into the car.

"What honeymoon? I'm not marrying you, Grady," Al objected, sliding into the driver's seat.

"You'll marry me." He smiled at her, showing her every inch of the happiness in his heart. "Who knows you better than me?"

Shaking her head, she started the car. "We've spent what … a few days together. You can't know me that well."

"You don't get to know someone by counting off the days on a calendar, baby; you get to know them by letting them into your heart."

She paused, smirked, and then put the car into gear. "I can't argue with you there."

"That's a first," he snickered under his breath.

As Al's BMW pulled away from the curb, he took in the lively crowds gathered about the sidewalks, feeling that indefinable enthusiasm the French Quarter seemed to arouse. As if seeing the city for the first time, Grady realized Doug had been right. Despite its corrupt nature and seedy ways, New Orleans held a fascinating beauty. There was just something about it that grabbed hold of you and never let go. He could understand why the natives loved it so, and knew he would never be able to leave. Grady had finally reached the end of his travels. He had come home.

Epilogue

Standing before the black gate of the imposing French Quarter mansion on Esplanade Avenue, the brown-haired man gripped a suitcase in one hand while adjusting the strap of the duffel bag over his shoulder with the other. He reached for the entrance button on the side of the gate and pressed it, waiting to gain access.

Gazing upward, the stranger's brown eyes explored the large french windows, wrought iron-wrapped balconies, and the round cupola atop the steep, sloping roof.

"Cool, a cupola."

"Yeah?" a woman's sultry voice came over the speaker beside the gate.

"Hi, I'm Mitch Levy. I'm the new tenant," the rugged, well-built man said, as a ripple of defined muscles peeked out from under his short-sleeved shirt.

"I'm comin' down," the woman's voice proclaimed.

Mitch Levy wiped away the faint film of sweat collecting on his brow as the late summer sun climbed higher in the mid-morning sky.

A rustle of a door opening before him made Mitch look up to the dark oak and etched glass doors of the home. When a beautiful blonde with long, slender legs stepped out from the doorway, clad in a revealing nightgown and barely-there cream silk robe, his eyes nearly popped out of his head.

"You're the new guy, right? For apartment C?"

Mitch nodded while his eyes traveled down the woman's large breasts and slender hips.

"I'm Suzie," she told him, approaching the gate. Her brown eyes drank in his impressive figure. "Wow, you're really tall," she added.

Mitch bashfully dipped his head to the side. "Yeah, just about six foot five."

Suzie opened the black gate. "You're a dancer, right?"

"Stripper, yeah. I'll be over at The Flesh Factory for four months."

"Well, I might just have to check out your show, Mitch." She held the gate open as Mitch struggled to get his bags through the narrow gateway. "You've been dancin' on the circuit for a while?"

Mitch nodded. "Two years."

Suzie fell in step beside him as they made their way up the narrow walkway.

"Long time to be on the road." Suzie played with the lapel of her robe. "I used to do the circuit, but I've been dancin' steady in New Orleans for over two years now. I've got a great agent keeps me workin' in the clubs here."

Mitch climbed the cement steps to the doors. "Who's your agent?"

Suzie walked behind him, studying the round curve of his ass. "Grady Paulson."

Mitch turned to her. "Yeah, me too. I just signed with him a few months back. Heard he is the up and coming guy for dancers."

Suzie smiled, showing off her pearly white teeth, "He's the best."

Mitch waited and Suzie pushed one of the oak and glass doors open. "He's the one who got me this place," he told her.

Suzie tittered lightly and rolled her eyes. "I know." She watched as he hobbled in the door with his bags. "You're gonna be on the second floor right down from me." She grinned, ogling his wide shoulders and thick arms. "Isn't that convenient?"

Mitch admired the brightly lit entrance and beaded drop chandelier. "Yeah, great."

Suzie climbed the dark oak stairs, making sure to accentuate the swing of her hips for his viewing pleasure.

"Al, the owner, asked me to give you your keys." Suzie flashed a set of silver keys in her manicured hand. "I'm to show you to your place and give you the ground rules."

Mitch's brown eyes went wide. "Ground rules? You're kidding?"

Halfway up the steps, Suzie turned to him. "Why does everyone say that? Yes, Little Al's got a few ground rules for all of her tenants."

"Little Al?"

Suzie rounded the top of the stairs and waited for Mitch to catch up. "Allison Wagner; she owns the place, and we all call her Little Al. She's real particular about noise. Likes to keep it quiet around here, so no loud music, loud parties, or any other loud disturbances that keep people up at night, you know?"

Mitch joined her on the second-floor landing. "Got it."

Suzie turned and headed down the hallway. Then a door closing on the floor above echoed along the landing.

"You'll be on the second floor along with me, Jason, and Barry. I'm in apartment D, Jason's in E. He dances at the Cock Fight Club, and Barry will be dancin' with you at The Flesh Factory, and he's in apartment F."

Walking next to her, Mitch struggled with his suitcases and duffel bag. "What about the third floor?"

"No tenants are allowed above the second floor," she instructed.

"What about the cupola? Can we go up there?"

"The cupola is off limits to all tenants," a man's voice affirmed from the landing.

* * *

Mitch and Suzie both turned to see a tall, muscular man with small blues eyes and short-cropped blond hair coming toward them. Dressed in a fitted black suit and black tie, with a shiny stainless steel watch on his right wrist, he seemed like any other businessman heading to work.

"Ah, there he is," Suzie chirped. "Mitch, you know Grady Paulson."

Mitch dropped his suitcase on the floor. "I didn't know you'd be here," Mitch declared, holding out his hand to Grady.

Grady gave his hand a firm shake. "I live on the third floor."

Mitch's brown eyes vacillated from Grady to Suzie, seeming slightly confused. "You live here?"

"Grady is Al Wagner's husband," Suzie explained.

It was then Mitch noticed the gold band on the third finger of Grady's left hand. "Your wife's name is Wagner?"

"It is … for now." Grady grimaced slightly. "I'm still working on getting her to take my name. She's kind of stubborn."

"Kind of stubborn?" Suzie snorted and turned to Mitch. "You'd better just call her Wagner," she advised. "Consider it another one of those ground rules."

Grady waved ahead to Mitch's apartment door. "Well, I'll be close by in case anything comes up." He waited while Mitch picked up his bag and started down the hallway once more. "You'll like it here. I came to this building over a year ago as a dancer."

Mitch gave him a quizzical side-glance. "Really? How did you go from being a dancer to an agent?"

Grady smiled. "That's a long story."

"Grady?" a woman's musical voice called from the third floor.

"I'm down here, darling."

All three turned and listened as a door closed and footfalls could be heard coming down the stairs from the third floor.

Grady dashed up the steps. When he emerged from the shadows on the stairs, he was holding the hand of a petite woman with long blonde hair. Her white stretch pants and black T-shirt barely covered her very large belly.

"I told you, no going up and down the stairs without me, Allison," Grady fussed.

"I'm not disabled, Grady; I'm pregnant. I can get around without your help."

When they reached the last step together, Grady squeezed her hand. "Just try to humor me, okay?"

"I'll think about it," she muttered.

As they came around the front of the landing, Suzie's brown eyes focused on Al's belly. "Lord, I think you're bigger than you were yesterday, Al."

Al rubbed her hand over the black T-shirt covering her midsection. "I don't think I can wait two more weeks for the C-section. I feel like I am going to pop at any moment."

"Congratulations," Mitch remarked, nodding to her belly.

Grady motioned to Mitch. "This is Mitch Levy, the new dancer and tenant I told you about, Allison."

Al smiled for him. "Welcome. I hope you like it here."

"I'm sure I will. It's a great old house," Mitch commented.

"Yes, it is," Grady agreed. "You'll be in my old apartment. I lived in C when I first moved in here. It holds a lot of great memories for us," he added with a mischievous grin to his wife.

Al elbowed Grady. "If you need anything, just check with Suzie. She'll be covering for me until the bruiser comes along."

"The bruiser?" Mitch inquired.

Grady smiled proudly. "It's a boy, a big one."

Mitch gave him a heartfelt grin. "Any idea what you're going to name him?"

"Douglas Matthew," Al told him.

"I just love that name," Suzie sniffed, wiping her hand over her left eye.

"Don't start crying again, Suzie," Al pleaded. "I can't have you crying every time we say his name." She turned to Grady. "Don't forget to pick up my chocolate ice cream before you come home."

Grady playfully rolled his blue eyes for Mitch. "Cravings. They're driving me crazy."

Al nodded to Mitch. "We should let you get settled." She kissed Grady's cheek and began waddling back toward the stairs.

"I'll see you up," Grady clucked, and then jogged to catch up to her side.

"I can make it," she insisted.

"Allison, stop arguing with me." He took her hand and led her toward the stairs.

Al watched as Mitch and Suzie entered apartment C. "He reminds me of you."

Grady squeezed her hand. "He's nothing like me. For one, he's a better dancer."

"He has the same look in his eyes that you had when we first met."

"What look was that?"

"That lost look, like a man in search of a place to hang up his suitcase."

"I did not look lost," Grady contended.

She paused before the stairs and smiled into his blue eyes. "Yes, you did. You looked like I felt at the time. I think that was the moment I knew you were going to be much more than just another tenant."

His fingertips caressed her pink cheek. "You had a funny way of showing it, baby."

"Well, I couldn't make it easy for you."

Grady chuckled. "I'm glad you didn't."

"You are?"

He put his arm around her. "Someone once said, 'Sometimes a man needs to go through a good bit of hell before a woman can let him know heaven.'"

"Who said that?" Al asked, crinkling her brow.

He basked in the love shining from her gray eyes. "You did."

The End

Alexandrea Weis is an advanced practice registered nurse who was born and raised in New Orleans. Having been brought up in the motion picture industry, she learned to tell stories from a different perspective and began writing at the age of eight. Infusing the rich tapestry of her hometown into her award-winning novels, she believes that creating vivid characters makes a story moving and memorable. A permitted/certified wildlife rehabber with the Louisiana Wildlife and Fisheries, Weis rescues orphaned and injured wildlife. She lives with her husband and pets in New Orleans.

To read more about Alexandrea Weis or her books, you can go to the following sites:
Website: http://www.alexandreaweis.com/
Facebook: http://www.facebook.com/authoralexandreaweis
Twitter: https://twitter.com/alexandreaweis
Goodreads:
http://www.goodreads.com/author/show/1211671.Alexandrea_Weis
TSU: https://www.tsu.co/alexandreaweis

Made in the USA
Middletown, DE
18 November 2015